T0146555

Pleasure Cruise

A Smuggler's Tale

Anthony J Broughton

authorHOUSE®

AuthorHouse™ UK
1663 Liberty Drive
Bloomington, IN 47403 USA
www.authorhouse.co.uk
Phone: 0800.197.4150

Published by AuthorHouse 01/13/2017

ISBN: 978-1-5246-6605-7 (sc)
ISBN: 978-1-5246-6606-4 (hc)
ISBN: 978-1-5246-6604-0 (e)

By the same author

Time To Act: A Mercenary Tale
published by Minerva Press 2000

Vertical Challenge: A Harrier Encounter
published by Book Guild Publishing 2007

Island Of Vengeance: A Story of Revenge
published by Raider Publishing International 2010

Sparkle of Death: A Tale of Revenge
published by Raider Publishing International 2012

The Exchange: A Story of Deceit
Published by Troubador Publishing Ltd 2014

Learn more about the author at his website:-
www.anthonyjbroughton.co.uk

Acknowledgements

I would like to thank Monica Enticknap and David Luxford for their enthusiasm and encouragement for me to continue writing and publishing my novels. Also to my wife Linda for her patience in giving me the time to pursue my writing ambitions. I dedicate this novel to the loving memory of my cousin Gladys Scott who recently died at the age of 103.

List of Main Characters

SUZIE DRAKE, ex-mercenary, co-owns SMJ Boatyard Ltd

MIKE RANDLE, ex-mercenary, co-owns SMJ Boatyard Ltd, fiancé of Suzie Drake

SIR JOSEPH STERLING, diplomat troubleshooter in FCO for security matters

COLIN BROOKE, DI in Special Branch

JIM & JENNY STERLING, son & his wife of Sir Joseph Sterling, co-owners of SMJ Boatyard Ltd

CAPTAIN PAUL WOODLEY, skipper of coastguard motor launch

GRANT PATCHAM, first mate on the coastguard launch

INSPECTOR FAIRBOURNE, policeman in charge of the murders aboard *Quester II*

SGT ENDERBY, the inspector's colleague

SIR JEREMY PENDLETON MBE, millionaire playboy. HENRY, his chauffeur

MR GROOMBRIDGE, insurance agent

KHURRAM & KASHIF PHADKAR, drugs boss twin brothers, owners of 'The Rosy Cheeks Nightclub'. CRUSHER, LEFTY, JAKE CROSSMAN their thugs. ANGIE, the receptionist.

GILES HARMAN, rival boat builder

RAY TEAL & JOHN GREEN, DC's in Metropolitan Police Special Branch

REG ASHDOWN, foreman at SMJ boatyard. GEORGE, Reg's helper

DI MAIDLEY, policeman at SMJ Boatyard investigation

ALASTAIRE BIGNOR, film director. RACHEL, one of his stars who resembles Suzie.

MO, drug dealer. DEVEN, his minder.

VIKTOR BELANOV, a Russian hit man.

ZENON HORAK, a Ukrainian hit man

SERGEANT BILL NEWLANDS, police informant

Chapter One

Adrift

In the still of the night, stars twinkled brightly against the dark heavens. On the water below, a sixty-foot yacht silently drifted along on the rolling waves of the English Channel. Banks of clouds, their shape ever changing, trickled across the charcoal sky partially blotting out the dull yellow moon and the stars. The inky black water, cold and uninviting, lapped against the side of the yacht as a gentle breeze brushed the flapping sails against the mast. The vessel gently rose and fell with the swell producing shafts of dull reflections that danced on the water's surface on this Saturday night, late in the month of May.

In the far distance appeared the glow of lights accompanying the engine throb of a motor launch stirring the night air. The volume increased as it neared the yacht, drifting gently on the waves and making no headway.

On the far side from the launch, masked by the yacht, a small sailing boat with an outboard motor silently slipped away under the cover of darkness and vanished into the night. A break in the clouds brought a flicker of light from the moon and bathed the area with an incandescent glow, allowing a momentary reflection from the yacht to glisten on the shimmering water.

A searchlight, mounted high on the coastguard's motor launch, cut a path through the darkness seeking its target. The luminescent beam scanned a vast area of sea towards the fleeting reflection. Silence was broken when shouts erupted as a ray of light fell on the drifting vessel and fingers were pointed in her direction. The throaty roar of the launch's engines increased in volume as she sped towards their discovery.

'That could be her,' pronounced Captain Paul Woodley to his six-man team.

The well-built, six-foot-plus captain had skippered the coastguard launch for nearly twenty years, was a man who had spent all his working life at sea, and his bronzed deep-lined suntanned face bore witness to that fact. He was born into a family of sailors who had battled with the sea for as many generations as he could remember; it was in his blood and was the only career he had ever considered.

'Yeah, it looks as if the tip-off was genuine. She's running without lights, and looks to be drifting. I can't see any movement aboard,' declared Grant Patcham, the six-foot tall gangly framed first mate of the launch, staring hard into the darkness through his binoculars.

The launch came alongside and the two craft gently bumped together. One crewman jumped aboard, a line was thrown across and the yacht secured before Patcham and one other crewman boarded her.

'Go careful,' warned the skipper caressing his full beard; a beard he first grew as a young man, and had never shaved off even though it had now turned mainly grey. 'I'm not sure what we should expect. I always get a bit nervous when we receive an anonymous tip-off.'

'Okay, skip,' Patcham responded.

With flashlights illuminating a path before them, the three men first checked the top deck of the yacht and found nothing out of place. Entering the wheelhouse, everything looked in order until the flashlight beam fell on the radio equipment; smashed beyond repair. With the entrance to the cabin area closed, Patcham grabbed the handle and yanked, pulling the unlocked door open. He drew back at the distinctly foul aroma that escaped from below.

'I'm not sure what's down there, but it doesn't smell too good,' he declared.

Patcham descended the three steps into eerie silence following the beam from his flashlight as it shone upon the interior of the cabin. Broken furniture and dark, shiny pools were visible on the floor. Stepping into the cabin, Patcham shone a light around the galley and lounge area and took in the scene before him. Illuminated in the beam were the bodies of three men spreadeagled on the floor. Each one had been shot. Patcham then realised what the dark patches on the floor were; it was their congealed blood.

'There are three bodies down here! You'd better tell the skipper what we've found and ask him to come aboard,' Patcham called out.

'Aye, aye, number one, I'll get him,' replied the crewman, backing out of the cabin with undue haste.

The skipper boarded the yacht. 'What a stink, and what an unholy mess,' he declared, turning up his nose and removing his peak cap to scratch his head of thick wavy hair.

'We'd better not touch anything. The police forensic team will want to check this yacht for clues,' stated Patcham.

'Right. But first we'd better make sure there are no more bodies hidden here in all this mess.'

The pair searched the rest of what were previously the bedroom cabins, bathroom and laundry. All of the cabins had been torn apart and wrecked almost beyond repair.

'Somebody was obviously looking for something, and didn't give a damn about how they went about it or how much damage they caused while doing it,' Patcham stated.

'At least it doesn't look as if there are any more bodies lying around,' added Woodley, pulling the smashed door to a wardrobe aside and flicking his flashlight beam on the interior.

'Thank goodness for that.'

Woodley moved a broken shelf aside and suddenly froze. The light fell on a canister lashed to a timing device with a hand ticking around the face of a clock, and stood alongside a can of diesel fuel.

'Shit! You don't know how to defuse a bomb, do you?' asked the skipper.

'I had basic police training, but that didn't extend to defusing explosives. I left that to the bomb squad. Why?'

'Take a look.'

Patcham shone a beam on the can of fuel, moved it to the canister and across to the clock, its seconds hand flicking past the number six.

'Christ! It looks like an explosive device coupled to a timer, and it doesn't take an expert to see that this little lot is due to go off in less than thirty seconds.'

'Let's get out of here fast,' said the skipper, scrambling from the cabin and heading for the steps.

Patcham turned, then stopped. He turned back, grabbed the explosives and headed for the exit. Scurrying across smashed woodwork, he leaped up the steps and dashed from the wheelhouse to bowl the canister as far as his cricketing arm would allow.

'Get down!' yelled Woodley.

The crewmen all watched the canister loop across the night sky, and to a man dropped to the deck. The bomb plunged into the sea and exploded, sending a torrent of water high into the air, raining down on the two vessels.

'Phew! That was a close thing,' declared the skipper, eyeing his first mate as they got to their feet. 'Are you always this damn stupid?'

'I guess it's the latent policeman instinct in me. Leaving the force hasn't dulled my enthusiasm to catch criminals, especially when it's murder we're looking at. I didn't want all this evidence to be wiped out. The forensic boys will want to get fingerprints and the like, and that little incendiary device would have quickly started a fire with diesel spread everywhere. It would have sunk this vessel in no time, destroying everything.'

'Aye, including us if we'd stayed aboard. Somebody didn't want this yacht found intact,' declared Captain Woodley.

'If we hadn't discovered her so quickly, we might have thought it was an unfortunate accident.'

'Hmm,' mused the skipper. 'Or even got us blown sky high if we'd have come alongside at the wrong moment.'

Patcham grinned. He was more familiar with facing such dangerous situations during his time in the police force. The two men brushed themselves down and returned to the lounge cabin.

'Have you taken a good look at this body?' asked Patcham, an ex-Metropolitan police detective with an eye for detail.

'No. Why?' asked the skipper.

'Because he's the only one who's been tied up, and one of his fingers has been unceremoniously chopped off. It's here on the floor,' he stated, pointing the beam of light on the severed digit. 'He was also shot in the chest and the leg, probably the leg first, unlike the others who were shot in the chest and would have certainly died straight away.'

Woodley screwed his face up in disgust. 'Why do you think they did that?'

'I reckon they were trying to get some information out of him. He must have been the skipper.'

'Poor chap. I imagine he was in agony before he died. It was probably a release when they killed him.'

'Yeah. This has all the hallmarks of a drugs run, so I presume the stuff was hidden somewhere aboard, and whoever killed them and left that bomb, tried to force the location from him first. Looking around, I imagine they had quite a job and probably didn't succeed.'

'That would explain the state of this yacht. Whoever did this has wrecked practically everything in their search.'

'Yes, it's a shame. This was once a quality motor yacht. I wonder if they did find what they were looking for before they scarpered?' mused Patcham, looking around the dishevelled cabin.

'That's not our concern. Try starting the engines, otherwise we'll have to tow her into the harbour. I'll radio the police and let them know what we've found.'

'Okay, skipper.'

'Did you notice the name of this yacht?'

'Yeah. It's *Quester Two*.'

'*Quester Two*. Okay. The police should have no problems in tracing her owners. We can help them with that.'

While Captain Woodley returned to his launch to contact the police, Patcham checked the wheelhouse. The key was still inserted in the ignition. Twisting it illuminated a red light.

'So far, so good,' he muttered to himself.

His finger hovered over the starter button for a few seconds before he pressed it, half wondering if the killers had been clever and left more than one set of explosives to blow the yacht to pieces. To his relief they had not, and the engine fired up immediately.

Switching on the lights, Patcham called across to the skipper, 'Everything seems to be in working order.'

'Good. Follow us in slowly to Littlehampton Harbour. The police will be waiting for us there when we arrive.'

Nodding, Patcham span the wheel and followed his skipper in the wrecked floating coffin that was once a luxury motor yacht named *Quester II*.

Chapter Two

Discovery

A white police car, with yellow Day-Glow stripes emblazoned on each side between red hatched lines, was driven through the archway into the Hamble yard of SMJ Boatyard Ltd, and drew to a halt in the visitor's parking bay. A blue flashing light unit sat on the roof that, for the time being was dormant.

Two policemen, one an inspector and the other a sergeant, stepped from the vehicle into the early morning sunlight. The inspector straightened his crumpled jacket, brushed back his thinning dark hair and donned his cap. The sergeant brushed down his uniform, adjusted his tie and left his helmet in the car. The two policemen glanced at the yachts in the workshops as they wandered across the yard to the office building. Pushing their way through the glass fronted doors, they approached Carol, the receptionist sitting behind the counter.

Removing his cap, the inspector said, 'Good morning. I'm Inspector Fairbourne and this is Sergeant Enderby, we're from the Sussex Constabulary. We made an appointment earlier this morning to see Mr Randle and Miss Drake at eleven o'clock.'

The receptionist smiled. 'Please take a seat gentlemen. I'll let them know you've arrived,' she stated, gesturing towards the row of six empty chairs waiting behind a low table that held an assortment of boating magazines. Carol picked up the telephone and announced the new arrivals to the person on the other end of the line.

A few moments later Suzie Drake, dressed in a lightweight beige suit and a white V-neck T-shirt, descended the wooden stairs to greet her visitors. She was an attractive woman in her mid-thirties, with a slim athletic figure, shoulder length black hair and a button nose. She and her fiancé Mike Randle were co-owners and directors of SMJ Boatyard Ltd with their friends Jim and Jenny Sterling. She extended her hand.

'Good morning, inspector. Would you gentlemen like to follow me to our office?'

The inspector shook hands. He and his sergeant followed the female director to the first floor office where Mike Randle was already waiting. He rose from behind his desk when they entered the room and exchanged greetings with them. The policemen were invited to sit down on comfortable chairs located behind a coffee table.

'Would you like a cup of tea or coffee?' Suzie asked.

'Coffee please, black with no sugar for me,' said the inspector.

'White coffee with two spoonfuls,' stated the sergeant, placing a briefcase on the floor beside him as he sat down.

'Top-up?' Suzie asked Mike.

'Yes, please,' he replied, handing her his cup and moving to sit at the coffee table.

Mike was a good-looking muscular man who had an eye for the women. He and Suzie met when they were both mercenaries, after Mike finished a long spell in the army. Their relationship grew over the following years, and they gave up their dangerous fighting careers and settled down to a more sedate life in the boatbuilding business. Their intimacy continued and Mike was finally persuaded to ask Suzie to marry him or chance losing her, though in truth she would not have left him, but was careful not to let him be too confident of this.

While Suzie poured the coffees, Mike asked, 'To what do we owe the pleasure of this visit, inspector? It sounded important on the telephone, but you were reluctant to give us any details.'

'Yes, that's right. I wanted to speak with you in person about this problem. It's a little delicate and is too important to discuss over the telephone,' he stated.

Mike and Suzie looked at each other with concern as she handed the men their coffees. Suzie placed her drink on the coffee table and sat next to Mike. 'It must be something very serious then.'

'It is,' the inspector said, looking at his sergeant. 'Where to begin?'

'Try the beginning,' suggested Mike.

'Yes, right. Well, I have been asked to investigate a case that has recently come to our attention, and I would like your help.'

'We're only too willing to help the police,' stated Mike.

'I suppose the whole thing really started when an anonymous telephone call was received at the Selsey Bill coastguard station. The informer said a motor yacht would try to sneak past the coastguard patrolling their area of the English Channel that evening.'

'When was this?' asked Suzie.

'Two nights ago, Miss, on Saturday.'

'And what is it they were they trying to smuggle? I presume that is why they wanted to sneak past the coastguard?' Mike asked.

'Yes, we think so. We are fairly certain it was to smuggle drugs. That seems to be the most popular and financially rewarding crime of this type at the moment.'

'Fairly certain?' questioned Mike.

'Yes. You'll see why we aren't absolutely sure when I've explained things in more detail.'

'Right. Do go on,' said Mike, sipping his coffee.

'The coastguard patrol kept a more than usual careful watch that evening and they came across a motor yacht that was drifting in the channel without any lights showing. The crew boarded her and discovered all the interior had been badly smashed and found the bodies of three men on the floor. All had been shot.'

'Wow! Somebody was ruthless!' exclaimed Suzie. 'It has all the hallmarks of a gang war.'

'Yes, that is possible. One of the men had been tortured as well, and had one of his fingers cut off.'

'That's horrible! It sounds as if they either wanted to send a message to someone or they wanted some information from him,' suggested Mike.

'That's the conclusion we came to as well. If the yacht was used to smuggle drugs, their location seems to be the most likely thing.'

'Hmm, could be. But why are you telling us this? We are a respectable boatyard, we don't smuggle drugs,' said Suzie.

'No, but you do hire out your motor yachts?'

'Yes,' she hesitatingly replied glancing at Mike, her tone indicating she was aware of a possible problem.

'And one of them is named *Quester Two*?'

'Yes, that's right, she's out on hire at the moment,' said Suzie.

'Don't tell me the vessel you're talking about is *Quester*?' Mike frustratingly asked.

'I'm afraid it is.'

'Shit! And the cabins are all smashed up?'

'The hull and engines look okay, but there's a lot of damage done to the lounge, the galley and all the bedroom cabins. In fact, most of the inside has been totally wrecked.'

Mike jumped to his feet in anger. 'The bastards! That is a very expensive motor yacht and will take a long time and a lot of money to repair.'

'Calm down, Mike,' Suzie implored, touching his hand. 'We do have insurance.'

'The radio equipment in the wheelhouse was also smashed, and the galley equipment seems to have suffered as well, but the engines are okay and the vessel is still seaworthy.'

'I suppose that's something, but why should the galley equipment be damaged?'

'It looks as if someone was very angry and has gone round smashing everything in a temper, possibly because they couldn't find what they wanted.'

'I'd like to get my hands on the bastard who did that,' snarled Mike.

'So would we. Though I must say, we have to thank the bravery of Grant Patcham, who's an ex-Metropolitan police detective, for all the evidence we have with which to locate these murderers.'

'Oh! Why's that?' asked Mike.

'The culprits left an incendiary device on board coupled to a timer. He and the coastguard skipper found it, and Patcham bravely carried it on deck and threw it overboard a few seconds before it went off. If he hadn't done so, the bomb would have exploded next to a can of diesel fuel, and the whole yacht would have caught fire and probably burned to a cinder and sunk.'

'Phew! Good for him. We must thank Mr Patcham for his actions,' stated Suzie, looking at Mike.

He nodded in agreement. 'Yes, we will. Where is our yacht, inspector, and what's happening to her at the moment?'

'Your yacht is in our holding berth in Littlehampton Harbour, and the police forensic boys are going over her at the moment to see what they can find. We're hoping they will turn up something to identify the killers.'

'So do I,' said Suzie. 'This is awful.'

'I presume the yacht is hired out regularly?' the inspector asked.

Suzie nodded. 'Yes, it is. We acquired her a few years ago and renamed her *Quester Two* after the original *Quester* yacht we were using was sunk. She was in a bit of a state so we completely refurbished her and used her as a show yacht in exhibitions. We have hired her out many times to clients who want a seafaring holiday.'

'So the yacht has had many people on board?'

9

'Yes, many hundreds I would think. Lots of people have looked her over at boating exhibitions.'

'That means the forensic boys are going to have a difficult time trying to get any clues to the men who did these terrible murders.'

'I would think so.'

'I presume you have records of the last person who hired the yacht from you?' asked the inspector.

'Yes, but if it was hired to smuggle drugs, the information is likely to be false,' suggested Mike.

'Nevertheless, I'd like to have a copy of those details.'

'I'll sort that out,' said Suzie, moving to her desk and logging on to her computer.

She keyed in the information, selected the correct pages with the mouse and declared, '*Quester* was hire by a Mr Glen Shoenieurr, for five days and was due back later today. He gave his address as Walthamstow in London.'

'That's a strange name,' said the sergeant, the first time he had spoken. 'It sounds foreign. How do you spell it?'

'It's spelt S H O E N I E U R R,' stated Suzie, 'I'll give you a printout of the booking form.'

The sergeant made a note in his book. 'Thank you, Miss, that would be helpful.'

'Yes, he was a strange sort of man as I recall,' stated Mike. 'I handled the booking. He was dark skinned and looked middle eastern or was perhaps from the Far East, India or Pakistan. As I recall he unusually paid the deposit in cash when he booked the yacht and also paid cash when he collected it.'

'What denomination did he pay you with?'

'Fifty pound notes I believe. Why?'

'Do you still have them?'

'No, not any longer. They would have been taken to the bank last Friday. We don't keep a great deal of cash here on the premises, only a few hundred pounds in petty cash in the safe.'

'I see. I only asked because there have been a spate of forged fifty pound notes circulating recently.'

'The bank accepted the money and we've not heard of any problems.'

The printer on Suzie desk clattered out a copy of the booking form, which she collected and handed to the policeman. 'There you are inspector, that's his details. You will notice he paid with cash. All the information he gave us is shown there.'

10

'Thank you, Miss Drake,' said the inspector, taking the sheet and handing it to his sergeant who slipped it into his brief case and extracted several photographs, each one in a plastic see-through folder.

'Would you like to take a look at these to see if you recognise anyone?' he said, handing the photographs to Mike.

Thumbing through them Mike said, 'I presume these are of the dead men you found aboard *Quester*?'

'Yes, that's right.'

Mike held one of the photographs up. 'That's him. He's the bloke who hired the yacht.'

Sergeant Enderby retrieved it and glanced at the back of the photograph. 'No name on this one, sir,' he directed to the inspector, 'but he's the one who was tortured.'

Handing the other photographs back, Mike stated, 'I don't recognise either of these two men. They may have been with him when he collected the yacht, but only Mr Shoenieurr came into the office to make the payment.'

'Okay. Never mind. You've been very helpful. Thank you. I'll leave you my card so that you can get in touch with me to find out how things are progressing with your yacht,' he said, handing a card to Suzie.'

'How long is it likely to be before *Quester* is returned to us?' she asked.

'I'm not sure. The yacht will be returned after the forensic boys have made certain there are no more clues to be found aboard her. I would think it's likely to be several days yet, possibly more. We'll let you know,' said the inspector rising from his seat.

A glum expression crossed Mike's face as he nodded his acceptance of the unwelcome news. 'I'd better get on to our insurance company. They'll want to see the yacht before we start any repair work.'

'They'll have to wait until we've finished with the yacht I'm afraid. We can't have people tramping all over our crime scene.'

'No. Right.'

'I'll show you gentlemen out,' smiled Suzie.

The two policemen shook hands with Mike and thanked them for the drinks. They followed Suzie down to the reception and returned to their car. Suzie watched them drive out of the boatyard before climbing the stairs back to the office.

'That's a blow to our schedule. We have another customer who's booked *Quester* for their holiday. What are we going to do?' she asked.

'How long is it before she was due to go out again?'

Checking her computer, she responded, 'About a week and a half; Saturday, the weekend after next.'

'Hmm … if we get her back by this weekend, we might be able to get her repaired in time, if the men are willing to work overtime on her.'

'I'm sure they will, especially if Reg encourages them to.'

'I'll have a word with him. Also, we'd better order replacements for the galley and radio equipment. They might take a while to be delivered.'

'Good idea. I'll ask Jenny to look up *Quester*'s specification and get that in hand straight away.'

'Is there any way we can put pressure on the police to return the yacht any quicker?'

'I could have a word with Jeremy,' suggested Suzie.

'Your friend, Sir Jeremy Pendleton MBE. Is he still trying to get into your knickers again?' asked Mike in a mocking gesture.

'Not quite so much since you bought me this wonderful engagement ring,' she stated, admiring the five stone diamond studded ring on her finger. 'Though as it's been a while since I received it, and we haven't set a date for the wedding yet, he's starting to find excuses to contact me more and more and is making comments with double meanings, if you know what I mean.'

'I know what you mean. So, he's still interested in you. Perhaps he thinks we've forgotten about the dirty trick he tried to play on us in Cannes in an attempt to split us up.'

'Oh, I don't think so. Whenever he gets too fruity with his remarks, I remind him of it, and he backs away – just a little.'

'Do you think he will help us?'

'I'm certain he will do everything he can. But, you must realise that if he is successful in getting *Quester* returned to us earlier, he will try to make use of that success.'

'Hmm,' pondered Mike. 'Then I'll have to trust you will be able to fend off his amorous advances yet again. Won't I?'

'You will,' smiled Suzie, picking up the telephone. 'I'll ask Jenny to do that ordering before I ring Jeremy.'

'And I'll speak to Reg about the overtime,' said Mike, disappearing through the doorway to visit the boatyard foreman in the workshops, and give him and the workmen the bad news.

Chapter Three

Back To Base

Following a visit by the police to SMJ Boatyard with news that their yacht *Quester II* was found drifting in the English Channel with three bodies aboard, Mike and Suzie were both angered and shocked. When they heard that the inside of the vessel was badly damaged and it would be returned only after the police forensics team had finished their work, they were further dismayed. Their yacht was booked to be hired out again soon, and Mike and Suzie needed her to be returned quickly in order to have a chance to repair the vessel in time for the next customer.

Suzie rang Sir Jeremy Pendleton MBE, a handsome millionaire friend in his early forties and notorious womaniser. She wished to seek his help in securing the return of their yacht a little quicker, and gave him their bad news.

'… and of course, we have other clients who have booked the yacht for their holidays, and we'd like to get her back as soon as possible, so that we can start work on the repairs.'

'Yes, I can see that, Suzie. Of course I will do whatever I can to help you, but you must understand that I have limited influence with the police. However, I do know the Chief Constable of this area personally, and will have a private word with him about your predicament.'

'Thank you, Jeremy. That's very kind of you.'

'You know I'm only too willing to help a lovely lady like you in distress, Suzie,' Pendleton gushed, in his most compelling manner, running a finger across his moustache, a habit he acquired when chatting up the ladies.

'I wouldn't exactly say I was in distress, Jeremy, but I would be most grateful if you are able to speed things up for us.'

'How grateful?'

'What do you mean? You're not expecting me to let you into my bed again, are you?'

'No, of course not – not yet anyway. I merely thought you might possibly allow me to take you out for a meal.'

'I'm not sure that Mike, my fiancé, would care for that very much. He knows what happened after our last meal out together, and he's not forgotten about the underhanded trick you tried to play on us in Cannes in trying to spit us up.'

'Fiancé. Right, okay, I get the picture. Cannes was too recent and Mike has a long memory it seems, and is unforgiving.'

'Very long for that sort of underhanded trick.'

'Then I shall do my best for you anyway and hope it softens his opinion towards me.'

Suzie replaced the telephone with a smile on her attractive face. Jeremy Pendleton, she acknowledged, was a good-looking millionaire playboy who revelled in his conquest of beautiful women. He would try hard to please Suzie in order to get her into his clutches once again. During a previous meeting, while needing to distract Pendleton for a short while, Suzie used her charms and his infatuation for her to good effect. Having tasted the heady sexual encounter with her once had fuelled Pendleton's enthusiasm to repeat the experience at the first opportunity. Trying to split her and Mike up had been a disaster he came to regret as it severely lessened his chances of repeating his conquest. In the meantime, he would do all he could to get back into favour with both of them and this request was an unmissable opportunity for him to do just that.

Mike spoke to their boatyard foreman Reg, a man in his fifties with heavy lined suntanned features, who had been around boats all his working life. He appreciated their anxiety about the situation and had a word with the men about working overtime on *Quester II* after the police had released her and she was able to return to the yard. He received positive responses from most of them. The small workforce enjoyed a family type of association with the boatyard's owners and foreman, and the men were happy to both help out and add more pay to their weekly earnings.

During the afternoon there was much to discuss between the four directors of the yard. Mike, Suzie, Jim and his wife Jenny, along with their foreman Reg met around the table in their boardroom. A list of all the items that were required urgently to repair *Quester II* in time, were drawn up for urgent orders to be placed. Details of the work required to repair the inside would have to wait until the yacht was returned and the damage assessed.

When their discussions were finished, Suzie remarked, 'Right, that sorts that little lot out.'

'Let's hope we can get all the equipment delivered in time,' remarked Jim.

'I placed the orders for the galley and radio equipment straight away, but I have to say that I'm not confident we will receive all of it in time,' stated Jenny. 'The suppliers usually expect deliveries to take at least two weeks. I've explained the situation and asked them to do what they can.'

'Okay, well done. We can't ask any more than that,' said Jim.

'Mike, have you noticed something funny about the name of the man who hired out *Quester*?' asked Suzie.

'No. I thought it was a funny name, but I put that down to him being a foreigner.'

'What was the name?' asked Jenny.

'Shoenieurr, spelt S H O E N I E U R R.'

Jenny wrote the name down. She stared at it for a few minutes. 'Is it an anagram?'

'Yes, I believe it could be,' replied Suzie.

Scribbling for a few moments, Jenny exclaimed, 'Yes! I know what it is. It's an anagram of 'heroin user', isn't it?'

'Yes, that's right. I wonder if the police have spotted that as well. I think I'll ring Inspector Fairbourne and let him into the secret.'

'Very clever of you both. I bet the inspector won't be amused if they've not managed to decipher that,' suggested Mike.

'Probably not, but I think I should tell him anyway.'

Inspector Fairbourne was not amused. He had not recognised the name as an anagram and neither had any of the other policemen working on the case. He took it as a personal insult by the criminals. It did however confirm that the murdered men were trafficking in drugs, and was a question now of whether the drugs were discovered by the killers or whether they were still aboard the yacht. The search by the forensic team continued.

At the end of the day, the four boatyard directors went home with various thoughts about the problems facing them because of the activity their yacht was illegally involved in. Much of this included the desire to see how bad the damage was, and to know how soon their vessel would be returned to them.

15

*   *   *

Two days later on Wednesday morning, the telephone on Suzie Drake's desk rang.

'Inspector Fairbourne, this is a surprise. How are you getting along with your forensic checks aboard *Quester*.'

'Quite well, but we have not discovered any drugs and would prefer to have a little more time to make sure nothing has been missed. However, it seems we have been instructed to return the vessel to you without further delay.'

'That's good news, inspector.'

'There was pressure from the chief constable to hurry us up. Someone must have had a word with him.'

'Really? Well, whatever the reason, SMJ Boatyard is very grateful that *Quester* is to be returned to us so quickly. I'm sure you understand that we wish to begin the repairs to her as soon as possible. Exactly when can we expect to collect her?'

'At the moment, your boat is tied up in the harbour at Littlehampton, in the police compound. Is it possible for you to collect the yacht from there?'

'I believe you said she is seaworthy?'

'Yes, that's right. The engines were found to be working okay and the yacht was motored into the harbour by the coastguard.'

'Good, then yes, of course we can collect her. What time will be convenient to you?'

'Tomorrow morning?'

'I was rather thinking we'd like to get her back today so we can assess what work needs to be done, and the men can start preparatory work on her straight away,' Suzie stated in a business like manner.

'Some time this afternoon then?'

'That sounds good.'

'Shall we say five o'clock.'

'How about three o'clock?' suggested Suzie, aware the policeman was trying to keep hold of the vessel for as long as possible.

'Right, okay, three o'clock it is then. I'll see you by the quayside this afternoon.'

'Good. Thank you inspector. We'll see you at three.'

Replacing the receiver, Suzie went to the window that overlooked the yard and saw Mike chatting to Reg about a repair job they were working on.

She flung the window open wide and called out, 'Mike, we can collect *Quester* this afternoon.'

Looking up, shielding his eyes from the sun he exclaimed, 'That's great!'

Turning to Reg he said, 'Will you tell the men they can start working overtime tonight if they'd like to, please, Reg.'

'I'm sure some of them will be happy to earn the extra money.'

'Good,' said Mike, finishing his conversation and hurrying towards the office.

He took the stairs two at a time in his buoyant mood and entered the room. 'Who rang?'

'Inspector Fairbourne, and he wasn't very happy about it. It seems Jeremy did his stuff and persuaded the chief constable to put pressure on them to release *Quester* straight away.'

'So, your telephone call to him did some good after all.'

'Yes, and he won't be slow to remind us of it.'

'Never mind that, when do we get her back?'

'We can collect her at three o'clock this afternoon from the police compound in Littlehampton harbour.'

Grabbing the telephone, Mike said, 'I'll get the insurance agent to meet us there. He'll want to look over her before we start the repairs, and it also means we can get the compensation claim under way immediately.'

*　*　*

At the appointed hour, Mike and Suzie arrived at the quayside of Littlehampton Harbour, a small South Coast commercial port situated at the mouth of the River Arun. The harbour, which has strong tides, has moorings for yachts and motorboats and is able to accommodate vessels up to seventy metres in length. Its close proximity to SMJ Boatyard made it a convenient location for them.

Sounding its throaty roar as the vehicle approached, Mike parked their Aston Martin DB9, watched by the inspector who was waiting for them.

'Our insurance agent will be here shortly,' Mike informed him. 'We'd like him to make an initial assessment of the damage.'

'As I told you on my visit, the damage is quite extensive.'

Mike nodded. 'The lads at our boatyard have agreed to work overtime to get her repaired quickly and some of them will start as soon as we get *Quester* back to the yard tonight.'

As he spoke, a black BMW drew to a halt nearby. The driver, a balding man, smartly dressed in a dark single breasted suit locked the car and with an attaché case held firmly in his grasp walked towards them.

Mike extended his hand. 'Mr Groombridge, thank you for coming at such short notice.'

'Not at all, Mr Randle. It's all part of the service,' he stated, shaking hands. 'Good afternoon, Miss Drake,' he nodded.

Suzie smiled at him. 'This is Inspector Fairbourne. He will be releasing the vessel to us after you've done your initial assessment of the damage.'

'Good afternoon, inspector. I have my camera with me. Shall we proceed?'

'Yes, of course,' he replied. 'Kindly follow me.'

The inspector led them to the berth where *Quester II* was moored.

'She looks in reasonably good shape from the outside at least,' stated Mike.

They followed the inspector aboard and entered the wheelhouse. 'Look at that damn radio equipment,' Mike swore. 'All smashed to bits needlessly.' They descended the steps to the cabin. 'Bloody hell!' he exclaimed, stepping into what once was the lounge and galley area. 'I know you said there was a lot of damage, but you didn't tell us that almost the whole of the inside was totally demolished. There's hardly anything left except firewood.'

'If we'd had more time, then some of this would have been cleared up,' said the inspector, seemingly still annoyed at the haste with which he was obliged to return the vessel.

Mr Groombridge started taking photographs. 'All of the cabin areas will have to be rebuilt from scratch,' he proclaimed. 'Whoever did this looks to have taken a sledgehammer to the cabin walls. Why would they do that?'

'Presumably to check that nothing was hidden in the cavities,' suggested the inspector.

'Then I'm surprised they didn't rip up the floors as well,' Groombridge stated.

'Perhaps they didn't have time,' the inspector said. 'Just like we haven't had the time either.'

'This little lot will be expensive to replace and will take quite a while,' said Mike, ignoring the inspector's obvious annoyance.

'Yes, and I doubt if our lads will be able to complete it before she's due to go out again on hire next week,' suggested Suzie. 'There's far too much work to be done.'

Nodding in agreement, Mr Groombridge asked, 'What's that sticky stuff on the floor?'

'That's the dried blood of the men who were killed,' answered the inspector. 'It would also have been cleaned up if we'd had the time.'

Mr Groombridge pulled a face, stepped over the offending stains and continued to take photographs of what remained of the other cabins. The flash unit on his camera lit the yacht in staccato pulses as he moved from the shell of one cabin to the next.

'Have you managed to determine why the men were killed and the yacht wrecked, inspector?' asked Mike.

'No, not yet. We are still sifting through the clues we've found. The sniffer dogs were brought in, but they failed to find any trace of drugs, which was a bit of a surprise. I felt sure this was a raid on a rival drugs run, especially after the anagram name that you pointed out.'

'Perhaps whoever did this found the drugs,' suggested Mike.

'Yes, that's possible.'

The insurance agent completed his task of recording the damage and inspecting the yacht, and the group stepped ashore. Mike agreed to send an estimate of the repair costs to the insurance company and they said goodbye to Mr Groombridge who walked jauntily back to his car.

Turning to the inspector, Mike stated, 'We'll be on our way now. We want to get the men started on the repairs tonight if possible.'

'Yes, I understand that, Mr Randle. Please let me know if you find anything that might help us to track down theses culprits.'

'Yes, of course, though I don't imagine you've missed anything. There's nowhere left to hide anything among all that rubble.'

Mike and Suzie stepped aboard and Mike fired up the engine. 'At least this seems to be untouched,' he stated, tapping the fuel gauge to make sure there was enough diesel to get them back to the boatyard.

Suzie patted the yacht as if it was a pet. 'Homeward bound *Quester*. We'll soon have you back in shipshape once again.' She turned to Mike. 'I'll drive back and meet you at the boatyard.'

'Okay, luv. It shouldn't take me long. I'll see you there shortly.'

Suzie went ashore and drove back to their boatyard. Mike revved up the engine and steered the motor yacht out of Littlehampton harbour, heading for home on the River Hamble.

Chapter Four

The Search

Following Jeremy Pendleton's successful intervention to speed up the release of *Quester II* from the police, the vessel was inspected by the owner's insurance agent to assess the damage. Once this was complete the yacht was piloted by Mike Randle, from the police holding berth in Littlehampton harbour, back to SMJ Boatyard Ltd for the repairs to be started. On arrival at the jetty the sixty-foot motor yacht was lifted into the workshop by their overhead crane and supported on chocks. This enabled the small workforce to begin the task of stripping out the damaged cabins in her in an attempt to get the motor yacht repaired in time for the next customer who had booked the vessel for hire.

'What is your estimate of when she'll be ready?' Suzie asked their foreman Reg after he had taken a preliminary look over the yacht.

He grimaced with dismay at the damage inflicted on her. 'It's a bit early to say yet, Miss. There's a lot of damage. Ask me again tomorrow afternoon. By then we should have cleared out all the broken bits and I'll be able to see if there's anything stopping us from erecting the new lounge, galley and cabins. Getting the wood and making the cupboards and kitchen units is no problem, but takes time. Finishing the job may well come down to the delivery times of the new equipment for the galley and wheelhouse. If I'm honest with you, I think it's doubtful we'll have her ready in time for our next customers.'

'Hmm, yes, I'm sorry to say I must agree. That's exactly what I was thinking as well when I saw the extent of the damage. Okay, Reg. Thank you. Just do whatever you can.'

'Yes, Miss. George is checking and servicing the engine. He's going to change the oil and make sure everything's there is okay. It's just a precaution, because somebody's definitely been into the engine room.'

'It was probably the police looking for clues.'

'Perhaps, Miss. I couldn't say.'

* * *

Several of the men worked overtime on the yacht until ten o'clock that evening and by later the following afternoon the whole of the inside was gutted with all of the internal smashed partitions and fittings removed. The men were busy preparing the woodwork to hold the new partitions, doors and cupboards. The floor had been stripped to get rid of the damage and unwanted blood stains and a new wooden floor was in the process of being laid.

Mike looked in at the progress the men were making. 'This looks so much better,' he proclaimed. 'You lads are doing a great job.'

The men smiled in appreciation of their efforts.

Reg boarded the yacht and approached. 'Can I have a word with you in private please, Mr Randle.'

'Yes, certainly, Reg. Come into the office,' he replied, surprised at the unusually formal request.

The foreman followed Mike up the stairs to the first floor office that each of the four co-directors used. He carried a plastic supermarket bag, which he handed to Mike. 'I didn't want to speak of this in front of the men,' he began.

'Oh, why? Is there a problem?'

'For you perhaps, yes. This package was found by George, in the engine sump of *Quester* when he was changing the oil. I've told him not to say anything to any of the other men.'

Mike took the bag. 'It's quite heavy. About twenty pounds I reckon,' he said, weighing it in his hand. He placed the bag on the coffee table and opened it to reveal a package covered in a black, heavy, waterproof plastic wrapping and tightly bound with string.

'I've wiped most of the oil off, but I haven't opened the package. I thought I'd leave that to you,' suggested Reg.

'Right. Okay. I wonder if this is what those killers were looking for.'

'Seems likely to me.'

'If that's the case, and if our guess is right, there are probably drugs in here.'

21

'Yep, I reckon so.'

'Well, there's only one way to find out,' said Mike, sitting down and pulling the package towards him.

Suzie and Jim walked into the office at that moment. 'It's going home time …,' Suzie's voice trailed off. 'What's that?' she asked.

'George found it in *Quester*'s sump when he was changing the oil. I'm about to open it and find out. We reckon it's probably the drugs those killers were after. We should soon know if we're right.'

'That's a strange place to hide a package. It means they had to drop the sump in order to put it in there. That could turn out to be a messy job while you're at sea,' suggested Jim.

'Yes, I agree, so they might have drained the oil and took the sump off while the yacht was docked somewhere. They could have used sail to get to the rendezvous, collected the drugs and hid the package, bolted the sump back on and filled the engine with fresh oil,' Mike surmised. 'That way, if the coastguard stopped them and did a search, it was almost impossible for them to find the drugs.'

'That would tie in with what George told me. He said the oil looked new and hardly needed changing,' Reg said.

With all eyes on the package, Mike slowly removed the string and peeled back the outer plastic covering.

'It's not likely to be dangerous, is it, Mr Randle?' asked Reg.

'No, I shouldn't think so, but it pays to be careful.'

All layers of the outer wrapping were carefully removed to reveal ten clear plastic packages, each one containing a white powder.

'Would you hand me the letter opener,' asked Mike. Suzie obliged and Mike made a small slit in one of the packages, dipped his finger in the powder and tasted a small quantity. 'Pure heroin, if I'm not mistaken, and quite a lot of it.'

'So, our anagram man had the right name,' said Suzie.

'It seems so. Once this lot is refined, this stuff must be worth a great deal of money on the open market,' Mike suggested.

'Enough to kill for?' asked Jim.

'I reckon so. There are ten packages here.'

'The point is, what are we going to do with them?' Jim questioned.

Mike glanced at each of them and said, 'Well, I don't know how or where to legitimately sell this stuff, and I wouldn't want to see it get on to the streets for drug addicts to use, so I guess we'd better hand it over to the police.'

'Good idea,' said Suzie. 'We don't want to have anything to do with drugs, especially when there's murder attached to them.'

Mike glanced at the wall clock. 'It's a bit late, but I'll try ringing Inspector Fairbourne. He'll be pleased we've found it. It confirms his theory that the yacht was being used for drug smuggling.'

'And add to the annoyance he felt on being instructed to return *Quester* before they'd had time to check the yacht over properly,' suggested Suzie.

'Yes, you're probably right,' agreed Mike, grabbing the telephone. He lifted the instrument to his ear then promptly returned it to its cradle. 'The reception's shut and Carol's gone home. I'll have to dial the call myself. Have we got the inspector's card?'

Grabbing a box file, Suzie rummaged through, produce the calling card they received and handed it to Mike.

'I'll get back to the workshop now,' said the foreman.

'Okay, Reg, thanks,' said Mike, punching the buttons on the telephone. 'And not a word to anyone about this.'

'My lips are sealed, Mr Randle,' the foreman stated shutting the door behind him.

After speaking to the police station receptionist for a few minutes Mike replaced the telephone. 'I expect you gathered most of that?' he asked.

'Yes. The inspector's gone home,' stated Jim.

'That's right. I'll ring him in the morning. In the meantime, I'll take this stuff home with us and lock it in our safe. That way I can hand it in at the police station on the way in to work tomorrow morning.'

Mike wrapped the package up and grabbed Suzie's hand. 'Come on it's late. Let's go home.'

Reg agreed to supervise the men working on the late shift until they finished at ten o'clock. Jim collected his wife Jenny and Mike locked the director's office.

He and Suzie piled into their DB9 and motored to their coast home on the outskirts of Bosham Hoe in West Sussex. Jim and Jenny drove their Rolls Royce Phantom to their Surrey home in Weybridge. Both couples discussed their hopes for *Quester II*, and speculated on the drugs find during their homeward journey.

Another eventful day had passed. *Quester II* was returned to her berth in the boatyard and had given up her hidden package. She was again receiving expert care in rebuilding her and would soon look like the graceful motor yacht she once was, before the drug smugglers had wrecked her in their search for the ten expensive packages of deadly white powder.

Chapter Five

Lost Cargo

With a badly damaged *Quester II* now back at SMJ Boatyard, many of the workforce took the opportunity to put in extra hours and earn themselves a bonus. They were endeavouring to get her repaired in time for the next customers, but knew it was a race against time they were likely to lose, despite work being carried out on her throughout the day and evening on both shifts.

The sky had turned jet black, and the sound of the water lapping against the jetty mixed with the distant traffic noise of vehicles that motored past on the M27. It was half past ten on Thursday evening, and after locking the main office and setting the alarm, Reg puffed out a lungful of air as he wearily locked the gates to the boatyard following a long day's work. He began his day by arriving ten minutes before the men who were working on the early shift started drifting in at six o'clock and stayed until the men on the late shift finished for the day and left for home ten o'clock. He was tired, and now all he wanted to do was drive home to his wife who would already be in bed, and lay his weary body down on a soft mattress. He shoved the yard keys in his pocket after extracting his car ignition key and turned to see a vehicle drive up and halt a few feet in front of him.

Shielding his eyes from the glare of the Mercedes headlights, Reg saw the outline of two figures alight from the front seats of the car. 'It's late and we're closed until tomorrow morning,' he called out.

'Not for us,' exclaimed a heavy set man with a pug face, courtesy of a broken nose. He shoved Reg back into the gate. 'Open up.'

'Why? What do you want?'

A small, dark skinned man in his fifties, barely five feet three inches in height and with a wiry frame, stepped forward from the rear seat of the car. The two minders peeled apart allowing him to confront Reg.

Speaking in a quiet but menacing tone, with a distinct inflection of his native Pakistan, the man declared, 'We were not expecting to see anybody here this late. But as we have, you should know that I am not a man who deals in … unnecessary violence Mr …?'

'Reg. I'm the foreman here.'

'Well, Mr Reg, as I was saying, I do not like unnecessary violence, but I wish to inspect one of your boats and I do not take no for an answer. Do you understand? Am I making myself perfectly clear to you?'

'I think so. If I don't show you what you want, one of your men will start hitting me.'

A forced smile crossed his lips. 'Something like that.'

'Which yacht do you want to see. I bet it's *Quester*.'

'Yes, it is, how clever of you. Why do you think that is the one I wish to look over?'

'Because we've only just got her back from the police after she was involved in a drug smuggling run – or so the police seem to think.'

'Do they now? That is very interesting. And did they find any drugs on board this boat?'

'Yacht,' corrected Reg. 'And I've no idea. They didn't confide that information to me. I'm only the foreman around here.'

'So you said. You seem to be working very late.'

'The inside of the yacht was smashed to bits, and we've been trying to repair her in time for the next client who's hired her, so we've had a late shift working to repair her.'

'Hmm… I see. Come on, open up,' the man instructed, pointing at the padlocked gate.

Reg looked at the men and realised there was no point in him resisting. He knew they could take the key from him easily, so he delved into his pocket, pulled out a bunch of keys and unlocked the gates.

One of the minders shoved him inside the yard and thrust a gun into his ribs. 'Where's this boat?' he demanded to know.

Pointing to the old workshop, Reg stated, 'The yacht is in there. She's the one on chocks to the left.'

The light blue Mercedes was driven into the yard and two more men emerged from the rear seat of the car. They all moved into the old workshop, a timber framed building erected in the early 1900s with a wood tiled sloping apex roof covered in felt, with the main structure open at each end. The building was fortunate to be still standing after a new workshop that was originally erected in the 1930s and was situated alongside, had to be rebuilt after an explosion and fire wrecked it a few years earlier. The fire brigade were quick to put the blaze out saving the older building and both workshops were now in constant use. At the rear of the workshops was the quayside on the Hamble River where the vessels arrived and departed before sailing out into the English Channel.

The yard was covered by floodlights, which were activated by movement and had blazed into life with the workshops remaining in darkness.

'Lights,' demanded the boss man.

Reg banged down the switch on the fuse box and the fluorescent workshop lights, scattered around the wooden beams, flickered several times before bursting into life. *Quester II* and two other smaller craft were illuminated, cradled by heavy wooden chocks holding them in an upright position.

'Take a look in the engine room,' pug face man was instructed.

He obediently climbed the narrow wooden ladder up to the yacht's deck with some difficulty. He was a big man and wobbled precariously as he stepped over the side and disappeared below. Reg knew what he was looking for, and also knew he was not going to find it.

Reappearing a few minutes later, the pug face man declared, 'The engine's been taken apart, boss. The sump's off and the package is missing,' he said, leaning over the side of the yacht.

The boss man turned to Reg. 'Who has dismantled the engine?'

'We've done that here today to check it over and fill it up with fresh oil, but nothing was found,' he lied.

'I do not believe you. I arranged specifically where the goods were to be hidden, with my nephew … now my late Nephew. He was a good boy and always did as he was told.'

'Perhaps the raiders found the drugs,' said Reg.

'No, that is not possible. My man was waiting for the boat to arrive and saw it motor into Littlehampton Harbour piloted by the coastguard, so the sump and oil could not have been removed. The engine was still in working order.'

'The police had the vessel for several days. Maybe they found it when they searched the yacht, and refitted the sump so we could motor our yacht back to the yard,' suggested Reg, trying hard to find an explanation that would fit the situation.

'No, I do not think so. They did not have the boat for very long, and you could have used sail to get her back to do the repairs if the engine could not be used.'

'I don't know then.'

The boss signalled to pug man who climbed down the ladder.

'See if you can persuade Mr Reg to tell me the truth, Crusher.'

'Crusher!' exclaimed Reg.

'A name my man has acquired because he likes to crush people's bones. If you do not want yours crushed, I suggest you start telling me the truth.'

It was useless to lie any longer, Reg could see that. This man was big and powerful enough to do him serious damage.

'Okay, okay. I was instructed to check the engine and change the oil. I found a package containing the drugs in the sump and handed them over to Mr Randle,' he said, not wanting to implicate George in the discovery.

'Who is this, Mr Randle?' asked the boss.

'He's one of the owners and directors of this boatyard.'

'How do you know they were drugs in the package?'

'Mr Randle opened one of them and tried a small sample.'

'Did he! So, what did Mr Randle do with this package?'

'I'm not sure. He said he was going to hand it over to the police.'

'To the police! And did he?'

'I imagine so. He took the package with him when he left, so I presume he dropped it off at the police station on his way home.'

'Hmm, you presume. Perhaps that is so. I think we should take a look around anyway, just in case you were wrong – or lying.'

The boss man turned to his men. 'Okay, I want you all to search the place.' He opened his hand to Reg. 'Give me the keys to the main offices,' he demanded.

Giving him a cold stare, Reg slapped his bunch of keys into the palm of the man's hand.

'Is the office alarmed?' he asked.

It was a silent alarm that rang in the local police station, and Reg was tempted to say 'no'. But that might bring a lone policeman to investigate and both of them could end up hurt, or even dead; he had already seen one man with a gun. The risk was not worth it.

He nodded, 'Yes, it is.'

'As you are the last to leave, I presume you know how to turn it off?'

'I do,' said Reg, who was pushed in the direction of the office.

Opening the main doors to the office block, the alarm began to flash a hidden red lamp under the reception desk until Reg punched the code into the alarm console to turn it off. He knew that hidden security cameras, which had only recently been fitted, were recording the break-in. If the men did not spot them they would be caught on camera. At least that would give the police a fighting chance to discover who they were.

After turning off the alarm, and leaving the boss to search the offices, Reg was taken back outside. He had to stand around helpless, while the men began searching the workshops, turning everything over and throwing things to the ground.

'Hey, mind what you're doing. You don't need to go smashing everything,' protested Reg.

His voice fell on deaf ears as the men continued throwing aside anything that was in their way. They climbed into several other yachts that were being repaired, and Reg cringed as he heard things being smashed in their search for drugs that were not there to be found. A mental picture of what *Quester II* looked like when he first saw the damage, came to mind. He hoped that less carnage would be inflicted on her and the other yachts this time. Even so, this would end once and for all their chances of getting the yacht ready in time. There would be a lot of repair work to be done afterwards. It was now more important than ever for the men to work overtime.

The boss returned from the offices and approached Reg. 'What is the combination of the office safe?'

'I don't know that. That's in the director's office. Only they have access to the safe. My job is to manage the workshops.'

'Crusher,' called the boss, 'see if you can persuade Mr Reg to give us the combination of the safe.'

'Right, boss,' he exclaimed, eager to inflict pain on anyone he was asked to. It was a sadistic pleasure he enjoyed.

One of the men grabbed the foreman and held his arms behind his back, while crusher smashed him in the stomach. Reg, a man in his fifties, crumpled immediately to the floor, only to be hit again by a stinging blow to his face. Blood seeped from the corner of his mouth as he drifted into semi-consciousness. Crusher raised his fist to strike him again and was halted.

'That is enough, Crusher,' his boss said. 'We do not want to kill the man.'

Crusher looked disappointed. He had hardly begun to enjoy himself.

'Lefty, can you open that safe?' the boss asked.

'I'm not sure, boss. It's a fairly sophisticated safe and it may take me quite a time to crack it,' confessed the small gang member in a thick Irish accent.

'Okay. Jake, have you brought your tools with you?' he asked.

'Of course, Mr Phadkar. I'll get them.'

His boss frowned at the mention of his name, and gave him an angry glance. 'I want you to drill through the lock of the safe in the upstairs office,' he instructed, pointing to the office block.

After collecting his tools from the boot of the car, Jake Crossman, a close shaven-headed crook with a chin covered in stubble, who had spent many of his 35 years in jail and who aspired to greater criminal heights and greater criminal wealth, went to work on the safe.

'This is a bloody tough safe!' he exclaimed to his boss, standing over him and watching him struggle to drill through the lock. It took almost half an hour before he finally broke through and prized the safe door open. To Phadkar's disappointment, there were no drugs in the safe, only a small amount of petty cash and papers.

'Perhaps he was telling the truth after all,' he complained, throwing the papers in the air in disgust.

Crossman pocketed the cash while Phadkar broke open desk drawers and rummaged through a filing cabinet looking for the private address of Mike Randle. He was disappointed to find only business addresses on the correspondence, and returned to the workshop where Reg had recovered and was sitting on the floor with one of the men watching over him.

'What is the address of this Mr Randle who you think has handed the packages to the police?'

'He lives somewhere on the Sussex coast, but I'm only an employee. I've never visited his house so I don't know the exact address,' insisted Reg.

Phadkar pursed his lips in thought and silence prevailed for a moment while he contemplated his next move. 'Tie him up. There is nothing more we can do here tonight.'

Crusher tied Reg's hands and feet behind his back, and when his boss was not looking gave him a kick in the ribs in frustration as the foreman lay on the floor. The gang returned to their car and drove off leaving the gates wide open and a battered and bruised foreman struggling to get free from his bonds.

Try as he may, Reg did not have the energy to extract himself from the well tied ropes that bound him and he eventually gave up and resigned himself to lay there until the early shift arrived in the morning. His wife would be asleep by now and, knowing that he was working a long day, would think he had stayed the night at the boatyard and slept in one of the yacht's cabins. It was something he had done in the past when the yard was very busy. Reg was uncomfortable and despite his tiredness managed only to doze off for a few minutes at a time before the discomfort woke him. He was destined to endure a long, uncomfortable night.

Chapter Six

Unwelcome Visitors

Mike Randle and Suzie Drake, ex-mercenaries who had given up their soldiering days and now co-owned SMJ Boatyard with their friends Jim and Jenny Sterling, were dreaming. They were fast asleep on their water bed in the front master bedroom of their large, detached, four bedroom house on the West Sussex coast. Suzie was relaxed in a peaceful sleep, while Mike tossed and turned. His dreams were more vivid and disturbing, becoming close to a nightmare that reflected the traumatic times he had endured in the army and as a mercenary. While in the British army he fought in the battle for the Falkland Islands, and as part of 2 Para was among the first to land at San Carlos, which led to the victory at Goose Green. Now, those traumatic days left him with bad dreams about the friends who died or were badly injured in that battle. Mike was rudely awoken with a start when the telephone on the bedside cabinet rang.

Looking at the green fluorescent numbers on the radio alarm clock, Mike swore. 'Who the bloody hell is ringing us at this time of the morning. It's not even six o'clock yet,' he complained, grabbing the receiver.

Suzie muttered something about wishing he did not get angry quite so quickly and turned over. It would be time to rise soon and she wanted to extract the last few minutes of slumber she could.

Mike listened to the caller; one of the men on the early shift at the yard. 'Oh, hello George, what's wrong?' he asked, surmising that something unexpected must have happened for him to make the call that early in the morning.

Mike tapped Suzie to wake her.

'What! … Is he all right? … Have you rung the ambulance and the police? … Then do so straight away, I'll be there in about forty-five minutes,' he stated, replacing the receiver.

'What's wrong?' Suzie asked, stifling a yawn as Mike leaped out of bed.

'The yard was broken into last night. Reg has been beaten and left tied up all night. I'm going there straight away.'

'Oh! That's awful. Poor Reg. How is he?'

'I'm not sure. I hope he's not badly hurt. I told George to call an ambulance and the police.'

'What are we going to do about our meeting in London this morning, Mike?'

'Oh hell! I'd forgotten about that. You'll have to go on your own, unless Jim or Jenny can go with you. Could you give them a ring and explain what's happened?'

'Of course, but do you think I should cancel it and go with you.'

'No, I don't think so. This meeting could be important. With *Quester* out of action for a few weeks we could do with another source of income to make up for it. We might not get a chance to bid for the contract if we don't attend the meeting – however good our excuse is.'

'Okay. I'll ring Jenny,' said Suzie, jumping out of bed and slipping on a silk kimono to cover her naked body.

Mike had a quick shower, grabbed his leathers and shoved his feet into his motorbike boots. He gave Suzie a quick kiss. 'Got to dash. I'm taking *Bonnie*, it'll be quicker.'

'So I see. Be careful. Don't go too fast.'

'Okay,' he replied, grabbing his crash helmet and jacket. He dashed down the stairs two at a time.

Stepping on to the landing, Suzie shouted, 'And give me a ring on my mobile when you get there so I know what's happened.'

'Will do,' Mike said, punching the buttons on the hall console to disable the intruder alarm. 'Bye,' he shouted, slamming the front door behind him.

Standing by the balcony at the top of the stairs, Suzie listened to the roar of Mike's Triumph Bonneville motorcycle rev up and crunch its way over the gravel driveway and fade into the early morning mist. Mike fast disappeared along the coast road, leaving the electronic wrought iron gates to clang shut behind him.

Silence returned to the house.

Suzie rang Jenny to give her the distressing news. ' ... and Mike thinks I should still go to the meeting because it might be important for our boatyard, especially as it looks as if *Quester* is unlikely to be ready in time for our next customer.'

'Yes, I can see that.'

'He suggested I ask you or Jim to accompany me in his place, if one of you hasn't got anything else arranged for today.'

'Jim has, but I haven't. And yes of course, I'd love to go with you to London. I've given Jim the news. He's going to dash down to the boatyard as soon as he's dressed. I hope poor Reg is okay.'

'So do I. Mike's going to ring me when he gets there and sees what's happened for himself.'

'Do ring me and let me know as well.'

'Of course, and I'll pick you up at around ten o'clock.'

After making the telephone call Suzie dressed. She went for her usual jog along the nearby beach with her mobile phone clipped to her waist in readiness for Mike's call.

Despite his fiancée's appeal, Mike drove at well over the speed limit along the M27 to their Hamble boatyard taking the view that this early in the morning there were not likely to be many police cars patrolling the motorway looking for speeding motorcyclists. With luck on his side, the first police car he saw was when he sped into the boatyard in time to follow their vehicle through the archway.

An ambulance was already there, and Reg was sitting inside with his shirt having been removed for his wounds to be attended to. George was nearby keeping him company.

Mike dumped his crash helmet on the motorcycle seat and rushed over to him. 'What the hell happened to you?' he asked, looking at the cuts and the bruises on Reg's face and body that had turned a dark mauve since Crusher was let loose on him.

'A gang of men wanted to search *Quester*. They were looking for that package we found, and I think they've ransacked your office and safe looking for it as well, Mr Randle,' Reg said, deliberately omitting to say what the packet contained.

'Never mind that, the office can be fixed. How about you?'

'I'm okay. I've just got a few cuts and bruises. Nothing that won't heal quite quickly.'

'You may have cracked ribs,' stated the ambulance man, prodding his body gently. 'We'll have to take you back to the hospital for an X-ray.'

'I think they may have damaged some of the yachts as well,' Reg added.

'We'll be able to fix those, so don't worry about it. You look after yourself and get better.'

A second police car pulled into the yard and a plain clothes policeman stepped from the vehicle to join them. 'Well, hello. We meet again, Mr Randle,' he stated.

'Oh, hello Inspector …?'

'Detective Inspector Maidley,' the six-foot two gangly policeman reminded him.

'Oh, yes, DI Maidley. It's been a while since we last met. How are you?'

'I'm well thank you, Mr Randle, and I trust you will not be running away from me this time,' he said, referring to a previous investigation when Mike and Suzie promised to see him but failed to keep the appointment, an act that annoyed him.

'Right, yes. I'm sorry about that. Events dictated that course of action. It was nothing personal you understand, and as it happens turned out to be the right decision in the end. We simply didn't have time for explanations and red tape etcetera.'

'I understand. I was told everything worked out satisfactorily in the end.'

'Yes, it did, more or less.'

'More or less?'

'The main culprit avoided punishment for his crimes, but we've not forgotten what he did and our time will come. He will not get away with it.'

'I see. I hope you are not contemplating doing anything that's against the law, Mr Randle.'

'Perish the thought, inspector.'

'Hmm. Your boatyard seems to attract trouble, but at least nobody's been shot this time, or so I'm led to believe.'

'No, that's right. After Pete and Barry were killed we decided not to have guards on patrol overnight, and installed security cameras and floodlights instead.'

DI Maidley looked around. 'I don't see the cameras.'

'They're quite well hidden. The man from the security firm who supplied them said we had two choices. Either to make them very prominent, in order to dissuade would-be burglars, or to hide them and the recorder to stop the buggers who break in from ransacking the place to find the recorder and destroying it. From what Reg has told me, it hasn't made that much difference.'

The inspector's expression did not alter, he had heard it all before.

He approached Reg. 'I'll get a full statement from you after you've been checked at the hospital, Mr?'

'Ashdown. Reg Ashdown.'

'Well, Mr Ashdown, if you could give me a few of the salient facts now that would help.'

'Of course,' said Reg, wincing at pain that shot through him, despite the ambulance man trying hard to be gentle as he wound strapping around his chest.

'Sorry,' he said, seeing Reg stiffen.

The inspector got out his notebook. 'How many of them were there?'

'Five men. Four heavies and a boss man. They arrived in a light blue Mercedes. The one who beat me up was called Crusher, and one of the other men was called Lefty, and another Jake. I think he called the boss man Mr Phadkar, or something like that. I was a bit dazed, so I'm not absolutely sure.'

'Did he? That was careless. Well done for remembering. We should be able to trace them quite easily,' said the inspector, licking the point of his pencil and scribbling in his notebook. 'What time did they arrive?'

'About ten-thirty last night, just as I was locking up.'

'Ten-thirty? That's very late,' suggested the inspector.

'We've a lot of work to do on our yacht *Quester*, so we have two shifts working and the late shift doesn't go home until ten o'clock,' said Mike. 'So Reg stays each night to look after the men who work on the late shift, and he locks up when they've all gone home.'

'I see. Do you know what these crooks were after? Have they stolen anything?'

Reg looked at his boss with a question in his eyes.

Mike Randle replied. 'Yes. They were looking for drugs that were hidden in the engine sump of our yacht *Quester*.'

'Oh really! Drugs eh! How do you know that?'

'Because that's where we found them late yesterday afternoon. I rang the police station to inform Inspector Fairbourne of our discovery, but he'd already gone home so I took the drugs home and intended to contact him and hand them over this morning on my way into the boatyard.'

'I see. How did the drugs get there in the first place, and how is Inspector Fairbourne involved in all this?'

'Our yacht *Quester* was hired out to a man who said he wanted a short yachting holiday with friends. It turns out that he and two other men used our yacht to smuggle drugs. The yacht was apprehended by the coastguard who boarded her and discovered three bodies, and the inside of the yacht wrecked. Our yacht was taken into Littlehampton harbour where she was searched by the police forensics men before we got her back. Inspector Fairbourne is the Sussex policeman in charge of the investigation.'

'I see. Obviously, neither the police nor the villains found the drugs and they came here last night to regain them.'

'That's looks about it,' agreed Mike.

'And where are the drugs now?'

'At home, in my safe. In my rush to get here this morning, after I'd heard what happened to Reg, I forgot to bring them with me.'

'We ought to get this man to hospital,' the ambulance medic interrupted.

'Yes, of course. Just one more question. Were the cameras recording this break-in?'

'Yes, they are on a timer,' stated Mike.

'So, did the men realise they were on camera?' he asked Reg.

'No, I don't think so. I'm sure they would have wanted to know where the recorder was hidden otherwise. That might also have been a bit painful for me as well, inspector.'

The inspector nodded. 'Good, then we should have some pictures of them. Could you check on that for me please, Mr Randle.'

'Yes, of course.' He smiled at Reg as the ambulance doors were about to close. 'You take it easy, and give us a ring when you feel fit and able to return. George will run you home after your X-ray.'

Mike looked at George. 'Is that okay?'

'Yes, of course, Mr Randle. I'll see to it.'

He patted George on the shoulder. 'Thanks, George.'

Mike, followed by the inspector and a constable, wandered into the office block and climbed the stairs to the director's room. The lock had been broken and the door was wide open. They stepped into the office and were confronted with broken furniture and papers strewn across the floor. All the desk drawers had been forced open and the contents, along with those of the filing cabinets, were scattered to the four corners of the room.

'What a mess! It'll take ages to clear this lot up and get it back into some sort of order,' Mike stated. He looked at the safe, wide open with iron filings on the floor where the lock had been drilled out.

The inspector approached. 'Someone knew what they were doing to get that open.'

'Yes. It's supposed to be a good make of safe that's not easy to get into,' stated Mike, picking up the telephone. 'I'd like to ring my fiancée and let her know what's happening and how Reg is.'

'Of course, go right ahead.'

Mike rang Suzie's mobile. She stopped jogging for a moment while he gave her the details, telling her that Reg was battered and bruised, but was a tough old soldier and was on his way to hospital and would be okay. She was relieved to hear it.

'Did you manage to contact Jim and Jenny?' Mike asked.

'Yes. Jenny will accompany me to London and Jim is on his way there to the boatyard.'

'Okay. Thanks luv. I'll ring you later to see how the meeting went.'

Mike returned the telephone to its cradle while Suzie rang Jenny to pass on the news.

'It looks as if they searched everything. Does anything immediately strike you as missing, Mr Randle?' the policeman asked.

'No, only the petty cash from the safe,' he answered, looking at the empty cashbox on the floor that was discarded after the money was taken.

'How much was in there?'

'About £250. We keep it mainly for entertaining clients.'

'I understand. Did they find the recorder?'

'It's hidden in a false bottom to this cupboard,' Mike said, lifting out a shelf to reveal the recorder. 'It's still here and looks okay. The timer starts recording at six in the evening and goes on until eight the next morning. We haven't got around to changing the timers since the men started the two shifts.'

'I see.'

Jim Sterling came barging into the room. 'I got here as quickly as I could, Mike. What a mess!' he stated, looking around the room.

'Yes, they've certainly buggered up our filing system.'

'At least the computers look as if they're okay, but the printer's smashed to bits,' he said, picking up several pieces from the floor. 'It'll take the girls ages to clear this lot up and get the paperwork back into some sort of order.'

'Oh! Jim, this is DI Maidley.'

Offering his hand he stated, 'I'm Jim Sterling, co-owner of this mess.'

The two men shook hands. 'I'm pleased to meet you, Mr Sterling,' the inspector stated, smiling at this slightly overweight man with brown eyes, a mop of blonde hair that had turned to a mousy colour and who he quickly assessed possessed a bubbly character. He sported an unshaven look because of his hurried departure from home that morning.

'You couldn't get a speeding ticket squashed for me could you? I got one rushing hear this morning,' stated Jim.

'No, I'm sorry, that's not my department I'm afraid.'

'Okay, I just thought I'd ask. It's not the money I'm worried about you understand, it's the penalty points on my licence.'

'You'll simply have to go more slowly in future,' suggested the policeman, in a tone of voice making Jim aware he was concerned with the break-in and not his speeding fine.

'Right. How's poor old Reg?' Jim asked Mike.

'He's been taken to hospital in the ambulance for a check up. They think he's probably got fractured ribs, but he'll be okay,' Mike said. 'We're just about to look at the security pictures.'

'Right.'

Mike ejected the DVD disc from the machine. He grabbed a nearby box and took a new disc out, inserted it and closed the recorder. Moving to his desk he switched on his computer and loaded the disc.

The disc automatically accessed the DVD and ran the program. Mike fast forwarded the recording until the clock showed ten-thirty. They watched the gang on the 4-way split screen come into the boatyard followed by the Mercedes car. All the men were caught on camera clearly and were easily identifiable as was the car number plate.

Scribbling in his notebook, Maidley stated, 'I'll get that number plate checked straight away.' He handed a note to the constable. 'Radio this in and see if you can find out who the owner is.'

'Right away, sir,' the PC said, taking the note and moving aside to the window to call in the request on his mobile phone.

'Can you get a print of these pictures?' the policeman asked.

'Yes, but I'll have to take the disc home to do that. Our printer's in pieces all over the floor.'

'Then perhaps I could borrow the disc and get the lab boys at the office to print them for me. I'll let you have it back later on. The forensic boys will be here shortly to see if they can find any fingerprints. Please ask your men not to touch anything in the meantime.'

'Okay, inspector. I'll take a copy of the disc first.'

'And I'll talk to the men,' offered Jim, disappearing from the room.

While Mike copied the disc, Jim addressed the men who had gathered in the yard. He explained the situation, though they mostly gathered what had happened and he asked them to take the rest of the day off telling them they would not loose any wages.

Jim continued, 'If the police forensic team finish in time, the late shift will be asked to start clearing up the damage. Nothing is to be touched by anyone in the meantime.'

Returning to the inspector, Jim arrived in time to see the recording of Crusher slamming his fist into Reg's stomach. 'Ouch! I can see that hurt. Poor old Reg. No wonder he's got cracked ribs.'

'Once we've identified these thugs, we can get them for unlawful entry and GBH.'

'That means they'll probably get a fine,' suggested Mike.

The inspector sighed. 'You could be right. Sometimes I wonder why on earth I bother to catch these criminals. The sentences they get often doesn't seem to warrant the time and effort it took to apprehend them.'

Mike smiled in agreement.

The constable interrupted, 'I've had the car number plate checked sir, and it's false. It belongs to a Ford Escort that was stolen several months ago and was never recovered.'

The inspector sighed. 'Righto constable, thank you.' He turned to Mike. 'No luck there I'm afraid but with these pictures we should be able to trace them, especially if they've got a police record.'

'I hope so, inspector. Damage to the yachts is expensive but can be fixed. Hitting an older man like Reg can damage him for life.'

'Very true. I presume you will be handing the drugs over to Inspector Fairbourne some time today?'

'Yes, I will. As soon as your forensic blokes have finished, and we can get the place cleaned up, I'll go home and collect them.'

'As these crimes are interlinked, I'll contact Inspector Fairbourne and liaise with him. I'll tell him to expect a visit from you.'

The inspector collected the DVD disc and left after having a few words with the forensic team as they arrived.

'I'm supposed to be meeting Mr Calizares for lunch,' stated Jim. 'We're getting together to discuss his requirements for the yacht we're hoping he'll commission us to build for him.'

'Yes, that's right. In all this confusion, I'd quite forgotten about that appointment. You go ahead, Jim. It's important you don't disappoint him. We need the work more than ever after this setback. I'll stay here and look after things until the police have finished.'

'Thanks, Mike. It's a good job I took the folder home containing all the paperwork for this bid to refresh my memory. I would never have found it in all this mess, but fortunately it's still in my study. I'll motor back and collect it. It'll give me an opportunity to have a shave and a clean up before our meeting.'

'Okay, Jim. It seems we both came out in a rush and forgot everything else,' said Mike, rubbing the stubble on his chin. 'When she gets here I'll ask Carol to remain on the reception to take the calls and explain what's happened to any visitors.'

'Good idea.'

'Drive home a bit more slowly this time. You don't want to pick up another ticket.'

'Too true. If I get too many penalty points they'll ban me from driving for a few months and I'll have to get Mr Charlie to chauffer me around everywhere. He'd like that.'

'I'm sure he would. How is he and Mrs Charlie?'

'They're fine. I'm not sure we really need a full-time housekeeper and chauffer stroke gardener now that Jenny and I are married, but I couldn't bear to let them go now.'

'At least it allows you and Jenny to work without having to worry about housekeeping, like Suzie and I do.'

'That's true. It's only because of my lottery win that allows us such luxuries.'

'But that doesn't exclude you from getting speeding tickets,' reminded Mike.

'No, more's the pity. I'm sure they only stopped me because I was driving a Rolls Royce.'

'What speed were you doing?'

'I was on the M3 motorway and only doing 90 … ish,' protested Jim.

'Hmm. 90ish eh?'

Jim shrugged his shoulders. 'I gather Jenny is going to accompany Suzie to the London meeting.'

'That's right. We ought not to miss out on this seminar in case it turns out to be worthwhile.'

'Right. I'll pop back later on after my meeting with Mr Calizares to see how things are progressing.'

'Okay. See you later, Jim,' said Mike, slapping him on the back.

Jim Sterling left to freshen up and meet his client for lunch.

The workmen had all wandered home. Mike remained to keep an eye on things and rang Suzie to give her the latest news. She was coming to the end of her jog, and confirmed she had arranged to collect Jenny on the way to London and drive on to the meeting.

Suzie said hello to Mr Lockhart and his dog Rex as she passed them on her climb up the wooden steps that lead from the beach to the cliff top. He was a retired widower who lived nearby and was a regular visitor to the beach with his Alsatian dog and often stopped for a chat.

Finishing his telephone call, Mike stood in his office among the papers strewn on the floor and looked out of the window at the yard. All was strangely quiet, apart from the three policemen all dressed in white overalls looking for clues and fingerprints.

It had been a bad start to the day.

Chapter Seven

London Seminar

While Mike waited for the police forensic team to finish checking the boatyard for clues in order for him to ask the afternoon shift to clear up the mess caused by the intruders, Jim was on his way home to have a shave before meeting a client. Suzie was on her way to Weybridge to collect Jenny. She had agreed to accompany her to an important seminar in the capital that Jeremy Pendleton had invited Suzie and Mike to attend. He was secretive about the objective of the seminar but said the organiser of the venue had invited many other boatyards representatives to the meeting, and insisted it would be a good opportunity to discover a new side to the business that SMJ Boatyard could financially benefit from. Suzie was intrigued by his comments and agreed that she and Mike would represent their boatyard at the venue. Because of the break-in, Jenny had agreed to attend the seminar in Mike's place.

The meeting was held in the conference room of 'The City Grande', a smart London hotel that had acquired a good reputation and was striving to become one of the top London hotels. After collecting Jenny from her home Suzie drove to London and parked her Aston Martin in the hotel's underground car park. The two women entered the plush hotel foyer of the newly refurbished Victorian building with high ceilings, ornate cornices and impressive chandeliers. They headed straight for the ladies powder room to freshen up before entering the venue. Suzie added some perfume to the top of her cleavage, peeking above the V-neckline of the white silk blouse she wore. It was one of several similar blouses Mike had bought her after a successful mission. Her outfit was completed by the beige London tailored trouser suit, giving her a smart executive look.

'Do you think my neckline is a bit low? Am I showing too much cleavage?' asked Jenny, who had a similar neckline to her designer dress, but had a fuller figure than Suzie.

'No, I don't think so, that's fine. I'm sure Jeremy will notice it straight away and it may encourage him to take more interest in any offer we choose to make,' suggested Suzie, 'assuming we decide to make an offer when we find out what all this is about.'

The two women finished checking their appearances in the powder room and followed the signs to the seminar. At the door Suzie produced their ticket for the man who wore a dark suit complimented with a black bow tie and white gloves. He took the ticket and smiled at the two women as they entered the room bristling with guests. Most were standing around, mainly in small groups, drinking and chatting. A waiter hovered with his tray of drinks and offered one to the two new arrivals. Both women took a glass but Suzie, who was driving, sipped only enough to get a hint of the taste of Champagne.

'Hmm, not the best Champagne I've ever tasted,' she remarked. 'Perhaps our mystery organiser has a tight budget.'

They wandered into the very brightly lit room, observing that the brightness came from floodlights held by a cameraman and his sound assistant who were filming the proceedings. Sir Jeremy Pendleton MBE, dressed immaculately in a dark Saville Row suit, looked up and saw Suzie and Jenny arrive. He hurriedly approached.

'Good morning, ladies. This is a nice surprise to see you two young lovely ladies. I was expecting to see Mike.'

'He was unavoidably detained on business,' explained Suzie.

'Well, no matter. I'm very glad you could both make it here today,' he gushed, in his usual flamboyant manner planting a kiss on Suzie's hand.

'This is Jenny Sterling, Sir Joseph Sterling's daughter-in-law. You met her at our boatyard last year during our discussions about the requirements for your yacht,' introduced Suzie.

Pendleton grabbed Jenny's hand and planted a kiss on the back. 'Yes, that's right. I recall seeing you at the meeting we had and have admired your beauty from afar,' he proclaimed.

Jenny, the attractive daughter of Jamaican parents who had emigrated to England in the 1950's, was slightly embarrassed at the gesture. 'Thank you,' she stated, looking at Suzie for help.

'That's a gorgeous dress you are wearing,' Pendleton drooled, finding it difficult to divert his eyes from her cleavage.

'Don't mind Jeremy,' suggested Suzie, 'he's always looking for another beauty to conquer, so he automatically goes into his smooth talking ways with his come-to-bed eyes, especially if he sees an attractive woman showing a touch of cleavage.'

'That's a little over-exaggerated Suzie but it worked with you I seem to remember. Or is that supposed to be a secret?' he asked, covering his mouth with a hand and looking wide-eyed at Jenny.

'No, it isn't. But the circumstances were a little different then, Jeremy,' Suzie defended.

'Circumstances may repeat themselves.'

'Unlikely,' she suggested.

Suzie glanced around the room. She recognised many of the attendees who were there; owners or managers of other boat building yards, mainly from the south of England. Her eyes settled on one individual and anger welled up inside her.

'Giles bloody Harman! What the hell is that rat doing here? I though you said you wouldn't be doing business with him after he resorted to theft and murder, Jeremy,' Suzie spat.

'I did, but although I am one of the financial backers of this project and have a strong influence, I don't have the final say about who gets the contract or who's invited to tender. That's Alastaire's domain. It may be better if you forgot about Harman and what he did. I've seen no actual proof that he was involved, I've only been told about it.'

'But that came from a very reliable source – Sir Joseph Sterling MBE no less, as I recall!' barked Suzie.

'That's very true, and I personally no longer have dealings with Harman and have naturally put in a very good word for you and your boatyard with Alastaire.'

Harman, a wiry man with a heavily lined angular face, deep set eyes and thinning hair was the director of a rival boatyard in Devon and was not concerned about the methods he used to gain new business. He saw Suzie and smiled at her with a sickly grin, knowing it would annoy her. She returned his glance with an icy stare. He ignored it and looked away. Suzie seethed. He was the last person she was expecting to see and was not about to forget what he had done. She vowed to get her revenge one day, on the man who hired the thugs to steal Pendleton's yacht from their boatyard. It was taken before SMJ Boatyard had the opportunity to deliver it, and the culprits murdered their night guards to get their hands on the vessel.

Pendleton quickly changed the subject. 'I'd like to introduce you to Alastaire Bignor. He's an independent film producer and will be giving you details of his project shortly,' he said, stepping between the two women and grabbing their arms to propel them forward.

'What sort of project are you talking about, Mr Pendleton?' asked Jenny, guided by him across the room.

'Do call me Jeremy. May I call you Jenny?'

Jenny was slightly perturbed by the request. 'Err … yes, I suppose that would be okay.'

'Good. Alastaire will announce all the details in a few moments,' he stated, chauffeuring the women towards a man in his mid-fifties, with a round face and receding hairline. He was dressed in a dark mauve blazer over a white shirt and sported a brightly coloured silk cravat. Perched on his nose were thick multicoloured framed dark glasses and he was smoking a cigarette through a long black holder.

'Alastaire, I'd like you to meet Suzie Drake and Jenny Sterling, two lovely ladies from SMJ Boatyard in Hamble. That's the boatyard I told you about where my luxury yacht *Julia* was designed and built.'

Blowing out a lungful of smoke he pursed his lips. 'Ah! Yes, Jeremy. I remember,' said Bignor, looking them both up and down. 'Well, hello ladies. If you're ever short of work come and see me. I can use attractive women like you in my productions,' he gushed, removing his glasses and putting the end of one arm between his lips.

'We're both gainfully employed, thank you,' replied Suzie.

'Pity,' Bignor stated, looking at Pendleton and replacing his glasses. 'It must be about time for me to make my important announcement, Jeremy.'

Pendleton glanced around the room, which had around two dozen guests milling about chatting and drinking the free champagne that was on offer. 'I think everyone is here now, Alastaire. Perhaps we should begin. Please excuse us ladies.'

Pendleton padded to the end of the room where a heavy oak, cloth covered table holding a stack of papers and folders waited. The cameraman moved into position to record the event. Standing behind the table, Pendleton gave it a sharp rap with his fist and made his announcement.

'Ladies and gentlemen,' he began with a raised voice, silencing the general murmuring coming from the guests. 'Thank you all for taking the time to attend this seminar. We realise you are all busy people and are wondering what this gathering is about. We intend to keep you in suspense no longer. If you would like to take a seat our host, Mr Alastaire Bignor, will explain the purpose of today's meeting.'

Most of the guests wandered over to the comfortable armchairs facing the table and sat down, including Suzie and Jenny, after glancing around to make sure Harman was not nearby. A few others stood at the rear behind the chairs sipping their Champagne.

Bignor approached the table and nodded. 'Thank you, Jeremy.' He addressed the guests. 'Good morning ladies and gentlemen. I trust you've all been offered a glass of bubbly.'

A general murmur of thanks issued from the attendees.

'Good. I shan't keep you very long. I know you all have busy boatyards to manage and are anxious to get back to them, and many of you have travelled quite a long way to get here this morning.'

There were murmurs of agreement and heads nodding from a few of the guests.

'No doubt some of you may not be familiar with me or my work?'

The room remained silent, with no one having heard of this host.

Bignor gave a slightly embarrassed smile and continued. 'I am an independent film producer and have made a number of films for the cinema and television, including 'My Life With The Eskimos', 'Another Day By The Sea' and the hard-hitting television documentary 'Internet Scams In Your Street' ...'

The producer went on to list other films and television programmes he had been associated with. Nobody in the room had heard of any of the films, and only a few recognised the television shows he named, though a few grunts of recognition were made to break the embarrassing silence that hung over the proceedings.

Bignor continued, 'Having successfully completed those projects, I now have a new one that I am working on, which I am sure will be successful and will be snapped up by the television companies. This is where you come in. I have written the script and I am preparing to film a pilot show and I need to establish some locations etcetera. The show concerns two good-looking millionaire friends and rivals who each own a luxury motor yacht, travel around the world on them, and who find themselves in various scrapes and difficulties.'

'Like detectives you mean?' asked one man.

'Yes, sort of. They become involved in other peoples problems and with panache and expertise, plus a few fights and scrapes, help them to resolve their problem. They are accompanied by mainly scantily clad attractive females who enjoy their company and like to sail from country to country on a luxury yacht visiting exotic places beneath a sun-kissed sky,' he expounded, stretching a hand out into the air to suggest the beauty of an attractive balmy scene.

'So that's the sort of production he wants us for,' whispered Suzie to Jenny.

She smiled. 'Scantily clad on a luxury yacht. And I bet he doesn't even pay very much. One has to be satisfied with exotic places under a sun-kissed sky,' she mocked.

'What I am looking for is a working, typically English boatyard location,' stated Bignor, 'that has a picturesque outlook and which is suitable for my camera equipment. I will also need the use of another luxury yacht for some of the filming. Sir Jeremy Pendleton MBE,' he turned and smiled at him, 'has kindly agreed to put his yacht *Julia* at my disposal but I will naturally require the use of a second one for the series. One for each of my main characters,' he explained.

'So, not only scantily clad but on our own luxury yacht,' suggested Jenny.

The two women tried to hide their smiles but Pendleton saw them and wondered what they were joking about.

'I'm sure you must have a few questions to ask,' suggested Bignor.

'How long will you need this yacht and boatyard for?' asked Suzie.

'Initially, I will need the boatyard for a few days, providing the weather is good and filming is not held up. The yacht I will need for a little longer, about three to four weeks to get the pilot show in the can. The completed episode will last about an hour so that should give me enough time to get all the shots I need.'

'And after that?'

'That will depend on whether the television companies decide to go ahead with a series.'

'So, you are not sure of filming anything other than the pilot show?' Suzie pressed.

'No, not at the moment, though I am certain that if the pilot is well produced the TV companies will look on a series favourably. I have already had preliminary discussions with them about the format of the show and I received a positive response.'

'How much are you paying for the use of a boatyard and a luxury yacht for three or four weeks?' asked Harman, standing near the back and ever thinking about the financial side of the arrangement.

'Payment will be made following discussions with the boatyard owners, not forgetting that my film will be shown on national television and will give you much sort-after free advertising for your business.'

'Does that mean you are not going to pay very much?' suggested Harman.

'Why don't you send a couple of thugs round like you did to our boatyard, to see if you can batter him into agreeing to pay more?' suggested Suzie in a loud aggressive voice making sure everyone in the room heard.

Harman looked embarrassed and Jeremy Pendleton stepped in to temper the situation before it got out of hand. 'I'm sure we don't want to get into any arguments about how much the payments will be. As Mr Bignor has explained, it is a matter for negotiation with each boatyard that is suitable and willing to take advantage of this unique offer.'

It was Harman's turn to seethe. Many of the boatyard owners had heard rumours about his underhanded tactics, but thought it unlikely to be true that his hirelings had resorted to murder to achieve his aim. Hearing Suzie's uncompromising allegation made them realise that for her it was real and was probably true, and she was not about to let Harman forget it. The guests turned to stare at him. He looked around at the sea of faces challenging him to deny the accusations.

He turned and headed for the exit. 'You'll hear from my lawyers in the morning, Miss Drake,' he thundered.

'Good. I look forward to that,' Suzie shouted in reply as he marched towards the door. Harman stormed from the room, slamming shut the door behind him. Suzie looked at Pendleton. 'I'm sorry about that, Jeremy, but he's a crook and he makes my blood boil and I couldn't resist the opportunity to have a go at him.'

'Good for you,' one guest announced. 'I've had dealings with him and he's not a very nice man.'

A couple of other men grunted their agreement. 'Yeah, that's right,' one added.

Pendleton took in a deep breath. 'Well, that's another issue entirely, so perhaps after that little spat we can all get back to discussing the reason why we are all here today.'

He smiled at Bignor who took up the conversation. 'Thank you, Jeremy. I think I've more or less given you all an outline of what I am looking for. Everything I've said about the project is contained in these notes,' he said, tapping a pile of papers on the table, 'which I would like you to collect and read. If you wish to be considered for the project for either your boatyard or one of your yachts, please let me know as soon as possible so I can discuss it with you. There are details of how to get in touch with me in the notes. Are there any more questions?'

'When do you expect to start filming?' one guest asked.

'If a suitable location can be found quickly and financial agreement reached with the boatyard owners, we could start filming within the next few weeks. I need good weather for the English boatyard scenes but much of the filming will be done abroad, in picturesque locations where there is a better chance of the sun shining for most of the day. It will also add a touch of class to the show.'

'Where abroad?' the guest persisted. 'This presumably means the yacht will be needed for quite a long time if you are given a series and won't be available for sale or hire.'

'Probably the Mediterranean island of Ibiza. I am still negotiating with an owner to rent his villa for a few days. And yes, if a series is booked, the yacht will be required for a few months. The cost for that will be a matter for negotiation.'

'Separate to the pilot show negotiations?'

'Yes, separate.'

Pendleton added, 'You should also realise that if the series is a big success, as I would expect, then your yacht will become much more desirable to hire out the rest of the year. People like to boast that their holiday was taken aboard a famous yacht used in a television series.'

The room remained quiet. Many of the guests looked as if they were not sure this was a good idea to get involved with.

'Any more questions?' asked Bignor. Nobody else spoke up. 'In that case ladies and gentlemen, thank you for your time. I look forward to hearing from some of you quite soon. If any of you want to discuss anything in more detail with me now, I will be available for the next half an hour or so.'

Murmurs broke the silence as the attendees stood and collected their notes. Some wandered to the exit in groups discussing what they had heard while others chatted to Bignor. Pendleton stepped over to Suzie and Jenny who were picking up their notes.

'Would you ladies do me the honour of accompanying me to lunch? We could discuss Alastaire's project in more detail.'

'Thank you, Jeremy. That is very nice of you, but we had a break-in at the boatyard last night and I think we should return to see what progress the police are making,' suggested Suzie, looking for a good reason to fend off Pendleton's advances. 'That's the reason why Jenny has joined me today instead of Mike.'

'Oh, I see. I'm sorry about your problem. Your boatyard seems to attract trouble, Suzie. Still, it meant I was able to see both of you two lovely ladies here this morning so it's not all bad news.'

Suzie smiled. 'Perhaps, when we've looked at the project in more detail, if we are interested then we may take you up on your offer to discuss the matter over lunch.'

'Good. I look forward to that.'

Suzie and Jenny left the hotel. 'Pendleton doesn't give up easily, does he?' Jenny asked.

'No, he doesn't. Don't tell Mike, but I rather enjoy our little exchanges. Crossing swords with Jeremy has become a bit of a challenge to keep him at bay.'

'Rather you than me. I don't know what Jim would say if he thought someone else was making advances towards me in order to get me into his bed.'

The two women laughed at the situation as they returned to their car.

Back in the hotel conference room, Alastaire Bignor put a hand on Jeremy Pendleton's shoulder. 'Tell me a little more about that good looking feisty woman, Jeremy.'

'Do you mean Suzie Drake from SMJ Boatyard?'

'Yes, that's the one. I could do with a woman like that in my production. She interests me.'

Chapter Eight

Break-In

After fending off Jeremy Pendleton's advances at a London seminar organised to find a suitable luxury yacht and boatyard location for Alastaire Bignor's television pilot show, Suzie and Jenny wandered into a nearby restaurant. Among the ceaseless hubbub of chatter they watched London traffic and pedestrians bustle pass by as they discussed the project over a quick lunch. They sat at one of the few spare seats in the restaurant with nearby office workers, many of them with a regular booking, filling most of the tables.

With lunch over, Suzie drove them back to her south coast home. 'I need to pick up a few papers before we go to the boatyard,' she told Jenny.

'Okay. That's fine. Jim's meeting me at the yard later this afternoon after he's seen a customer.'

'Who's he seeing?'

'Mr Calizares. Jim's put a lot of effort into persuading him to have his yacht built at our yard instead of at your old enemy Harman's yard in Devon.'

'Harman! Well I hope he succeeds and Harman knows which yard has beaten him.'

'I'm sure he will. Jim tells me that Harman has offered Mr Calizares certain incentives, which amount to bribes to get him to place the order with them. Jim's reading of Mr Calizares is that he's a straightforward honest man and hopefully has been put off by Harman's unprincipled tactics.'

'Let's hope he's right. It would give me great pleasure to see that rat beaten to a lucrative contract.'

Leaving the A27 dual carriageway and motoring along the winding coast road, they approached the large detached house that Mike and Suzie had purchased after their return from a mission in Africa. The property was surrounded by a ten foot high wall and enclosed behind an electronic wrought iron gate, courtesy of the previous owner who had valuables he wished to protect. Suzie pressed a button on the remote control to open the gate and had to brake hard when it unexpectedly remained closed. Her car screeched to a halt.

'That's strange. It worked okay this morning when I left. The battery must be flat. What a nuisance,' she declared, slapping the remote and pressing the button several times again, but to no avail.

'The gate doesn't look to be shut properly,' observed Jenny.

The two women stepped from the car and approached. They discovered the gate was slightly ajar.

Inspecting the lock, Suzie declared, 'The gate's been forced open. The lock is broken.'

'There's a car partially hidden, parked at the side of the house,' pointed Jenny.

'Yes, I see it. We must have burglars. I'll ring Mike to let him know,' said Suzie, punching the buttons on her mobile.

'Hello, luv. How did your meeting go?' Mike asked, seeing the familiar number displayed on his phone.

'I'll tell you about that later. I'm standing outside our gate. It didn't open when I pressed the remote and on closer inspection, Jenny and I can see it's been forced open. Someone's inside our house. There's a car hidden by the side, I can just see the front of the bonnet. Do you think I should call the police or go in?'

'No, don't go in. What make of car is it? Can you tell?'

'I can see the badge, it's a Mercedes.'

'What colour?'

'I can't quite make that out, but it's light, either white or possibly light blue.'

'That sounds as if it's the car that Reg described driven by the hooligans who beat him up and ransacked our yard.'

'What were they looking for – the drugs?'

'Yes, that's right. The drugs we found in *Quester*'s engine. I brought them home last night and in the rush to get here this morning I forgot about them. They're still in the safe – or were. It has to be the same gang. They must still be looking for them and may have found them by now. If they're doing the same sort of damage they did to our yacht and offices, I wouldn't like to think what out home will look like afterwards.'

'That settles it. The police will take too long to get here. I've got a gun in the car. I'm going to confront them.'

'No! Don't! Wait until I get there. I was just about to leave anyway.'

'You hurry here as quickly as you can. I'm not going to let some thugs smash up my home if I can help it. I'm going in.'

'I'm coming with you,' declared Jenny.

'Jenny's coming in with me,' stated Suzie.

'I'm on my way. I'll be there as quick as I can,' Mike said slapping his mobile shut, grabbing his leather jacket and dashing to his motorcycle.

He met Jim in the yard, returning from his meeting with Mr Calizares.

'Suzie's just rung me. There's a break-in at our house and the intruders are still inside. The two girls are there and are armed. They're going in to investigate. I'm hurrying home on *Bonnie*,' he said, revving up the motorbike.

'I'll be right behind you,' said Jim, dashing towards his Rolls Royce as Mike's motorbike flew out of the yard with the tyres squealing and smoke from the burning rubber trailing behind.

At the house Suzie pocketed her mobile. She opened a hidden compartment behind the glove box in their car and pulled out two Walther PPK pistols.

'Your driveway's very open. Someone may see us sneaking in,' Jenny observed.

'That's true but I know another way in. There's a tree branch that hangs over the wall around the side. I've got my keys so we can get in through the back door,' Suzie said.

They scrambled back into the car and Suzie drove around to the side of the house and parked beneath the branch of an oak tree that jutted out above the wall. Climbing on to the car roof, the two women clutched the overhanging branch, swung over the wall and dropped to the ground.

The large rear garden, mainly covered by lawn, was bordered by shrubs and perennials. A garden shed stood in one corner and a purpose built gazebo, situated near the opposite corner, stood alongside a pond stocked with many goldfish. Mike and Suzie had little time for gardening and employed a man to visit once a week to keep the garden tidy and mow the lawn. They enjoyed relaxing in the gazebo during the better weather, usually while sipping a Pimms and watching the fish swim about.

'We would have to be dressed in our best clothes while doing this, wouldn't we?' complained Suzie.

'Not to worry, it'll be a good reason to persuade Mike to but you a new outfit,' suggested Jenny.

'Hmm, that's true! The alarm isn't ringing, so they must have disabled it,' Suzie declared. 'That means I should be able to unlock the back door without them hearing us, if I'm quiet enough.'

Jenny nodded and the two women bent low, scurried to the rear of the house and crouched near the back door.

'So far, so good,' Suzie declared.

She inserted the key into the lock, gently twisted it and heard the tongue snap back. Gently pushing the door open, Suzie moved into a utility area housing a freezer, washing machine and an assortment of outdoor items including several pairs of boots, black for him and green for her, and garden shoes that were nearly new due to the owners wearing them so infrequently.

'We're in luck. The door into the hallway is still closed,' she whispered, tiptoeing through the room. Jenny followed.

Checking her gun, Suzie slowly pressed down the handle of the door, pulled it open a few inches and peered into the hallway. Nobody was visible but she could hear crashing noises coming from the living room and voices from men upstairs, rummaging through the bedrooms.

Suzie turned to Jenny, 'You watch my back. There's someone in the living room and more of them upstairs. I'm going to tackled whoever's down here first.'

'Okay. Be careful,' she implored.

Both Suzie and Jenny had experience of operating under difficult conditions when on active service in Africa, and found their latent skills rising to the fore at the first sign of danger. Suzie crept into the hallway clasping her gun in both hands with arms extended. Jenny did the same, pointing at the stairway. They moved shoulder to shoulder in unison towards the living room and stopped at the open doorway.

Suzie glanced at Jenny. 'Ready?' she whispered.

She nodded without taking her eyes from the stairs, as she listened to the movement of someone in the bedrooms above.

Smartly entering the living room with her gun at the ready Suzie saw a man with his back to her, bent over while rummaging through drawers in the sideboard and throwing everything out that was of no interest. Anger welled up in her as she glanced at the senseless mess and destruction being wrought on her home.

Kashif Phadkar froze when the cold barrel of a gun touched the back of his neck.

'One slight twitch and I'll blow your bloody head off,' whispered Suzie, with gritted teeth in a tone of voice that left the man in no doubt she was very angry and meant every word of it.

With eyes wide open at the sudden knowledge any careless movement could bring sudden death, the man slowly stood up. Suzie's gun came crashing down on his head knocking him unconscious. He dropped to the floor, falling forwards and colliding into the sideboard as he fell, breaking ornaments and sending them crashing to the floor.

'Shit! The others might hear that,' cursed Suzie, turning to see Jenny in the doorway, glancing in to investigation the noise and see for herself that everything was okay.

'Can't you kill him a bit more quietly?' she asked in a loud whisper, stepping into the room.

'I didn't kill him; I've just knocked him out. I didn't know what else to do, with more of them upstairs.'

From the corner of her eye, Suzie saw movement and looked up to see two men descending the stairs brandishing guns. 'Look out!' she cried, as she and Jenny scrambled to either side of the living room doorway.

The men on the stairs saw them and let loose with a volley of shots. The bullets gouged lumps out of the doorframe and zipped into the room. Suzie whipped an arm around the doorway and fired back a volley of shots blindly in the direction of the men. One of her bullets nicked the side of Crusher's leg. He screamed out in pain, lost his balance and crashed down each step to the bottom of the stairs. His accomplice scrambled down behind him firing wildly into the room to prevent any return fire. At the bottom he grabbed Crusher and helped him to his feet.

While Suzie and Jenny waited for the shooting to stop, unseen by them Phadkar regained consciousness. Suzie cautiously peered around the door frame and saw a limping Crusher leaning on his mate Lefty, who helped him towards the front door. Seeing Suzie he thrust a gun in her direction. She turned back sharply, and was confronted by Phadkar who had sneaked up behind a preoccupied Jenny and dug his gun into her side.

'Drop your weapon,' he demanded.

Jenny looked at Suzie with an apologetic look for allowing the man to sneak up behind her. She dropped her gun to the floor.

'Now kick it away.'

Jenny kicked the gun away. Phadkar was not tall enough to put an arm right around her neck and instead stood behind Jenny and clutched her Adam's apple. He held his gun to her head.

'Drop your weapon or I'll kill her,' he told Suzie.

'I don't think so. If you shoot her you'll have lost your protection and I will put a bullet in your head,' stated Suzie.

She was playing mind games. It was a skill she learnt in her chequered past, and was good at. She needed to be, she was gambling with Jenny's life.

'If you drop your gun you will live. If you don't you will almost certainly die.'

Kashif Phadkar hesitated. He wondered what he should do, peering over Jenny's shoulder at this attractive but deadly woman holding a gun, a weapon she held with authority and he knew she was not afraid to use. With only a quarter of his face showing he made his move, deciding his best chance of survival was to attack.

Swinging his gun round to aim at Suzie, removed some of his cover. It was a move she had anticipated. She was expecting him to take the gamble and try to shoot her. His judgement was wrong, and with one swift movement Suzie jerked her gun into position and fired. The bullet ploughed into the right side of Phadkar's forehead. The impact spun his body round and slammed him backwards, crashing to the floor and pulling Jenny with him.

The front door was banged open wide as the two thugs scrambled to their car while wondering what the shot had meant for their boss.

Suzie helped a blood spattered Jenny to her feet.

'Are you okay?' she asked.

'Yes, thanks. That bugger hurt me with his grip,' Jenny said holding her throat and wiping away some of the blood from her face.

'Sorry about that. I had no choice.'

'I know. That was a close thing. It's a good job your aim is still true,' she remarked. 'I was so concerned with the men firing at us from the hallway that I didn't see him sneak up on me.'

The Mercedes revved up and roared off down the driveway showering gravel in all directions. The wheels spun furiously as the tyres fought to grip the surface with the driver struggling to keep the car in a straight line. It smashed through the unlocked gates, crashing them back against the uprights. Suzie dashed to the front door with her gun ready to fire, but she was too late. She lowered her gun and watched the car speed off down the coast road towards the dual carriageway before wandering back to the dining room. Jenny was looking shivery.

'Are you sure you're okay?' she asked.

'I feel a bit shaky and my throat hurts like hell, he gripped it so tightly.'

'Sit down in the armchair. I'll get you a drink.'

Suzie helped Jenny to the chair and poured her a large brandy.

'Sip it slowly. It'll ease the pain and calm you down.' Jenny took a few sips. 'Okay, now?'

'Yes, thanks, I'm fine. It's been quite a while since I was involved in a shooting. I'd almost forgotten how horrible it is to see someone killed this close up,' she said, looking at the blood spattered body of Phadkar.

'Yes, I understand. The last time must have been when we were in the African jungle fighting those rebel soldiers,' Suzie stated.

'Yes, that's right.'

'I seem to remember your aim was very good that day.'

'That was the last time I fired a gun until today, and my target that day was at a distance. I've given up rifle shooting since Jim and I were married.'

'As a mercenary I became hardened to the killings I saw in Africa. It doesn't affect me as much as it does you, though I'm very glad to say that part of our lives is behind Mike and me.'

'That's where you met him, isn't it?'

'Yes. That was about the best thing that happened to me out there,' Suzie recalled, staring at the ring on her finger. 'Now all I've got to do is get him up the aisle.'

Jenny smiled, breaking the tension. 'And that might not be so easy.'

'You're right. He fancies that he's a bit of a ladies man and he's right, but at least I'm making some progress.'

'What are we going to do about this dead bloke?' Jenny asked.

'What do you think is best? Should we ring the police or wait for Mike? He should be here soon. Maybe it's best to ask Sir Joseph?'

'That's a good idea. I'll ring dad. He'll know what to do.'

'Mike's probably breaking the speed limit to get here. I'll ring him first to let him know what's happened and assure him we're both okay. I'll ask him to slow down, but it probably won't make much difference. That's if his mobile is on and connected into his helmet,' Suzie said grabbing the telephone.

Mike's mobile was on and he listened to Suzie's account of the fight while charging down the A27 at high speed. 'You're both okay though?'

'Yes, we're fine, but Jenny's a bit shaken. Don't go breaking your neck to get here quickly. Everything is under control, the other men have fled. Jenny's going to ring Sir Joseph to find out what's the best thing for us to do about the body.'

'Good idea.'

'Their Mercedes was light blue like you suggested, and it must have been damaged when they charged through our gates. They're hanging off the hinges now, and our alarm console in the hall has taken a bashing. All the wires have been ripped out.'

'Bastards! More expense. Our security system didn't do much good.'

'Perhaps we should get it changed?'

'Sounds like a good idea. I'm approaching the carriageway turnoff. Jim is right behind me. We should be there in a few minutes.'

'Okay, Mike.'

'Wait! There's a light blue Mercedes just exited the coast road and going like a bat out of hell, and there's damage to the front of the car. That must be our intruders. I'm going to follow them and see where they go.'

'Okay, but do be careful and keep in touch.'

'I will,' agreed Mike, pulling in to the side of the road and flagging Jim down. His Rolls screeched to a halt.

'I'm going to follow that Merc,' he said, pointing to a car on the far carriageway. 'I'm sure it's our intruder's car. There's been shooting at the house but the girls are both okay, though Jenny's had a bit of a rough time by the sounds of it. Can you check on them to make sure there's no problems?'

'Can do,' agreed Jim. 'Go careful.'

'I will,' said Mike, revving up the motorcycle.

He crossed the carriageway bridge and roared off after the Mercedes as it motored down the dual carriageway travelling westward, back in the direction Mike had come from. Jim put the Rolls into drive, and pressed on to the house, eager to make sure the women were unharmed.

Chapter Nine

Towards London

While Mike followed the Mercedes vehicle holding the suspected intruders who broke into his home to search for their drugs, Jenny rang her father-in-law Sir Joseph Sterling. She needed his advice on what they should do about the body of the intruder Suzie had killed at their home.

Sir Joseph was an ex-diplomat who was close to the end of his working career and after losing his wife a few years previously had taken a Whitehall desk job as a trouble shooter for the government on police, intelligence and security matters at the Foreign and Commonwealth Office in London. Jenny explained the situation and was relieved that he was both calm about the matter and able to say he would take care of things. This was not the first time he had been asked to sort out such a delicate problem for his son or daughter-in-law.

'I'll send Sandy round to collect the body. It'll probably take him a couple of hours or more to reach you and I'll get Colin Brooke to sort things out with the relevant authorities afterwards,' he said, dropping his rimless glasses on the desk blotting pad and running a hand through his thick grey hair.

'Thanks, Dad.'

'Does this have anything to do with the break-in at your boatyard last night?'

'Yes, we think so. News travels fast. How do you know about that?'

'I've been keeping an eye on things since I learned that your yacht *Quester* was involved in that drug smuggling incident with the coastguard. Jim told me what happened.'

'Oh, I see. Did he tell you we found drugs in the *Quester's* engine sump yesterday afternoon while we were repairing her? That's what they were after when poor Reg was beaten up.'

'No, I didn't know that. It could explain recent events,' he said, slipping on his glasses and making a note on his jotter pad.

'Mike was unable to reach the policeman in charge of the case last evening so he took the drugs home and locked them in the safe. Reg was forced to tell them Mike took the drugs with him when he left the yard so we suspect that's what these men were looking for here.'

'Yes, it seems likely. Do you know if they found them?'

'No, I don't. Suzie hasn't looked yet. She's surveying the damage they've done to almost every room in the house in their search for them.'

'Let me know when she does.'

'Okay. There's something else.'

'More?'

'Yes. Suzie rang Mike to tell him about the break-in. While he was racing here on his motorbike, he thinks he saw the car with the other two men escaping. They drove on to the A27 and he's following them.'

'Do you know which direction they're heading?'

'No, not until we contact Mike.'

'Try to find out. If they're coming into the London area tell him not to go charging in when they get to their destination, but to let me know. I'll ask Colin Brooke to organise a police raid on the premises. We need to catch these drug smugglers and close down their operation before any more of that awful stuff gets on to the streets.'

'Okay, Dad. Thanks very much. I'll ring again when I've more news. 'Bye.'

Colin Brooke was a tough-looking detective inspector with Special Branch, who stood over six-foot tall, and over time had become a friend of Sir Joseph as well as a work colleague. His friendly grey eyes, clef chin and dark complexion gave him a handsome appearance that women found attractive, though he had remained a bachelor. This was mainly because of the unsociable hours he was sometimes obliged to keep because of his job. It was a job he cherished and would not give up easily.

Suzie descended the stairs and wandered into the living room with a blanket to cover Phadkar's body. 'Everything okay?' she asked.

'Yes. Dad said he'd sort things out. Sandy's on his way to collect the body, but it'll take him a while to get here,' Jenny said, staring at the shape of Kashif Phadkar's crumpled corpse with the blanket now draped over him.

'Okay, that's good. I'm not sure what I'd do without his help sometimes.'

'He wants Mike to contact him when the men he's following get to their destination if it's in the London area, so that Colin Brooke can organise a police raid on their premises.'

'I'll let Mike know.'

'He'd also like to know if they found the drugs.'

'Yes, they did. It looks as if they had an easier job getting into this safe than the one at the boatyard. It's a combination safe and it's wide open.'

'One of them must be a safecracker.'

'Yes, probably. They've wrecked upstairs, and obviously had a quite a job to find the safe in the first place.'

'Why? Where's it hidden?'

'Underneath the bed in the spare back bedroom.'

'Under the bed! That's an unusual place for a safe, isn't it?'

'Yes. It was fitted there by our strange and cautious previous owner to protect his coins and banknotes. It seems he wanted to be near them at night in case burglars got into the house.'

'I bet he kept a gun under his pillow as well,' chuckled Jenny.

'You're probably right and that sounds like a good idea. I'll have to start doing that again I reckon now that we've had two break-ins.'

'And talking of guns,' Jenny picked up her gun and handed it back to Suzie.

'Thanks. I'd better put these back in the car, and see what sort of damage those crooks have done to the gate.'

'I'll have a wash and clean up,' said Jenny, looking in the mirror at the blood spattered on her face and shoulder. 'I doubt if I'll get these blood stains out of my dress. But then, after what's happened I don't think I'd want to wear it again anyway.'

'Like we suggested before, it'll also give you a good excuse to tell Jim that you need a new outfit,' Suzie said, heading for the front door, 'and it might be better if we went into the kitchen so we don't have to be near that body.'

'Good idea.'

Suzie returned the guns to their hiding place, and drove their car into the garage as Jim's Rolls Royce sped through the open gateway and skidded to a halt on the gravel.

He jumped from the vehicle. 'Are you girls okay? Mike said there'd been shooting.'

'Of course we are. We know how to take care of ourselves,' Suzie maintained.

They entered the house. Jenny rushed to her husband and they hugged each other.

'What happened?' he asked. 'Your neck looks very red.'

'This man grabbed me by the throat and was threatening to shoot me. Suzie shot him. He's dead,' Jenny said, glancing through the doorway at the body lying on the floor.

Jim looked at Phadkar's fallen shape and was a little shocked. 'I thought you'd left all that cloak and dagger stuff behind you.'

'So did I. It was a bit scary for a moment,' Jenny said.

'But you're okay?'

'Yes, I'm fine, just a little shaken,' she admitted, rubbing her throat.

The trio went into the kitchen and Suzie filled the kettle and switched it on. 'We could all probably do with a nice cup of tea,' she announced to nodding of heads. 'The gate has been practically knocked off its hinges, it must have done quite a bit of damaged to the front of their car. I'll ring Mike and bring him up to date on things and see which direction he's heading.'

Listening to Suzie on his mobile while he continued to follow the light blue Mercedes, Mike remarked, 'We're bombing along the A3 towards London. They must be in a great hurry 'cos they haven't done less than 85 mph since they reached the motorway.'

'You be careful,' exhorted Suzie.

'Me and *Bonnie* are fine. It's been a while since we had a good burn-up. She's loving it.'

'And so are you by the sounds of it.'

'Can't disagree with that.'

'Jim's arrived. He and Jenny are going to stay until Sandy gets here to collect the body.'

'Good.'

'Remember, telephone Sir Joseph when you get there and don't go charging in. I know what you're like. Let the police handle it.'

'Okay, luv. I'll ring you again when I arrive.'

Jenny passed the information on to Sir Joseph. After downing their cups of tea she, Jim and Suzie started to clean up the untidy state of the bedrooms.

'Look at this mess,' said Suzie, standing in her master bedroom surveying all the things that had been thrown onto the floor, including all their clothes from the wardrobe. 'They've emptied everything out of all my dressing table drawers.'

'We'll soon get it tidied up,' Jim said.

The three of them busied themselves replacing the unbroken items and clearing away the smashed things. They worked their way through the four bedrooms.

When they finished, Suzie said, 'Thanks very much you two. The whole place looks a lot better now.

'And it's helped me to do something while getting over the shock of what happened,' declared Jenny.

'Good. It must be time for another cup of tea.'

They returned to the kitchen and Suzie brewed them all a drink as they chatted about their terrible ordeal to Jim while they waited for Sandy to arrive. Suzie decided to postpone clearing up the mess in the living room until after the body had been removed.

It had been an eventful day with both the boatyard and their house broken into, Reg beaten up and in hospital, Suzie fending off the attentions of Jeremy Pendleton and annoying Giles Harman before shooting dead an intruder, and it was still only five o'clock in the afternoon.

Chapter Ten

The Rosy Cheeks Nightclub

With the knowledge that Suzie and Jenny were now safe and Jim had joined them, Mike raced along on his motorbike trailing the Mercedes on the A3 heading towards London. The car carried the men he was convinced had broken into his house looking for their drugs, and had created a lot of damage in their search.

Mike allowed several cars to stay between them to ensure they were unaware of the motorbike following them. The two occupants were so anxious to get back to base and so engrossed in discussing what had happened, the thought that anyone would be following in a car let alone on a motorcycle did not occur to them. This was especially so for Crusher who gave much of his attention to a painful leg wound that was bleeding. They travelled through Guildford and on to Wimbledon. The closer they came to Central London the more congested the traffic became and Lefty had to throttle back and slow down to 60 mph or less, much to their annoyance. While they journeyed the pair rehearsed their excuses in an attempt to explain their reasons for returning without Kashif Phadkar, uncertain what fate may have befallen him.

At Clapham they turned off the A3 on to the A2217. They motored through crowded streets where Mike had difficulty in remaining behind them because of the slow congested traffic that held up cars, but a motorcycle was able to weave through. The Mercedes turned on to a side road and pulled into a yard at the back entrance to 'The Rosy Cheeks Nightclub' in Brixton.

The name of the nightclub shone out from a bright red neon sign mounted above the entrance door next to the outline of a topless dancer lit in ever changing flashing colours. The nightclub catered for private members who wanted to drink into the early hours of the morning while watching the strippers going through their act. They enjoyed the attentions of the scantily-clad glamorous hostesses who did their best to persuade them to part with more of their cash. The nightclub had been raided by the police on several occasions in their search for drugs, but the owners were careful and none had been found.

Mike watched the Mercedes driven into the yard and parked by the back door. He stopped in a lay-by and observed Crusher limp into the nightclub helped by his mate, Lefty. It was nearly seven o'clock; the bright sunshine of the day had begun to recede as the first customers pushed their way through the front door of the nightclub and head to the bar for a drink. Soon the loud music would blare out, and the bar area would fill up with members and thick cigarette smoke. Because this was a private nightclub, the smoking ban did not have to be observed and customers were happy to puff away all night on their cigarettes and cigars. Soon the gambling machines would begin to rattle swallowing up the coins fed into them and members would be eager to see the strippers go through their erotic act.

Limping into the office past the sign on the door which read 'The Boss - knock and wait', Crusher and Lefty were greeted by Mr Khurram Phadkar who with his twin brother Kashif ran the nightclub and drugs operation.

Looking up from his desk he asked, 'What happened to you two, and where's my brother?'

'We don't know.'

'Don't know!' yelled Phadkar. 'What do you mean you don't know?'

In a shaky voice Crusher reported, 'We were searching the boatyard man's house like we were told, and we located a hidden safe in one of the bedrooms.'

'That's right,' chipped in Lefty, anxious to confirm Crusher's story. 'I cracked the combination and got it open. Inside we found the packages of drugs we were looking for.'

Crusher added, 'We collected them and were going down the stairs when we spotted two women in the dining room. The two women appeared from nowhere, and they were both armed with guns and started shooting at us,'

'Shooting? What happened?' said Phadkar getting to his feet, a worried frown crossing his brow.

'They both fired at us, and I got hit in the leg when we went down to help your brother,' maintained Crusher, in an attempt to diffuse the accusations he guessed would be levelled at them. 'And if it wasn't for Lefty here, I might not have got out of the house alive.'

'So, where is my brother?' Phadkar yelled, as if more volume would encourage an answer.

'He was searching downstairs in the living room where the two women were, while we checked upstairs in the bedrooms. We don't know what happened to him,' Crusher said.

'What do you mean you don't know? You mean to tell me you left my brother there to deal with two gun-toting women?' he raged.

'We didn't know what else to do. The women were firing at us from the living room so we thought he might have already got out and be waiting in the car, but when we reached it he wasn't there.'

'You idiots should have gone back for him.'

'I'd got hold of the packages we went for, but I was bleeding badly and we needed to get away,' Crusher said, pointing to his bloodstained trouser leg while offering the drugs to Phadkar in the hope it would temper his rage.

It did not.

'So, you turned and ran, and left my brother to deal with these two women on his own,' he complained, snatching the package.

'We waited outside the gate for a few minutes to see if he came out of the house, but he didn't,' lied Crusher.

Phadkar banged his fist down on the desk. 'Then bloody-well go back there and find out what's happened to him. And take Jake with you. He seems to be the only one around here who knows what he's doing.'

'I need to get my leg seen to,' pleaded Crusher.

'Aah! Get Angie to look at it,' he waved with a fist. 'She's done some nursing. Lefty, you go back with Jake. And do not come back until you find out what has happened to my brother. If the police have got him, I want to know.'

'Okay, boss,' Lefty said, happy to leave the room to find Jake Crossman.

Crusher was about to follow him when Phadkar called to him, 'Crusher, tell Lefty I checked the package and found you had snatched the wrong one. You didn't get the drugs after all. He's got a bit of a loose tongue, and I don't want people to know I have drugs on the premises. I will have to re-contact my buyer and let him know I've got them back and I am not sure when they will collect them. I don't like leaving drugs here in case there's another police raid, so it is better nobody else knows about it. Do you understand?' he asked, his native Pakistani accent stronger because of his anxiety.

'Yeah. Okay, boss.'

Crusher hobbled from the room to give Lefty the message and get his leg attended to by Angie. Phadkar waited until he closed the door before inspecting the package. He satisfied himself that it was the drugs before he opened his secret safe in which to hide them. He lifted a corner of the carpet and peeled it back to reveal wooden floorboards. Prizing up four short lengths exposed his safe. He stashed the drugs away and span the combination dial to make sure the safe was locked. He replaced the floorboards and carpet, treading it down with his foot to ensure it looked undisturbed.

Phadkar dumped his wiry frame into the chair at his desk, held his hands in his head and breathed out a frustrating sigh.

Jake Crossman barged into the office followed by Lefty. 'You want me and Lefty to find your brother?' he asked, to confirm the arrangement.

'Yes, Jake. I need someone who I can trust to do the job right. I don't know what the matter is all of a sudden. Nothing seems to be going smoothly,' he complained. 'First we get our shipment of drugs stolen and my nephew and two of our men are murdered, then we find out some boatyard owner has found the packages and taken them home, and when we go to retrieve them, there is shooting and my brother is left on his own to deal with two armed women. It has not been a good time these past few days.'

'I'll sort it out,' assured Crossman. 'I'll take the black Merc. The other one's got quite a lot of damage to the front. I don't want to be stopped by the police.'

'Good idea. I'll tell one of the boys to put the other one in the garage for repairs,' said Phadkar.

'Come on, Lefty. Let's go,' Crossman beckoned.

The pair left the nightclub to carry out their task.

*　　*　　*

While he waited outside the nightclub, Mike contacted Sir Joseph with the name and address and he in turn spoke with DI Colin Brooke to arrange a raid on the establishment.

From his vantage point across the road Mike watched Lefty accompanied by Crossman, pile into a black Mercedes, slam the doors shut and drive off. They were followed by another man who removed the blue Mercedes and drove it to the garage for repairs.

'I think I'll just pop inside and check the place out,' Mike told himself. 'There's no harm in that.' He locked his motorbike and wandered to the entrance.

Inside the front door, he was challenged by a tough looking heavy-set man who informed him he needed to become a member if he wanted to enter the nightclub. Mike agreed and was shown to a small table in the foyer where he was asked to fill in a registration form. He completed the form and was requested to pay a joining fee of £50 by Angie, an attractive woman in her late forties. She began working at the nightclub as a stripper many years previously, and now looked after the girls and helped with the daily running of the business. Angie eyed Mike up and down and saw a handsome man standing before her in his leathers.

'You're a biker then?'

'An occasional one,' Mike replied.

'I've not seen you around here before. Are you local?'

'No. I'm just visiting the area for a while,' Mike replied, finding it difficult to take his eyes off the large amount of cleavage and bosoms Angie was showing with her low cut, brightly coloured red dress with black feathery edges.

He filled in his home address as the flat he once owned in Surbiton, not wanting to reveal his real address as it might be recognise, knowing their men had recently visited his house. Mike had less than fifty pounds in cash on him so was obliged to use his correct name in order to use his credit card.

He handed Angie the form and card. She placed the card in the card holder and asked Mike to enter his pin number. Angie glanced up to the mirrored ceiling as he pressed the buttons and the machine beeped to confirm the transaction.

'I won't be a moment, I'll get you a member's card and receipt,' she purred, grabbing the credit card, disappearing into the nightclub and making for the general office.

She took a photocopy of the credit card for possible fraudulent use at a later date and made a note of Mike's pin number on it. She had learned the art of recognising and remembering which numbers were entered from the card holder reflection in the ceiling mirror. It was a habit the nightclub employees were required to do whenever the opportunity arose, though Angie cared little for the practise and found herself in trouble when she deliberately forgot a client's pin number. Thieving was restricted to small amounts at a time from newer nightclub members. Experience had shown that many of the members did not want to make a fuss and let it be known they visited a strip club, which was also known to have upstairs rooms where the girls were allowed to entertain a client after hours to earn themselves and the nightclub more cash.

Crusher hobbled into the general office. 'Ah, there you are, Angie. I've been looking for you. The boss said you were to bandage my bleeding leg.'

Angie looked at the blood soaked torn trousers, 'It's only a scratch. You could wash that yourself and put a plaster on it.'

Crusher, who took a fancy to Angie, an attraction that was not reciprocated, insisted, 'The boss said you were to do it.'

'Oh, okay. I'll just see to this new member first,' she said, dropping the photocopy of Mike's card and joining form on the desk and returning to the foyer.

For curiosity Crushed picked up the form and stared at the name. It seemed familiar somehow, but at first he could not remember where he had seen it before. All of a sudden it came to him. This was the same name as the boatyard owner whose house they had searched that afternoon; the house where the shooting took place. He hobbled into the boss's office waving the paper.

'What do you want, Crusher?' Phadkar said, in a tone that showed his anger had not subsided.

'Take a look at this, boss,' he said shoving the paper on the desk in front of him. 'This is a new member who's just come into the nightclub.'

'What of it! We get new members all the time.'

'The name on the form is the same name as the boatyard owner whose house we searched for the drugs this afternoon, and where we last saw your brother.'

'Are you sure?' Phadkar said grabbing the paper.

'I'm sure. The name's definitely the same. It's what that bloke at the boatyard told us though the home address is different, but that could be false.'

'It's too much of a coincidence, coming across two different men with exactly the same name on the same day.'

'He might have been shooting at us as well, and followed us here when we left his place,' suggested Crusher, continuing to make his excuse for not carrying out a very successful job for his boss.

'Then we had better have a word with Mr Mike Randle. He might know what has happened to my brother,' stated Phadkar, rising from his desk.

The pair peered into the nightclub as Angie showed Mike to the bar to receive a first free drink that was given to all new members.

'That must be the bloke,' Crusher said. 'He's in motorbike gear. And come to think of it, I remember seeing a motorbike behind us on our trip back, but I didn't take much notice of it.'

'That's no real surprise. It certainly sounds as if he is a man I need to talk to. Go and tell him I like to greet new members and invite him into my office. Then ring Jake and tell him to get back here. There's no point in him driving all the way to Randle's house on the south coast when he's obligingly walked in here. He can give me the answers I want, and if they've nabbed Kashif, I will use him to do an exchange.'

'Okay, boss.'

'And when you have done that, get a couple of the boys to join us. If he is who you say he is, he can keep us company. I want some answers right now and until I know what has happened to my brother I am not too fussed how I get them.'

Chapter Eleven

The Raid

After the break-in and shooting at his home, Mike followed Crusher and Lefty to 'The Rosy Cheeks Nightclub', a private strip club in Brixton, London. Curiosity got the better of him and after calling Sir Joseph on his mobile with the nightclub's location, he watched Crossman and Lefty leave the premises before he ventured inside. To enter the nightclub he had to become a member and pay a fee, which he did not expecting the name on his credit card to be recognised by anyone. However, Angie took a photocopy of his details and Crusher saw it and recognised the name. He explained his discovery to the boss, Khurram Phadkar, who now wanted to meet this newest nightclub member. He was anxious to get some answers about what had happened to his twin brother Kashif at the boatyard owner's home.

Mike was escorted to the bar by the attractive Angie and was approached by Crusher. 'I'm told you are our newest member?' he croaked.

'So I believe,' said Mike, noticing the blood on his trouser leg but not making his observation apparent.

'The nightclub owner, Mr Phadkar, likes to meet all new members. He wants to see you in his office, now,' Crusher stated, his approach less than eloquent.

Angie looked surprised at this request. Mike guessed there was more to the approach than it appeared. He recognised Crusher from the boatyard surveillance pictures and recalled Phadkar as the name that Reg had remembered. He knew what damage this man's fists were capable of but also knew there was no point in refusing the invitation, and besides, it was a way of gaining more information.

'After you,' Mike replied.

He followed a limping Crusher into Khurram Phadkar's office and stepped from the hard tiled floor of the bar and entrance area on to a good quality soft fitted carpet that sank beneath his feet. The window blinds were drawn and the room was sparsely furnished with two desks facing the door, a cocktail cabinet in one corner and a few chairs dotted around. The walls held several paintings, all reproductions of famous artworks of an erotic nature to reflect the nightclub's business of making money by exhibiting the naked flesh of attractive women.

Phadkar sat behind his desk in the dimly lit office, created by overhead diffused lighting and three brass table lamps with dark green shades. One stood on the cocktail cabinet, with the others on each of the two desks. Phadkar's lamp threw harsh shadows on to his face, giving him a slightly sinister look, which he was well aware of and put to good use. It balanced the inferiority complex he had due to his small stature as a boss of a gang of larger men.

Standing when Mike entered, Khurram Phadkar began, 'Welcome to our nightclub, Mr Randle. Please take a seat.' He said, the strong inflection of his native Pakistan apparent to Mike. Phadkar gestured to a chair waiting in front of the desk and made no offer to shake hands but returned to his seat.

'Thanks,' Mike nodded, dropping his muscular frame into the chair while anticipation that trouble was about to begin.

* * *

While Mike was meeting the co-owner of 'The Rosy Cheeks Nightclub', Crossman and Lefty were travelling towards his house in the Mercedes. Crossman was chatting to Lefty about their search of the house that afternoon. He was surprised to hear that, despite retrieving a package from the safe it turned out to be the wrong one and did not contain the drugs.

'Are you sure it was the wrong package?' asked Crossman.

'So Crusher said. Apparently the boss opened it and told him.'

'So you didn't examine it yourself before you took it?'

'Nah. It was the only package in the safe, so I assumed it was the right one. Randle must have hidden it elsewhere or handed it in to the police station like he said he was going to.'

'If it had been handed in our police informant would have let us know. He's been instructed to tell us if any valuable drugs are received locally, which means our boatyard owner must still have them.'

'I guess so,' confirmed Lefty, unsure what Crossman was fishing for with all his questions.

Jake Crossman knew his boss and also knew he regarded Lefty as having a bit of a loose tongue. He was reluctant to accept the information was correct but went along with it for the moment.

'What's this boatyard bloke's name?'

'Mike Randle.'

'Perhaps Randle wants to keep the stuff for himself. That little package must be worth quite a lot of money on the open market.'

'About half-a-million quid I understand, though you didn't hear that from me.'

'Sure,' replied Crossman, the hint of a smile parting his lips.

At that moment Crossman received a call on his mobile from Crusher, informing him that Mike Randle had entered the nightclub and would be persuaded to give Phadkar the information he wanted. They were to return immediately.

'It seems that our boatyard man has stepped from the frying pan into the fire. He's obligingly arrived at the nightclub and the boss is going to ask him a few questions, which some of the boys are going to see he answers. We've been instructed to return to the nightclub,' Crossman told Lefty.

'Suits me. I'm not all that keen on going back to his house. With those women there with guns, I could end up getting shot as well.'

*   *   *

At 'The Rosy Cheeks Nightclub', Mike sat in front of Phadkar's desk and felt a slight draft on the back of his neck as the door opened to allow two muscular guards to join Crusher. He instinctively knew what was happening behind him and had no need to look round.

'I understand you are a director of SMJ Boatyard on the Hamble River. Is that not so?' asked Phadkar.

'I don't remember putting that on my application form,' Mike replied.

'Even so, it is true, is it not?'

'Perhaps. But why should that concern you? Do you want to but a yacht?'

Phadkar scorned at Mike's flippancy. 'I merely wish to make sure that I am talking to the right man.'

'If you want to buy a yacht I'm the right man. We make them to order, or can sell you a second hand one if you can't afford that.'

'I do not wish to buy a yacht, Mr Randle. I only wish to establish that you are the right man to answer my questions,' Phadkar tersely replied, his frustration at Mike's unhelpful answers annoying him.

'Apparently, I'm the newest member to this nightclub. Does that make me the right man?'

Phadkar banged his fist on the desk, 'Let us not play games, Mr Randle. You have obviously followed my men here from your house.'

Shaking his head, Mike said, 'Not true. I haven't been home since I left early this morning to see one of my employees at the boatyard who was badly beaten up last night by a gang of thugs. I don't suppose you know anything about that?'

The question remained unanswered. 'So, am I expected to believe that you simply happened to come all the way to London tonight and by a sheer coincidence came into this establishment. The nightclub where the men who visited your home this afternoon returned to?'

'Your men went to my home did they? I trust my fiancée made them welcome.'

Phadkar again banged his fist on the desk, harder this time. 'Enough of this ridiculous bantering. Who are the two women who like to play with guns? And what happened to my brother at your house?' he raged.

'Have you lost him? That's very careless of you.'

Phadkar glanced up at his two guards. It signalled them to move forward and take up a position at the back of Mike's chair. He could feel their presence towering over him and took a quick glance up at the two heavies.

'Friends of yours?' Mike asked.

With eyes wide and gritted teeth Phadkar rose from his seat. A slight nod to his men was an indication for them to grab Mike. Each man took a hold of his upper arm and wrist, lifting him to his feet in a cross-like position with his arms stretched wide.

Leaning on his desk Phadkar thrust his face towards Mike and uttered, 'If you do not tell me what has happened to my brother at your house this afternoon, I will have my men pull your arms off,' he snarled, finishing his sentence in a loud voice.

'So, you think you can render me (h)armless?' joked Mike, tensing his muscles and tugging slightly.

Nobody laughed at his joke but both heavies as Mike predicted, tightened their grip on him. Without warning he dropped to one knee and yanked his arms down towards the floor. With each of the two men strongly gripping his arms, both were dragged down and crashed their foreheads on the desk top, knocking them senseless and releasing their grip on Mike.

He lashed out with his foot, catching the first man squarely in the face, propelling him into the wall where he slumped to the floor. Swivelling around quickly, he saw the second man regain some of his senses and charge at him. Sidestepping, Mike left his leg out and the man tripped over it and spread-eagled on the floor. As he rose, a sharp chop to the back of his neck rendered him unconscious and he slumped back down with his face pressed to the carpet.

Lounging by the door, Crusher saw the men floored and hobbled forwards as quickly as his injured leg would allow. Mike heard him approaching and grabbed Phadkar's desktop lamp. He swung round and smashed it into the head of the onrushing man. Crusher staggered to a standstill and promptly received a kick in the crutch that doubled him over in pain. Mike grabbed his chair and smashed it over the back of Crusher's head before throwing the broken pieces aside and turning to face Khurram Phadkar.

With all three of his men lying prostrate on the carpet, Phadkar's face turned to a sheepish grin. 'I am not a violent man. I did not really intend to do you any harm, Mr Randle' he cowered, 'I simply want to know what has happened to my brother, Kashif.'

'Is that the same not doing any harm that your thugs did to my boatyard foreman Reg, who's now in hospital with facial bruises and fractured ribs?'

'I am deeply sorry about your employee. I was not there, it was my twin brother who visited your boatyard and house. I will have a quiet word with him about that when he gets back.'

'I think you may find that a bit difficult.'

A frown crossed Phadkar's forehead posing a question.

'Like I said I wasn't there, but if what I was told is correct then one of your men was shot dead at my house. If your brother is the only one who's not returned then it doesn't look very good for him.'

Phadkar was shocked. His face paled and he slumped down on to his chair. 'Shot dead,' he muttered. 'I heard there were shots fired, but … dead? Are you sure?'

'Like I said, I was not there, so no, I'm not absolutely sure but I think it's very likely.'

The three men on the floor started to rouse. Mike opened the first man's jacket, and as expected saw a gun in his shoulder holster and grabbed it. He collected a gun from each of the two other men.

'For a man of non-violence it's strange that you let your thugs carry guns.'

Phadkar shook his head to clear his mind from the shock he received about his brother. 'They are security guards, not thugs. And when you run a strip club there are sometimes troublesome, and often drunk clients who in their stupor want to grab the girls. They have to be restrained and quietly evicted.'

'And your men need guns to do that?'

'We also take quite a lot of cash at the nightclub each evening and need protection for that.'

'With joining fees like the one I had to pay I'm not surprised.'

The two guards got to their feet and helped Crusher up. He nursed a bruise that rapidly appeared on his forehead. Mike gestured them to keep back waving a gun at them. With a slightly dazed look on their faces they moved away.

A commotion erupted in the nightclub and shouting came from the bar area. People could be heard rushing around and DI Brooke barged into the director's room.

'What's the meaning of this and who are you?' Phadkar demanded.

Brooke held up his identity card. 'I'm Detective Inspector Brooke from Special Branch. I have a warrant to search this establishment for drugs,' he said, waving a piece of paper. 'Who are you?'

'I am Khurram Phadkar, the boss and co-owner of this nightclub. Let me see that,' he demanded. Phadkar snatched the warrant and examined it. 'Bah! You won't find any drugs here inspector. This is a legitimate private nightclub with all the relevant licences from the local authority. Perhaps you should concentrate on arresting this man,' he pointed. 'He has a gun and is trying to rob me,' Phadkar insinuated. 'He may have even killed my brother if what he says is true.'

Brooke looked at the guns Mike was holding and eyed the men standing in the corner, all looking the worse for their encounter with the nightclub's newest member.

'Had a bit of trouble, Mike?' he asked.

'Nothing I couldn't handle, thanks, Colin,' he replied, offering the guns to Brooke. 'You might want to see if theses three have a ... relevant licence from the authority for these. And also perhaps check them against the bullets taken from the men who were killed aboard *Quester*.'

'Good idea,' said Brooke, taking the guns from Mike.

'Those were my men so the bullets will not match. Perhaps you should spend your efforts trying to catch the men who killed them,' Phadkar protested.

'So, it was your men who were on board a yacht carrying drugs,' Brooke stated.

'I know nothing about any drugs. My men were on a well earned holiday cruise and they were all murdered, including my nephew.'

'Hmm,' mused Brooke.

'And that is the man who beat up poor Reg last night,' said Mike, pointing at Crusher. 'I saw him on the recording slam a fist into poor Reg's stomach and kick him in the ribs before he left. That's probably what fractured them.'

Brooke stepped closer to Crusher and with their noses only a few inches apart declared, 'That's not nice; hitting an old man like Reg.'

Crusher's face coloured but he remained silent.

Mike took a DVD from his pocket. 'This is a copy of the boatyard security DVD. You'll be able to see exactly what I mean, and identify him.'

The three security guards were led away leaving Phadkar to suffer the indignity of having his nightclub, his desk and his room searched.

'Are you going to arrest me as well?' he asked Brooke.

'That depends on what we find. Do you have a safe, Mr Phadkar?'

'Behind that picture,' he pointed.

'Perhaps you'd be kind enough to open it for me? I'd hate to have to break into it.'

Phadkar took a bunch of keys from his pocket and opened the safe. 'Anything else?' he asked.

The question remained hanging in the air.

DC Green entered the room and handed Brooke a bunch of papers. 'Look what we found in the general office,' he said.

Brooke glanced at them. 'It seems you make photocopies of all the credit cards you get your hands on, Mr Phadkar.'

'It is merely a precaution to enable us to check and make sure the card is not stolen.'

'Really? How is it that each person's private pin numbers are listed here as well? You weren't thinking of using this information to help yourself to unauthorised payments were you?'

'I know nothing about any unauthorised payments. I leave the running of the general office to others. You must speak to Angie, she is in charge of the day to day running of the nightclub,' Phadkar stated, trying to remain above all the accusations he was faced with.

'I will. It seems there's a lot going on in your organisation you know nothing about.' Brooke turned to Mike. 'This one seems to be yours. That was a bit careless of you.'

'I had to pay an enormous fee just to get in. I didn't realise they'd taken a copy of the card.'

'So, you didn't tell them your pin number or give permission for them to copy the card?'

'Certainly not.'

'In that case it's illegal gathering of personal information and you Mr Phadkar, as boss and co-owner of this establishment, are under arrest. Take him away,' Brooke instructed Green.

Phadkar was led from the room with a scowl on his face.

'He'll ring his solicitor and will be back here in a few hours, I guarantee it,' Brooke told Mike.

'I saw two more of his men leave in a black Mercedes car. One of the men was in the car I followed here from my home.'

'Sir Joseph told me Suzie had a bit of trouble with some men who broke into your house. Those others will be back and I'll talk to them later,' Brooke stated.

'I wonder where they were going.' Mike murmured, more to himself than to Brooke. A horrible thought then crossed his mind. 'Phadkar was very concerned about what happened to his brother this afternoon at my house. I told him someone was killed there and it looks likely it was his brother. I wonder if he sent those men back there to find out. I'd better ring Suzie and warn her.'

'When did they leave?' asked Brooke.

'It must have been almost an hour ago.'

'You warn Suzie. The employees at this nightclub all seem to be carrying guns, so I'll get the local police to send some armed men to your place, just in case you're right.'

Mike and DI Brooke made their telephone calls. Suzie was slightly annoyed that Mike had ignored Sir Joseph's request not to venture into the nightclub, and said she would retrieve her gun from the car and keep it handy in case the armed men made a return visit before the police arrived.

In the nightclub, the wall safe was searched but the hidden safe under the floor remained undiscovered and the drugs were not found.

'No luck?' Mike asked.

'No, but now we know for sure they're involved with pedalling drugs, we can keep a closer eye on the place.'

'I'd better be getting back. Suzie may need some help clearing up. At least I know that now she's been warned she will be okay. Suzie can take care of herself, and fortunately Jim and Jenny are still with her. It's a long journey home so I'll be on my way.'

*   *   *

While the police raid was in progress, Crossman and Lefty were on their way back from Mike's house after they were recalled by Crusher. They reached the nightclub. On eyeing the police vehicles outside they parked the Mercedes a short way along the street where they could watch and wait. Mike and DI Brooke stepped through the back door and wandered into the street as they talked.

'I recognise that man in the motorbike gear,' Lefty said.

'Who is he?'

'He must be Randle, the man whose house we searched this afternoon. While I was looking around the place I saw a photograph of a man and a woman in army type gear with each of them holding a gun. It looked as if they were in the jungle and the man had his arm around the woman's waist. It was him, I'm sure of it. She must be one of the women who were firing at us. I bet it was him who brought the police here.'

'So, it seems that our boatyard man and his girlfriend are a bit more experienced fighters than we realised.'

Crossman and Lefty watched from their car as Mike crossed the road and walked towards his motorbike. He donned his crash helmet, revved up the motorcycle, signalled goodbye to Brooke and rode off.

'We can't go back into the nightclub while the police are still there so I think we'll follow our busybody intruder and take care of him,' said Crossman, pulling on his gloves and checking the clip on his gun before starting the engine and motoring after Mike as he disappeared down the road.

Chapter Twelve

The Chase

Leaving 'The Rosy Cheeks Nightclub' in Brixton, after DI Brooke and his men had searched the building and failed to find the drugs in a hidden safe, Mike started his drive home on *Bonnie*, his pride and joy 1977 Jubilee Special Triumph Bonneville T140V motorcycle. He switched on the headlights, revved her up on the electric start and drove off making his way back towards the A3. He was so delighted to be out riding his beloved motorcycle again, that in the gloom he failed to notice the Mercedes he had seen drive off not much more than an hour before pull out from behind a line of parked cars and follow him.

Lefty and Jake Crossman, who was driving the Mercedes, were unsuccessfully endeavouring to keep the motorcycle in their sights as it was driven through the bustling traffic of London.

'We can't keep up with him. There's far too much traffic. He's already way out of sight,' complained Lefty, straining to look past the mass of cars blocking their way.

'That's okay. It's nothing to worry about. You know where his house is, so we know which route he's likely to take. His motorbike is very distinctive and is easy to recognise. I'm sure we'll eventually catch him up and it looks as if he's heading for the A3.'

'That's the way we came back. He must be taking the same route home.'

Crossman took chances at changing traffic lights and cut up several cars, whose drivers blasted their horns in annoyance. By the time Mike drove clear of the congestion the Mercedes was far behind him. When Crossman reached the dual carriageway and had a clearer road in front of him, he jammed the accelerator pedal to the floor and the car sped up to over 90 mph racing along in the outside lane with headlights blazing to warn other drivers of his impending approach.

Travelling at a steady 45-50 mph, Mike was enjoying his pleasant drive home in the early evening, motoring into the dwindling light of a grey sky descending like a darkening mist over the roadway as a pink dusk gradually turned to night. The speeding Mercedes quickly shortened the distance between them until Mike's Bonneville was in sight.

'There his is. I knew we'd soon catch him up. We've got him now,' crowed Jake Crossman, driving up close behind Mike's Bonneville in the nearside lane.

The accelerating Mercedes, its headlights showing large in Mike's rear view mirror, thumped into the back of his motorbike causing it to wobble. Mike steadied the bike and accelerated hard. He noticed the distinctive Mercedes badge on the front of the car's bonnet in his mirror and immediately realised who was driving it, confirming his fears that the bump was no accident.

They were trying to kill him.

The Bonneville sped up to almost 110 mph, the motorbike's limit, with the Mercedes accelerating behind in an attempt to ram bike and rider off the road. Mike weaved the Bonneville back and forth across the road, dodging between surprised motorists and using the hard shoulder to keep clear of his pursuers by overtaking cars on the near side. Crossman blasted his car's horn to move aside any vehicle that was blocking his pursuit of the motorcycle, before racing past them on the nearside if it was quicker.

With no other vehicles on the road before him Mike turned off his motorcycle lights. Darkness had almost descended and with no street lighting on this section of the carriageway he became much more difficult to see. He took the calculated risk that he would see other traffic ahead of him in time to avoid a collision. Mike was thankful there were few cars on this stretch of the road, and it was mainly straight with only gentle bends, allowing him an early opportunity to see any vehicle he approached at the high speed he continued to maintain.

'Shit, where's he gone now?' moaned Crossman. 'He's turned his bloody lights off and I've lost sight of him,' he said, turning the car's headlights on to full beam.

A shadowy outline of bike and rider, hurtling along the nearside edge of the road, was picked out in the car's lights.

'There he is, practically off the road on the left hand edge,' pointed Lefty.

Crossman again stamped on the accelerator pedal, swerved the car across to the nearside and caught up with the motorcycle. Mike continued to weave across the road, frustrating Crossman's attempts to knock him off. The powerful Mercedes pulled alongside Mike and closed in, endeavouring to shove him into the central reservation. Braking his motorcycle hard caused the car to speed past him. The Mercedes brake lights glowed red, tyres squealed throwing up clouds of smoke as the car decelerated fast. Crossman swore profusely as Mike revved the bike up, streaked past them and hurtled down the road.

The one advantage his motorcycle had, was its ability to accelerate very fast, putting distance between them for a short while. The car's greater power soon cut the gap down and was close on his tail again.

'He's bloody good on that bike,' said Lefty. 'We're getting near to the turnoff into Guildford, and he's bound to take it into the city to try and loose us in the traffic. Are you going to get him in time?'

'I'll get him, whatever it takes.'

'We can't chance knocking him off when we get into a lit-up area. Somebody is bound to see us. I expect all those cars we shot past are wondering what on earth is going on.'

'I've had enough of this cat and mouse crap,' exclaimed Crossman, pulling a gun from its holster. 'I was hoping I could make it to look like an accident, but now I don't bloody care. I just want this meddling boat builder dead. With him out of the way retrieving the drugs should be a lot easier.'

The motorcycle and its pursuer charged along the road as the Mercedes electric window silently slipped down. The occasional motorist who they flashed past, looked on in horror at the speed they were travelling at and presumed the two were racing each other.

Each time Crossman came within range of Mike, he thrust his gun out of the window and began firing. A bullet hit Mike's crash helmet and ricocheted off. Another barely missed him and dug into the back seat of his motorbike. With this new threat to his life he weaved even more aggressively, desperately trying to keep out of the firing line while at the same time grimly trying to avoid being rammed into oblivion.

A signpost flashed past indicating the turnoff to Guildford was ahead. If Mike could reach it and pull off the dual carriageway on to side roads into the city with more traffic, he stood a better chance of eluding his attackers. Crossman, well away of that as well, let loose with a barrage of shots.

Mike's luck eventually ran out when one of the bullets sliced across the top of his shoulders. He flinched at the sudden searing pain and lost control of the motorcycle. The bike shook violently in a front wheel wobble. Mike tried desperately to correct it and braked hard, but his speed took him careering towards the central reservation at an uncontrollable rate.

He ploughed into the motorway central verge.

The Triumph hit the kerb and cartwheeled out of control throwing Mike into the air. He flew over the central reservation, crashing on to the opposite, northbound carriageway. An oncoming car swerved violently, skidding sideways and spun in a 180 degree turn, missing Mike in the outside lane by inches as he rolled over and over until he finally came to a stop. Broken pieces flew from his motorbike and littered the southbound carriageway as it smashed its way along the road, sparks flying from the bike gouging its way to an eventual standstill.

'That takes care of our meddling boat builder,' smiled Crossman. 'I'll be very surprised if he survives a smash at that speed but I think we ought to make sure.'

'Shame about the bike. There aren't that many of those Bonnevilles left now,' moaned Lefty.

Crossman stared at him with incredulity. 'We've just killed a bloke and you're more worried about his bloody motorbike.' He shook his head and jammed the brakes on, decelerating fast to exit at the approaching junction. Pulling off the road he negotiated the roundabout, drove under the bridge to the far side and returned the Mercedes to the northbound carriageway.

'What are you going to do?' Lefty asked.

'See if he's dead and if not, finish him off.'

'You mean you're going to run him over?'

'If that's what it takes. In this light it'll look like an accident.'

The Mercedes approached the spot where Mike lay prostrate on the road, but by this time two passing motorists had stopped near the crashed motorbike and crossed the carriageway to check on Mike. They were joined by others who were curious to see the body in the road. A 999 call to the police and ambulance was made by one of the men on his mobile phone.

Crossman cursed that he was not able to run over the body or inspect it unhindered. He parked his car on the nearside edge and wandered over.

'Is he dead?' he asked the man kneeling by Mike's body.

'No. He's still just alive, but pretty badly hurt. He was charging along at over 100 mph and shot past me like I was standing still. I imagine he's got quite a few broken bones.'

'Not enough for my liking,' cursed Crossman. He returned to his car.

'Is he dead?' asked Lefty.

'No, he's not. He's badly smashed up but still alive. It seems our boat builder is harder to kill than I thought. There'll be another opportunity though. At least it's put him out of action and he won't be bothering us for quite a while.'

Crossman revved up his car and sped back to London, dissatisfied that he had only temporarily put Mike out of action.

Chapter Thirteen

Revenge

After trying unsuccessfully to avoid being run off the carriageway by the Mercedes driven by Crossman and Lefty, Mike lay on the road near to unconsciousness. He was attended by motorists who had stopped and waited with him while the ambulance sped towards the accident. Having established that much to their annoyance Mike was still alive, Crossman motored back to 'The Rosy Cheeks Nightclub' in London.

The police had finished their search of the nightclub and returned to the police station, taking the credit card copies, and Khurram Phadkar and his three security guards with them.

They were questioned about the break-in at SMJ Boatyard and the copying of credit cards. Crusher was charged with causing grievous bodily harm to Mr Reginald Ashdown, the foreman of SMJ Boatyard Ltd. The boss Khurram Phadkar was charged with unauthorised copying of private information. While they were in the detention room they were joined by Sergeant Bill Newlands who volunteered to stand on guard by the door.

Phadkar spoke quietly to him. 'Has any valuable drugs been received by the police in the last couple of days?'

'No. None,' stated the informant. 'I would have heard of any large consignment being handed in and contacted you as we agreed.'

'I'd like you to check on a Mr Mike Randle. He runs SMJ boatyard in Hamble. I want to know all about him and the women he associates with.'

'I'll see what I can do. I'll check the police computer files and let you know.'

Phadkar's solicitor, a Pakistani man dressed in a well-cut made-to-measure brown suit, was quick to arrive at the police station. He arranged for all of them to be released pending a hearing, allowing them to return to the nightclub.

'You're back quickly,' announced Crossman, following Khurram Phadkar into his office. 'Angie told me the police took you and the boys in for questioning. I didn't expect to see you until tomorrow. How was it?'

Phadkar wearily dumped himself down on his desk chair. 'Very awkward. We are only back tonight thanks to my solicitor. The Hampshire police faxed them with photographs of everyone in the raid you did last night on that boatyard in Hamble. They must have security cameras there.'

'They must be well hidden then. I didn't see them or I would have made sure we destroyed the recordings.'

'I had a job to convince the police that it was my twin brother Kashif in the pictures and not me. Newlands, our informant, put in a good word for us and helped to get us released. He will want paying for that and for the information he got for me about our boatyard man.'

'I'll see to it. So, what happens now? Are the police going to take you to court?'

'I don't know. I'm not going to worry about it at the moment. That is what I pay the solicitor to handle. Let him worry about it. I am more concerned about what happened to my brother Kashif.'

'Have you learned anything about the kafuffle at Randle's house?'

'Yes, I think so. It seems fairly certain he was shot dead by either Randle, who said he was not there, or one of the other two women at his house after those two morons ran out and left him there on his own. That is what Randle told me. If so, those women will be sorry. I will make them all pay dearly for killing my brother.'

'He could have got it wrong. Your brother might simply be injured.'

'No, I do not think so. If he was taken to hospital, I would have been contacted by now so I have to assume the worse, that he is dead. The police would neither confirm or deny it. They said they are looking into it and will ring me in the morning. I did not get a chance to question Randle about it before the police arrived, but I am sure he is mixed up in it somehow.'

'Lefty and me took care of him, for a bit. He's all smashed up on the carriageway and is lucky to be alive still.'

'You did not eliminate him?'

'We tried to. He must have nine lives.'

'I want Kashif's killer, or killers dealt with. Crusher said both women were shooting at him. One was white and one was black. If my brother Kashif is dead, then I want all of them to pay heavily for that.'

'I can take care of it if you'd like me to,' suggested Crossman.

'No. I do not want any more trouble that will lead the police back to my nightclub. They already suspect we deal in drugs and are snooping around here. I am going to get a professional hit man to do the job. Hassan has got a lot of contacts, I will ring him, he is bound to know how to get hold of someone to do it.'

'A professional! That'll cost money.'

'I do not care. While I was at the police station Newlands made a few enquiries and discovered that our boat builder, Mr Michael Randle, was a soldier in the British Army paras, and then became a mercenary fighting in the African jungle. I should have guessed as much when he brushed aside the guards in my office. And his fiancée is Miss Susannah Drake, she was a troublemaker who tangled with the law when she was young and later she also became a mercenary.'

'They sound like trouble.'

'Yes, they are. This pair knows how to take care of themselves. I am sure that is why Kashif was shot. They are used to handling guns. The other woman may have been a mercenary as well, but he could not check because I do not know what her name is. I want a professional hit man to take care of them. No more slip-ups. They are all too dangerous.'

'Except when riding a motorbike on the Queen's highway,' sneered Crossman.

'Yes. At least Randle will be out of the way for the moment but I want to make that permanent for all of them. Kashif's death must be avenged.'

'Randle will be banged up in the hospital and in no fit state to argue. It would be a good time to get him.'

'Yes, you are right. Which hospital would they take him to?'

'Guildford General Hospital is the closest. He's probably been taken there.'

'Get Angie to ring the hospital and say she is a friend and has heard about the accident. See if she can discover if Randle is there and if he is, which ward he is in,' Phadkar instructed. 'Then make sure you do the job properly this time.'

Crossman hid his annoyance at the remark and simple replied, 'Okay.'

'I will put out a contract to take care of the other two women,' Phadkar stated, picking up the telephone.

Angie rang Guildford General Hospital and talked to a helpful receptionist. She passed the information on to Crossman. 'Randle is in Guildford General. He's got to undergo an operation. It seems he had an accident on his motorbike on the way home. How did you know about that?'

'I'm psychic,' suggested Crossman.

Angie gave him a hard stare as he walked away. Jake Crossman she thought, was too nasty for her liking. It was obvious to her that he was somehow involved in Randle's so-called accident.

'Randle's in Guildford General Hospital,' Crossman told Phadkar. 'I'll go there now and take care of things during the early hours. There'll be less people around to worry about then.'

'Take Lefty with you, and no mistakes this time,' Phadkar said.

Crossman nodded and left.

Phadkar meanwhile spoke to his gangland acquaintance who sent him an email detailing how to get in contact with the sort of professional he was looking for. He was given instructions on what method and wording was needed to put out a message on a particular internet website for a hit man to contact him. The wording had to be stated in a seemingly innocent way that would only be understood by those interested in that type of work, and on a site that had become a magnet for that kind of request. Phadkar gave details of Mike and Suzie without naming them.

'Frustrated employer seeks help to trace two employees to pass on a surprise package to them. Last known address was a boatyard in Southern England. Caution required as they are experienced and avoid easy contact. Send details of previous undertakings and rates for more information to kp@thercnclub.co.uk.'

Phadkar had to wait only a few hours before two answers came back requesting more details and stating a very high price, which shocked him even though he knew it would be costly.

'It is a high price, but it is for Kashif, so it is worth it,' he mumbled to himself as he replied to both requests.

In the meantime, Crossman collected Lefty and the pair motored to Guildford General Hospital to complete their unfinished task of eliminating Mike Randle.

Chapter Fourteen

Hard To Kill

After his motorcycle accident, deliberately caused by Crossman and Lefty, Mike Randle was rushed by ambulance to Guildford General Hospital. The emergency services were quick to arrive at the scene, summoned by a passing motorist. The police coned off one lane on each carriageway to prevent further mishaps on the northbound roadway around Mike and the ambulance, and on the southbound around the wreck of Mike's motorbike. The Triumph Bonneville was smashed into several tangled pieces and was scattered over a long length of the carriageway.

Several motorists had remained with Mike until the emergency services reached them, thwarting Crossman efforts to finish Mike off. The ambulance arrived amid wailing sirens and after a brief check on him by the paramedics he was carefully lifted into the ambulance and rushed to the hospital.

When two motorists were questioned by the police who were travelling on the southbound carriageway, they described seeing a car and a motorbike flash past them at well over 100 mph.

'I though they were racing each other at first, but then I saw the biker swerve his machine across the road on to the nearside and the car followed him,' said the first witness.

'And I saw him turn his lights off, as if he was deliberately trying not to be seen,' added the second witness, 'but the driver put his car headlights on full and charged after him again.'

'So, do you think the man was knocked off his bike deliberately?' asked the policeman looking at them both.

'Oh, I don't know about that! It's possible but I wouldn't like to swear to it,' said the bald headed accountant, anxious not to get himself too involved. The second witness shook his head in agreement.

'Did you see what make of car it was?' questioned the policeman.

'I think it was a Mercedes. But I couldn't be absolutely positive. It's very dark and there are no streetlights along this stretch of the carriageway.'

'Yes, it was definitely a Mercedes. I saw it clearly,' the second witness added. 'There were two men in the car. I once saw several flashes coming from the vehicle, but I don't know what that was. At first I thought I saw a hand poke out the window with a gun and fire it at the motorcyclist, but that's ridiculous – isn't it?'

The policeman scribbled a note in his book. 'Not if they were trying to kill him it isn't. It might be a gangland feud. Did either of you notice what the registration number of the vehicle was?'

Both men shook their heads. 'The car was moving too fast,' the accountant stated.

'What about the colour?'

He replied, 'It was a dark colour, possibly black.' Looking at his watch, he said, 'It's getting late and I'd like to get home to my wife. She gets a bit annoyed if my dinner is burnt. Is that all your questions?'

'Yes, I think so for the moment,' agreed the policeman. 'Well, thank you gentlemen. If we need to speak to you further we'll be in touch.'

The two witnesses smiled at each other and were quickly on their way. A pick-up truck arrived to collect the mangled motorbike and the broken pieces strewn along the road.

Meanwhile, the ambulance with blue lights flashing and the siren wailing loudly sped its way to Guildford General Hospital with the paramedic taking a few relevant details from Mike as they journeyed.

He was barely conscious and in a state of shock as the attendant wheeled him into a consulting room where he was transferred onto a bed and the curtains drawn around him. A nurse sat nearby and filled in a form with Mike's details while she waited for a doctor to arrive and make his examination. Mike was given a painkilling injection to reduce the torment and trauma his body was experiencing through the shock of the incident. The drug began to work and calmed him down as the internal, uncontrollable shaking his inside was generating, slowly subsided and a calm feeling permeated through his body.

'Would you please telephone my fiancée and let her know what has happened to me?' Mike asked, his mind in a dream like state created by the drug, but totally aware of what was happening around him, though feeling slightly detached from his numb body.

'Of course,' she replied. 'I'll just finish writing out your details first.'

*   *   *

Meanwhile, at her home near Bosham Hoe, Suzie was grateful that Sandy and his mate had arrived to collect Kashif Phadkar's body.

'He's in the living room,' Suzie told Sandy, a tall redhead dressed in a boiler suit.

He stepped through the front entrance and she showed him the blanket covered body lying lifeless on the living room carpet.

'Okay. We'll take care of it, Miss,' he promised.

Suzie returned to the kitchen where Jim and Jenny waited. They remained there until Sandy and his mate had placed the body in their van and left.

'I'm glad that's over,' Suzie remarked.

The three of them cleared up the broken things in the living room. 'What are you going to do about all that blood on the carpet?' Jenny asked.

'Get a new carpet. And I'll have to ask the decorators to come in and fill up all the bullet holes and repaint the hall. At least the grandfather clock is still in one piece.'

Suzie gave Jim and Jenny a hug before they started their journey home to Weybridge. 'Are you sure you'll be all right?' Jim asked Suzie.

'I'll be fine. Mike will be home soon. He rang to say he's on his way.'

It had been a harrowing experience for them all. Suzie waved them goodbye. Shortly afterwards a car crunched up the gravel driveway and two policemen, both armed, arrive at her house.

'Good evening, Miss Drake?'

'Yes.'

'We were asked by DI Brooke to call on you and make sure you are all right.'

'I'm fine, thank you. I was told you would be arriving but it's not really necessary,' stated Suzie. 'My fiancé will be home soon.'

'He said there's a possibility an armed gangster may be paying you a visit this evening and we've been asked to stay with you for a while – just as a precaution.'

'Then you'd better come in,' Suzie said, opening the door. 'I don't imagine anyone would be silly enough to try anything with your police car in the driveway.'

'Let's hope not, Miss.'

'Would you like a cup of tea?'

'That's very nice of you, two sugars please,' said the policeman.

'Just one sugar for me,' stated his mate.

With most of the clearing up now done, Suzie sat in the kitchen chatting to the policemen. Nearly two hours passed with no armed visitors arriving.

'It looks as if you two have had a wasted journey,' Suzie remarked.

'It's never a waster journey when we make sure than someone is protected and stays safe,' declared the policeman.

The kitchen telephone rang. It was the hospital nurse on the line with news of Mike's accident.

'Is he all right?' Suzie asked.

'He's conscious but is a bit shaken,' she reported. 'I'm sure he'll be okay. He looks to be a tough sort of guy.'

'Has he broken any bones?' anxiety colouring her voice.

'We think his wrists may be broken, and possibly his leg. We'll know more after the X-rays are taken.'

'Oh, God! Okay. I'll be there in about an hour,' she said, glancing up at the kitchen clock.

Suzie slammed down the telephone.

'My fiancé's had an accident. He's been taken to Guildford General Hospital, so I've got to leave right away.'

'Righto, Miss. We'll escort you to the hospital then get back to the station.'

'Thank you.'

Suzie grabbed the car keys from the hall table and dashed from the house, followed by the policemen.

*   *   *

At Guildford General Hospital, Mike waited patiently for the on call doctor to examine him. He arrived in a clean white coat with a stethoscope hung around his neck and emerged through the curtains.

'Let's see how much damage you've done to yourself,' he said.

Mike's leather trousers were cut off him, much to his annoyance. His protests that it was not necessary fell on deaf ears. The doctor insisted it was essential to lessen any movement that might cause further injuries as his leg had obviously been damaged in the crash. Mike was gently eased out of his jacket. He had the rest of his clothes removed and was covered with a gown. With this achieved the doctor checked him over, his warm hands gently probing Mike's body. After a quick assessment he asked the nurse to arrange for several X-rays to be taken.

'You're a bit old for thrashing around on a motorbike, aren't you?' the doctor suggested.

'Rubbish! I'm not even forty yet, and I wasn't thrashing around. Some bastard tried to kill me and deliberately knocked me off,' Mike replied.

'Come, come now! I'm sure you must be mistaken,' said the doctor in a condescending manner, continuing to probe Mike's body.

'I might be a bit broken up and in a bit of a daze because of your drugs, but I'm not senile,' Mike spat, angered that he was not taken seriously. 'And hang on to my leathers. I want them back. The jacket is evidence.'

'Evidence? Evidence of what?'

'Take a look at the back of my shoulder and you'll see.'

Mike was gently turned on his side.

'You've got a scratch across your shoulder. I imagine you caught yourself on something when you came off,' suggested the doctor.

'Wrong! That was caused by a bullet.'

'A bullet! Rubbish! You have a vivid imagination, Mr Randle.'

'Are the police here? I want to speak to them.'

'No, they're not! You calm down. I'm sure they've got better things to do than run around after careless speeding motorcyclists who conjure up imaginary motorway assassins in order to justify their reckless riding. Is that a story you made up for the insurance company?' he asked.

The question remained unanswered when at that moment DI Maidley accompanied by a DC, pushed his way through the consulting room curtain surrounding Mike's temporary bed.

'I'm sorry but you can't come in here, I'm seeing to a patient,' advised the doctor.

The detective held up his identity card. 'I'm Detective Inspector Maidley of the Hampshire Police.'

'Oh, right. What can I do for you?'

'At the moment I'd like a word with your patient. I'll talk to you later, if I may, doctor ...,'

'Jones, David Jones.'

'Davy Jones eh ? That's a good name for a doctor.'

'It's an old joke,' the doctor sighed.

'Hello, Mr Randle,' the inspector said, moving to Mike's bedside. 'We meet yet again in nasty circumstances. This is getting to be a bit of a habit.'

Mike forced a half smile. 'I won't shake hands if you don't mind inspector,' he said. His hands were crossed on top of his chest with his wrists resting at an awkward angle.

Maidley glanced at Mike's hands. 'I understand. How is our patient, doctor?'

'His reckless speeding hasn't done him any favours but he'll live. He's likely to have collected a few broken bones in the process though. I'm certain both of his wrists are broken and possible his leg. It's just a question of what other damage he's done to himself.'

DI Maidley nodded and looked at Mike. 'I was looking forward to getting an early night before the station night sergeant rang me. I'd told them to inform me if your name arose in connection with anything because of the break-in at your boatyard, but I didn't expect it to be this.'

'Sorry, detective. It was exactly my choice either,' Mike stated.

'When I was told that two witnesses said they thought you might have been deliberately run off the road, and one of them thought he might have even seen a gun fired at you, I knew it was time to pay you a visit and get your side of the story.'

Mike looked at the doctor with another half-smile.

With a sheepish look on his face Dr Jones said, 'Yes, well, don't take too long. Mr Randle is heavily drugged and is due to be wheeled down to the X-ray department very shortly.'

'Okay, doctor. Thank you.'

The doctor left the cubicle.

'So, what did happen? I imagine it wasn't an accident,' the policeman said.

'No, it certainly wasn't. It was two of the men from 'The Rosy Cheeks Nightclub' in London who were involved in last night's raid on our boatyard, I'm sure of it.'

'What makes you think that?'

'It was the same Mercedes car that I'd seen leaving the nightclub with them in earlier this evening, and I caught a quick glimpse of them when the car pulled alongside side me as the driver pointed his gun and fired at me.'

The DC scribbled in his notebook. DI Maidley opened his mouth to ask another question but stopped when his mobile phone rang.

'Sorry about this, excuse me,' he said, moving away and putting the phone to his ear. 'Good evening inspector. What can I do for you?...

That's okay. I've already had one late call this evening … Killed at Mr Randle's house. Is that so? Well, there's a coincidence. I'm at Guildford General Hospital talking to Mr Randle at this very moment.'

'I thought he was on his way home,' said DI Brooke.

'He was, but somebody decided to try and spread him all over the A3 carriageway.'

'Is he okay?'

'The doctor thinks he's probably got a few broken bones but says he'll live.'

'Thank goodness for that.'

'I'd let you talk to him, but I doubt if he could hold the phone at the moment. He may well have broken both his wrists.'

'These people don't seem to mind who they hurt or how much damage they do. It might be an idea if I came to see you inspector. I think we should pool our knowledge on this case,' suggested Brooke.

'Good idea. I'll ask Inspector Fairbourne to join us as well. He's also involved in this case. Shall we say, my office at nine tomorrow?' he suggested.

'Make it ten. I've a bit of a journey to get down there, and there's likely to be more traffic on the roads on a Saturday.'

'Okay inspector, ten it is. I'll see you tomorrow.'

At that moment the curtains parted and two attractive nurses entered pushing a trolley. 'I'm sorry but you gentleman will have to leave now. We have to get this patient to the X-ray department,' one nurse informed.

Closing his mobile, DI Maidley nodded to his DC to leave and said, 'I'll get myself a coffee and wait outside, Mr Randle. I'll talk again to you after your X-rays have been taken.'

'Okay, inspector.'

The policemen left and Mike was lifted gently by the sheet beneath him on to the trolley. He was wheeled down the almost empty echoing corridor to the X-ray department.

'You two lovely ladies are working late tonight,' Mike said, automatically turning on his charm, despite his condition.

'It's one of the joys of working in a hospital,' one replied.

'Yes, it means we get to see blokes like you brought in who are all smashed up and are drugged up to the eyeballs. Then we get to take all your clothes off so you can be operated on. It's all good fun,' said the other, both of them giggling as they pushed the trolley through the double swing doors into the room X-ray department.

*   *   *

Speeding into Guildford General Hospital car park, Suzie slammed the car door shut and waved a thank you to the two policemen who had escorted her there. She rushed to the A & E Department and hurried to the reception desk.

'My fiancé, Mike Randle, was brought in earlier this evening after an accident.'

Picking up a telephone the receptionist said, 'I'll enquire Miss …'

'Drake.'

'Miss Drake. Please take a seat.'

DI Maidley and his DC were in the waiting area getting themselves a cup of coffee from a vending machine. He wandered over to the waiting area.

'Hello, Miss Drake.'

'Oh, hello inspector. I didn't expect to see you here.'

'I heard about Mr Randle's accident and came straight over to speak with him. He has just been wheeled into the X-ray department,' he said, anticipating the question.

'How is he?'

'I'm sure he'll be all right. He seems remarkably cheerful considering what's happened to him.'

'What exactly did happen to him? He's a careful motorcycle rider, especially on his favourite Bonneville motorbike.'

'Careful he may be but, it looks as if he was deliberately knocked from his motorbike by a couple of thugs in a car.'

'What! You mean they tried to kill him?'

'It certainly looks that way. I'll know a bit more after I've spoken to him again and read the police accident report.'

'Was it a light-coloured Mercedes?'

'I don't know the colour, but Mr Randle said it was a Mercedes. He was sure he'd seen the car and the men earlier this evening at a nightclub in London.'

Suzie wandered over to a seat and sat down. 'It must be connected to the raid on our house and boatyard.'

'Highly likely. I'm due to meet DI Brooke and Inspector Fairbourne tomorrow at my office to discuss this case with them. We need to get to the bottom of this quickly, before any more innocent people get hurt.'

Suzie nodded in agreement.

'Would you care for a coffee, Miss Drake?'

'No, thank you. Not at the moment, inspector.'

The receptionist called out, 'Mr Randle will be out of X-ray in about five minute's time, Miss Drake. You'll only be able to see him for a few minutes though. He's heavily drugged and will be taken to the operating room shortly.'

Suzie wandered over to the desk. 'Okay. Thank you. Can I arrange for a private room for Mr Randle when he comes out of the operation?'

'Certainly. I'll ask the secretary to see you about the details.'

'Thank you.'

Mike was wheeled back to the admissions room, where Suzie and the inspector were able to talk with him for a short while. He explained about his visit to 'The Rosy Cheeks Nightclub' and told how he tried hard to avoid being shunted off the road by the Mercedes, but ran into the central reservation after a bullet creased his back.

A fresh faced clean-shaven man in his early forties entered holding the X-ray photographs that were taken. 'I'm Mr Craig, the surgeon who'll be patching you up shortly, Mr Randle.'

'What's the damage, doc?' asked Mike.

Holding the photos up to the light and staring at them he declared, 'The X-rays show the injury to both wrists of an anteriorly displaced comminuted fracture of the distal radius. The injury to your right knee consists of haemarthrosis of the knee and a fracture of the lateral tibial condyle with a 3cm laceration of the medial aspect of the upper tibia.'

'What's that in English?' asked Suzie.

The surgeon smiled. 'Basically it means that Mr Randle has two badly broken wrists, a fracture on his right knee and a gash on his right shin, plus several other cuts and bruises, and a nasty slash across the top of his back. I'm not sure how he managed to get that.'

'I am. So, what happens next?' asked Mike.

'We'll need to operate on your wrists. The fracture to your left wrist will be held in position with an Ellis butressing plate while it mends, but your right wrist is splintered into rather a lot of small pieces, which prevents us from fitting a plate. We will have to manipulate the break into place as best we can. The fracture on your right knee will mean your leg will be in traction for a while, before it is put in plaster.'

'Will all these bones mend okay?' asked Suzie, frowning at the news of Mike's injuries.

'Yes – in time. It will take many months before they are completely healed and will probably give aching problems in the future. It is also likely to start arthritis off.'

'Great!' said Mike. 'I go through soldering, being a mercenary, endure just a few minor injuries and bullet wounds, only to be knocked off my favourite motorbike by a couple of strip-joint thugs and end up a cripple on the operating table.'

'You're not a cripple. And at least you're still alive,' reminded Suzie.

'When did you eat last, Mr Randle?' the doctor asked.

'I had a snack at lunch time. Why? Are you going to feed me? I'm feeling a bit peckish now.'

'No, we are not going to feed you, not yet. But we do have to wait six hours from the time you last ate before you can be operated on. As that was quite a time ago, we can prepare to do the operation straight away.'

'Oh! I see,' Mike said, in a disappointing voice.

'You'll have plenty of time to savour hospital food later,' suggested Suzie.

'We have to get Mr Randle prepared for the operation soon. I'll give you a few more minutes then I'll have to ask you to leave,' explained the surgeon.

'How long will it be before Mike is able to talk again after the operation?' asked Suzie.

'Several hours, and as it's nearly eleven o'clock, I would give the hospital a ring in the morning to see how things are progressing if I were you, Miss.'

Suzie nodded. 'I'll see you afterwards,' she said, giving Mike a kiss.

'Okay, luv.'

'I've arranged for you to be transferred to a private room when you come out of the operating theatre.'

'Thanks, luv. At least I'll be able to get some quiet kip when this lot have finished cutting me up.'

'I'm sure you are in good hands. I'll see you later,' she said, carefully squeezing his arm.

'And I'll talk with you again tomorrow, Miss Drake. Here's my card. Ring me if you need any help or have any problems,' said DI Maidley, handing her his card and nodding to Mike before pushing his way through the curtain.

Suzie left the hospital. She sighed heavily and with damp eyes walked slowly back to her car watched by two other hidden pairs of dry eyes staring at her from a Mercedes vehicle hidden in a dark corner of the hospital car park.

Chapter Fifteen

The Visit

In Guildford General Hospital car park, Suzie wandered slowly back to her car. Mike was about to have an operation to repair the damage inflicted on him by Jake Crossman in his attempt to kill him by running him off the road. It was a worrying time with both Reg and now Mike suffering from the attentions of a drug smuggling gang. They seemed determined to recover their contraband and eliminate anyone who stood in their way, whatever the cost.

Crossman and Lefty sat in their Mercedes, parked in a dark corner of the hospital car park. They watched Suzie walk to her car.

'I recognise that woman,' said Lefty. 'She's the other woman in the photo I told you about, and she's one of the women at the house who was shooting at us. She must be Randle's woman. We could get her now.'

'We don't need to concern ourselves with her. From what I've heard she could be trouble, but her boyfriend's in no position to give us any bother. Anyway, the boss is going to put out a contract on her and her lady friend who shot his brother.'

'That'll cost him.'

'Yeah, but he can afford it. He's making a lot of money selling those drugs to Mo and his gang.'

Suzie opened her car door. She felt a tingle in the back of her neck and rubbed it. 'I must be getting tired,' she told herself, dumping her slim frame into the seat and twisting the ignition key. She listened to the sound of the DB9 as it revved up, delighting her every time she heard its throaty roar. The car glided across the tarmac car park and disappeared through the exit gate. Crossman and Lefty listened to the vehicle's roar diminish and finally fade away to nothing as the car melted into the night.

'Go and see if you can find out what's happening to Randle, and check which ward he's in,' instructed Crossman.

'Okay, Jake,' agreed Lefty, slamming the car door shut and thrusting both hands into his tattered jacket pockets. He scurried towards the hospital entrance.

After a few minutes he returned to the car. 'The receptionist says he's quite badly injured and has just been wheeled into the operating theatre, and it'll be an hour or more before they've finished doing the op.'

'It looks like we've got a bit of a wait then,' suggested Crossman, reclining his seat and settling back.

'She also said I wouldn't be able to talk to him for quite a while as he's heavily drugged and will be asleep for several hours after the operation is finished.'

'That's good. He won't be able to take any evasive action this time. He's as good as dead right now.'

'His woman's booked him into a private room. It's on the first floor. He's in the 'John Steed Ward', room number 15.'

'That suits me fine. It's better than him being in a general ward. There won't be other people around to get in the way,' Crossman yawned, closing his eyes. 'Wake me in a couple of hours.'

'Can I put the radio on?'

'No, I want a snooze.'

'Very quietly?'

'No!' Crossman stated, raising his voice. 'I want you to keep an eye out for any problems.'

Lefty sat in silence. He was starting to get cold and pulled the collar up on his jacket. He settled down in his seat and made himself as comfortable as he could.

He stared at the clock on the dashboard and sighed, 'Roll on one o'clock.'

* * *

Crossman opened his eyes and gazed at the car clock. It showed the time as nearly half past two. He thumped a snoozing Lefty on the arm.

'Wake up. You were supposed to wake me over an hour ago.'

A startled Lefty protested, 'You wouldn't let me have the radio on. I got fed up with just sitting here, it's cold and it's late. I'm tired as well.'

Shoving his hands into his leather gloves, Crossman took his gun from its holster. He checked the clip and slammed it home. 'You wait here, and don't go back to sleep. I won't be very long. This will be a lot easier than last time. Randle will still be out for the count, drugged to the eyeballs. This time I'm not going to miss him,' he declared, putting the safety catch on, screwing the silencer in place and stuffing the gun into his waistband.

'Do you always wear gloves when you handle your gun?' asked Lefty.

'Yeah. It's a precaution I got into after I lost a gun once and thought the police might find it with my fingerprints on.'

'And did they?'

'No. I was lucky that time. But ever since then I've made sure there is none of my prints on the gun as well as filing off the serial number, just in case.'

Slinking into the hospital, Crossman pushed his way through the glass doors and kept his head down. He was about to walk past the night receptionist when he was challenged.

'Can I help you, sir?' he asked.

'No, thanks,' Crossman replied, continuing to walk on with his head down. 'I'm visiting a friend.'

'The wards are closed. There's no visiting at this time, sir,' called the receptionist, watching him disappear down the corridor.

'He's in a private room,' Crossman called.

'Oh! That's okay then,' he agreed. 'Funny time to be visiting,' he said under his breath, watching the stranger walk straight past the notice requesting every person to clean their hands with the antiseptic hand wash provided. Crossman turn into the stairway.

Emerging at the top of the stairs he looked up and down the empty corridor bathed in subdued lighting and inhaled the antiseptic aroma that most hospitals possessed. He turned up his nose.

A sign on the opposite wall indicated which direction to take for the 'John Steed Ward'. Crossman smiled and quietly moved to his left. Following the signs at each intersection he arrived in the ward and stood at the door to room number 15.

Taking a further glance around to make sure that nobody had seen him, Crossman pulled the gun from his waistband. He checked the silencer was screwed on tightly and released the safety catch. Leaning forward, he put his ear to the door and listened. All was quiet.

Inside the room, lit only by a bedside light, Mike rested after his operation. Both arms were held aloft in slings and his right leg was in the air, held in traction from a pulley near the ceiling with a heavy weight dangling close to the floor.

Gently twisting the door handle, Crossman slowly pushed the door open a few inches and peered inside. The bedside chair was empty and he saw Randle in a deep sleep, induced by the effects of the anaesthetic.

With his gun at the ready, Crossman stepped inside the room and pointed the weapon at Mike. With his finger on the trigger, he pulled up sharply as a gun barrel pushed an indent into his cheeks.

'Drop that weapon right now, or I'll put a bullet right through your bloody head,' Suzie demanded with gritted teeth.

Crossman froze, fear welled up in him. This was totally unexpected. He guessed who it was, but he had seen her leave and assumed she must have returned while he and Lefty were both asleep. He would have a few harsh words to say to him if he missed her while he was snoozing. Crossman knew she was almost certainly the one who had killed his boss, and his weapon dropped with a clatter on the tiled floor. Suzie cautiously moved back out of reach.

'How did you know I'd come here for him?' Crossman said, turning to look at her.

'I had this tingling feeling in the back of my neck when I got into my car. That usually happens when someone is watching me, it's a sort of sixth sense I have, and I don't ignore those sorts of feelings, especially when I know someone is out to kill me or Mike.'

'But I saw you leave.'

'I drove around to the rear entrance and quietly cruised in the back way.'

'That's why I didn't hear the distinctive roar of your car.'

'I've been waiting in here for Mike to be returned from the operating room.'

'Very clever. What do you intend to do now?'

Suzie pulled her mobile phone from a pocket and flipped it open. 'I'm sure Detective Inspector Maidley would like to have a chat with you, and if you try anything funny I will have no qualms about shooting you after what you've done to Mike.'

At that moment the night nurse, carrying a tray holding a flannel and a bowl of water to wipe Mike's brow with, pushed her way into the room startling the occupants. Seeing a gun in Suzie hand she screamed. Crossman grabbed her arm and shoved her towards Suzie. She clattered into her and both women crashed to the ground with the nurse dropping the tray and showering the floor with water. Crossman dashed from the room and ran down the corridor as fast as his legs would carry him. By the time Suzie got to her feet and reached the door, the corridor was empty and only the echoing sound of Crossman's footsteps could be heard clattering down the stairs toward the exit as he made a hasty retreat, Suzie helped the nurse to her feet. 'Are you all right?'

'Yes, thank you. I'm sorry I screamed. It was a bit of a shock. Who was that man?'

'I don't know, but he was here to kill Mike.'

'Kill him? That's awful!'

'I'll ring the police,' said Suzie, retrieving her mobile phone.

'I'll get a mop to clear that water up,' the nurse said. She hurried from the room, her face flushed with shock.

Suzie picked up the gun Crossman had dropped, by the silencer and shoved it in the bedside cabinet drawer. 'His fingerprints may be on that,' she told herself.

DI Maidley's telephone rang for a long time before he wearily answered it. 'Yes, what is it at this time of the night?' he angrily protested.

Suzie apologised for calling him at that hour and explained what had happened.

'Sod! Perhaps I should have anticipated that after what those witnesses said. I'll get there as quickly as I can, Miss Drake. I'll bring an armed guard with me and post him outside the door.'

'Thank you, inspector' said Suzie. She closed her mobile and flopped down in the bedside chair.

Two nurses entered the room. One mopped up the spilt water and the other wiped Mike's brow and checked his pulse. 'He looks fine,' she stated. Suzie smiled in agreement. The nurses finished their tasks and left the room.

Suzie stared at Mike, still heavily sedated and totally unaware of all the drama that was going on around him. 'Perhaps it's better this way,' she decided. 'He needs rest to recuperate. He's experienced more than enough excitement for one day.'

Chapter Sixteen

Judas

It was 6 a.m. in the 'John Steed Ward' room 15 at Guildford General Hospital. Mike's eyes flickered open after he had undergone his operation. Suzie had remained in the room all night and grabbed a few short snatches of sleep in a bedside chair. Mike was still woozy from the effect of the drugs, but understood what Suzie was telling him.

'Hello, Randy, how do you feel?' Suzie asked.

Mike looked at the lovely face of his fiancée and her slim figure. 'Randy, but unable to do anything about it. Look at me, I'm a mess,' he said, glancing at both arms in above elbow plaster and his right leg lifted up in the air.

'You're not a mess, you're just a bit knocked about that's all and at least you're still alive. You should try to remember that.'

'I guess that's something to be thankful for, though at the moment it doesn't feel much like it. It feels like my whole body is either numb or hurting like hell. What time is it?'

'It's six o'clock and I'm sure you'll be up and about, jogging along the beach in no time at all.'

He smiled, 'If you say so.'

'But it might have been a bit different if I hadn't stayed the night,' said Suzie, putting a comforting hand on Mike.

'Why? What happened?'

Suzie explained about the gunman sneaking into his room in an attempt to finish what the men had failed to do on the motorway, and how he was able to escape when a nurse entered and disturbed them.

'I bet it's the same lot that knocked me off my bike. It's a good job you were to tackle him.'

'Yes, it was the same man I saw on our security recording. I was tired, so it took me a few moments to realise that somebody was watching me in the car park when I left. I'm pleased that my sixth sense is still working.'

'Amen to that.'

'I returned through the rear entrance.'

'Good thinking. What happened after this bloke fled?'

'I rang DI Maidley. At first he was a little angry and being woken up so early in the morning, but when I explained what had happened in the hospital he was very apologetic at not realising another attempt might be made by those gangsters. He turned up shortly afterwards with an armed guard. His man's sitting outside the door now.'

'It sounds as if he's a bit late. I doubt if they'll try a third time.'

'Maybe, but I wouldn't put it past them, having had the audacity to try twice. I'm much happier knowing he's sitting out there.'

'You should be on the lookout too. It's the same mob whose gang member you killed so they may be after you as well, and possibly Jenny as she was with you when you shot that bloke.'

'Yes, that's true. I'll give her a ring and warn her.'

'Good, and you be careful.'

'I can take care of myself and I'll keep my gun handy. And talking of guns, I gave DI Maidley the gun that our would-be killer dropped. If his fingerprints are on it, he should be able to find out who he is if he's got a record.'

'If his fingerprints are on the gun?' questioned Mike.

'Yes. I noticed he was wearing gloves, so he might have been cunning enough to clean the weapon to make sure his prints weren't on it.'

'Just tell DI Maidley to check on everyone at that London nightclub. I reckon that's where he'll find him.'

'I'll do that.'

'You look tired, luv.'

'It's been a long night, but I got a little sleep.'

'What happened at your London meeting yesterday?'

Suzie related Alastaire Bignor's proposals about his filming project to Mike. She added that Jeremy Pendleton had suggested discussing the matter with her over lunch, and he was likely to ring soon to try and persuade her to keep the appointment.

'Do you think I should suggest postponing that meeting?'

'Not at all. You should discuss the proposals with Jim and Jenny to see if they think the venture might be worth pursuing. Knowing the damage that was done to *Quester*, I'd say it doesn't look as if she'll be ready in time for us to hire her out next weekend, but she could be available in a few weeks time if this Alastaire bloke is interested in hiring her to do his filming.'

'True. And talking of being interested in her, reminds me that Jeremy Pendleton is likely to be at his most attentive. With you temporarily absent, and his influence in helping to get *Quester* returned to us quickly from the police, he may see this as an opportunity to try his luck with me again.'

'Then you'll have the job of fending him off again. Won't you?'

'I will. I hope he doesn't try using this new venture as a lever like he did the last time.'

'If he does you'll have to disappoint him and we'll manage without joining the filming set. Won't we?

'We will, but it could be a great advertising opportunity for our boatyard.'

'And we could do with the money,' suggested Mike.

'Money's not everything.'

'No, but it's a long way ahead of whatever's second.'

Suzie smiled, 'And I reckon I know what you think is second, Randy.'

'Hmm,' said Mike, 'I thought you might, and thinking about it, I may have to reverse those two.'

A nurse entered the room. 'So, you're awake, Mr Randle. How do you feel?'

'With my fingers usually,' quipped Mike.

'Mike!' chastised Suzie.

'Sorry. Apart from feeling like a punch bag, I'm fine thank you, nurse. I am a bit thirsty though. My mouth's very dry. Could I have something to drink, please?'

'No, I'm sorry, not for a while. Not until the anaesthetic has completely worn off. I'll let you have a sip of water to wet your mouth with when I return.'

Mike closed his eyes in acceptance, and was unable to stifle a yawn.

'You're also tired. Now I know that you're okay and there's a guard on the door, I'll leave you in peace for a while,' said Suzie.

'Okay, luv, but remember, watch your back.'

'I will. I'll be back to see you later on. No chasing the nurses now.'

Mike smiled. Suzie gave him a kiss and left the nurse to give him his sip of water. She returned home, watching carefully to make sure she was not followed. She saw nothing and kept a particularly sharp eye out for any Mercedes that were on the road. At home she rang Jim and

Jenny with news of Mike's troubles and the progress he was making. After warning Jenny to be on the lookout for trouble, she arranged to meet them later on to discuss Alastaire Bignor's project.

*   *   *

Later that morning, DI Brooke called at Suzie's house on the way to his meeting with DI Maidley and Inspector Fairbourne. He showed her the photos from the boatyard break-in he had printed from the security DVD he received from Mike. She identified Crossman as the man who had entered the hospital intending to finish the job of killing Mike. Afterwards Brooke kept his appointment with the two policemen and they pooled their information. Forensics discovered a partial fingerprint on the gun left at the hospital but were unable to match it with any they had on file. Jake Crossman kept well out of the way when the local police made another visit to the nightclub looking for him.

His home address was obtained from Angie and he was later questioned by Brooke's two DCs, Green and Teal, but denied visiting the hospital and produced several witnesses to state that he did not leave the nightclub until it closed at 3 a.m. It was his word against Suzie's and the police were unable to charge him with anything except illegal entry into SMJ boatyard. Crossman would be given a date when he would have to make his court appearance.

Jim and Jenny called in to see Suzie at her home to discuss Alastaire Bignor's project before they all travelled to visit Mike in hospital. The anaesthetic had worn off and he was experiencing more pain, and despite his suntan looked pale and in severe discomfort.

Suzie asked, 'How long will your arms be in these slings?'

'Just for a few days they tell me. Then my left arm plaster will be cut down to below the elbow so I can feed myself. At the moment the nurses have to do everything for me.'

'I bet you make the most of that.'

Mike smiled. 'It's not as glamorous as it sounds.'

'I bet,' said Suzie. 'Colin showed me a photo of a man named Jake Crossman who works at 'The Rosy Cheeks Nightclub'. He was the man I tackled in here this morning, but Colin said when he was questioned about it by his men, he produced several witnesses to say he was with them at time you were run off the road and when I tackled him here.'

'No doubt men who work for the nightclub.'

107

'So I believe. They gave him an alibi so it's his word against mine. He apparently refused to go to the station to have his fingerprints taken. He rang his solicitor who started to complain about police harassment of his clients who work at the nightclub when he was charged with illegal entry into our boatyard.'

'That's typical! I'm sure he's the one who knocked me off my bike.'

'Probably. But is seems the police are powerless to do anything about it at the moment.'

The three of them discussed Alastaire Bignor's proposals with Mike for almost an hour and could see by then he was becoming tired.

'You look as if you could do with a rest, Mike,' said Suzie, brushing hair from his brow. 'We're all agreed about pursuing this idea further so we'll go now and let you get some sleep.'

'Okay, luv.'

She gave him a kiss. 'The repair men are coming to fix the gates today and also the alarm console is being replaced later today, so our home will be locked up tight again.'

'Good. I'm pleased about that but still keep a sharp eye out, both of you.'

'We will. 'Bye.'

The trio left Mike to have his sleep in peace and quiet.

*   *   *

Having fled from the hospital without his gun, Crossman was now worried. Despite not leaving his fingerprints on the weapon and successfully refusing to be fingerprinted, he realised their ballistics experts were likely to check the bullets and may well discover a match with those that killed Phadkar's men aboard *Quester II*.

If this happened it was inevitable they would speak to his boss about this new piece of evidence as soon as it came to light. Knowing it was Jake Crossman who went to the hospital to kill Mike Randle, Phadkar would quickly realise his trusted gang member was the person responsible for trying to steal his drugs and it was he who killed the men on the yacht, including his nephew.

It was time for Crossman to make his move. He entered Khurram Phadkar's office.

'The police were here this morning,' Phadkar stated.

'Yes. I decided to make myself scarce until they'd gone. I saw no point in tempting fate, so I went home. I told Lefty to disappear for a while as well.'

'They have photos of you from the boatyard and asked me where you were. I told them you no longer worked here but you had better keep a watchful eye out for them. They will be back.'

'That's already sorted. They had my address and came around to my flat to interview me. They wanted me to go with them to the police station, but I refused. They've got no proof I tried to kill Randle and couldn't arrest me for anything. I'd already set up an alibi with a couple of the guards here at the nightclub and our solicitor made sure they left empty handed. I will probably have to make a court appearance to explain about the boatyard break in. I've already thought up an excuse to explain that.'

'Good.'

'Did they say anything about your brother?'

'Yes. It was as I feared,' sighed Phadkar. 'They told me he was killed last night breaking into a house but would not say which house it was or who it was that shot him.'

'Though we know who is responsible and where they live.'

'Yes. Kashif's body is in the local morgue. I am going to make the formal identification at eleven o'clock this morning,' he said, glancing at his watch.

Jake Crossman nodded, saying nothing.

'From what the police asked me, I presume you failed to take care of that meddling Randle person?' Phadkar said.

'No, his fiancée was waiting in the hospital room with a gun. I was lucky to escape. I'm sure it was her that killed your brother. She's no stranger to firearms.'

'So I understand. I have received two replies to my internet request for a hit man. I gave both of them some more information on our targets and one of them has agreed to take the contract on. He telephoned his acceptance to me this morning.'

'That's good,' said Crossman, settling in the chair in front of Phadkar's desk. It gave him the opportunity to pull out the gun stuffed in his waistband, unseen.

'I have transferred the payment to the man's account and sent him the rest of the details on Suzie Drake's home and business address. He will have to find out who the other female is. Everything is set for him to eliminate both women though he has got another contract to complete first, so it will be a week or so before he can take care of things.'

'Is that okay with you?'

'It is perfect. It gives me time to distance myself from the hit. I asked him to make it look like an accident if he could, but to be sure he takes care of them whatever way he has to.'

'What about Randle?'

'I thought you were going to take care of him, so I did not include him in the deal. If I want our man to add Randle to his hit list it will add to the cost.'

'It must be expensive,' suggested Crossman.

'It is, but it will be worth it to get my revenge. My brother did not deserve to be shot by a couple of gun happy females.'

'Has your buyer collected the drugs yet? I guess you'll need the money from that shipment to pay the hit man,' Crossman probed.

Phadkar raised his eyebrows. 'What makes you think I've got the drugs?'

'Lefty might be a trustworthy employee, but we both know he can't keep anything to himself. I reckon that's why you got Crusher to give him the misleading information that they grabbed the wrong package.'

'You are quite right. I did not want everyone to know I was keeping drugs here at the nightclub.'

'You must have been worried when the police raided the place?'

'A little, but the drugs are well hidden.'

'When does Mo and his men collect the stuff?'

'They will be here at three o'clock this afternoon.'

Jake Crossman had got the information he was after. He took his gloves from his pocket and slipped them on.

'What on earth are you doing, Jake?' his boss asked.

Crossman screwed the silencer on to his gun and pointed it at Phadkar. A look of shock transformed his expression.

'Well … you see, this is my backup gun. Unfortunately, I left the other one at the hospital when I was so rudely interrupted by that Drake woman.'

'So? You always tell me you make sure the gun is clean and has no fingerprints on it.'

'That is true, but the police ballistics experts are bound check it and may discover it was the gun used to kill your drug smuggling trio on that yacht.'

Phadkar's eyes opened wide and he jumped up from his chair. 'What! You Judas,' he yelled. 'You killed my men. Why?'

'That's simple – the rich rewards. The drugs are worth a great deal of money. The men all knew me so they didn't suspect anything. Killing them was quick and easy.'

'And my poor nephew?'

'He was more trouble. I needed to know where the drugs were hidden. They weigh quite a lot so I reckoned I would find them easily, but I was wrong. I tore the boat apart and couldn't find them, so I had to persuade him to tell me. His pain threshold was quite low. He squealed when I chopped his finger off.'

'You bastard!'

'Shut up and sit down,' demanded Crossman, pointing his gun at Phadkar. 'As you are well aware they were hidden in the engine sump, so I didn't have time to get them. The bloody coastguard arrived too quickly.'

'How did they know about the shipment?'

'I tipped them off. I expected to grab the drugs and be away in plenty of time. If the stupid coastguard had been a few minutes later spotting the yacht, it would have been blown to bits and nobody would have found anything. They would probably have though it was an accident, someone getting careless, and of course all the evidence would have been at the bottom of the channel.'

'You are a traitorous murderer. What is it that you want?'

'The drugs. Where are they? They must be close by for you to give them to your buyer this afternoon.'

'Go to hell!' Phadkar spat.

'I probably will, but not before you if you don't tell me where you've hidden those drugs,' Crossman replied, leaning across the desk and putting the gun to Phadkar's forehead.

'All right! All right! If I tell you, then what?'

'I get the drugs and the cash when I sell them to Mo for a good profit, and unlike your brother you get to live. That's a fair deal, isn't it?'

'I don't have much choice, do I?'

'No, you don't.'

Phadkar rose from his desk and wandered over to the corner of the room. He pulled back the carpet and lifted the floorboards to reveal the safe.

'Very clever. No wonder the police missed it.' Crossman stated. 'Open it.'

Spinning the tumblers to enter the combination, Phadkar twisted the handle and lifted the safe door open. Crossman watched him carefully. He needed to know the combination. The safe contained the drugs, some cash and a gun.

Phadkar looked at the gun and reached into the safe. 'These drugs are worth a lot of money,' he stated to distract. He grabbed the gun and pointed it at his renegade employee but was not quick enough to pull the trigger. Jake Crossman's weapon spat out a lethal bullet that hit Phadkar squarely in the chest and knocked him flying.

As a dying Phadkar slid down the office wall staining it red, the door opened and Crusher stepped into the room. 'Boss, I've con ....' His words trailed off as he took in the situation.

Crossman swung his gun round but did not fire as Crusher dashed from the room. He charged into the general office, where Angie was engrossed in counting the money from the previous evening's takings.

'Jake's killed the boss,' he blurted out.

'What!' Angie yelled.

'It's true. I saw him standing over the boss with a gun in his hand. Mr Phadkar had blood running down his shirt from a bullet hole.'

The door opened and Crossman stalked in, still holding his gun. Crusher hid behind Angie.

'What's this all about, Jake?' she asked, standing to face him.

'There's been a change in the management here. I'm in charge now. I'm the new boss.'

'And what happens to the rest of us?'

'Nothing. You can all continue as before as long as you keep your mouths shut. Nothing else has changed, only I'll be giving the orders from now on,' he stated, unscrewing the silencer from his gun and pocketing them both.

Crusher was still wide eyed and looked terrified.

'There's nothing for you to worry about, Crusher,' Crossman stated, pulling at the fingers of his gloves to remove them, 'as long as you do as you're told and keep quiet about what happened here today. Is that clear?' he said, slapping Angie's desk with his gloves to emphasise his demand.

Crusher jumped at the crack resounding from the gloves and nodded his head. 'Yes, Jake. I mean, boss.'

'Good. Then the first job for your new boss, is to get rid of the body of your old boss and to make sure the room is left clean without a trace of what's happened there,' he said.

'Yes, boss,' answered Crusher.

'And make sure the body is well hidden where nobody can find it.'

'I'll bury him in the old disused quarry.'

'Good. I like that. Get Lefty to help you.'

Moving slowly to the door, not taking his eyes from his new boss, Crusher hurried from the room to carry out his task.

Jake Crossman smiled. He had not exactly planned things this way but everything had worked out rather better than he could have hoped for. He now had control of the nightclub, control of the drug smuggling business and would be making himself a lot of money when Mo arrived with cash to buy the drugs that afternoon.

Chapter Seventeen

A New Boss

It was exactly three o'clock in the afternoon when three men barged into the new boss's office without knocking at 'The Rosy Cheeks Nightclub' in Brixton. The men were all natives from Caribbean islands. They carried themselves with assurance, as a reminder to everyone they meant business, and were surprised to see a rearranged office and Jake Crossman sitting behind the only remaining desk. One of the Phadkar brothers was killed by Suzie Drake and the other one shot by Jake Crossman. This left the way clear for him to assume control of the nightclub and drugs operation.

'I'm Mo. Where's Phadkar? I arranged to meet him here this afternoon,' growled the first man strutting into the office with his two helpers standing by the door to see they were not disturbed. One man held firmly on to an attaché case.

Crossman took his time to answer. He lit a cigar. His intention was to create the impression he was in complete charge, and would do things in his own time and not be rushed by anyone.

As Phadkar's bodyguard in case of trouble, Crossman was present at previous visits of Mo and his men. Now in charge, he gazed longingly at the attaché case he knew was stuffed full with wads of notes. He also knew it meant his face was not unfamiliar to them. On all the previous deals after the talk, the handover had been kept a secret. Crossman and Mo's men had been asked to leave the room before the deal was finalised, a move that had annoyed him.

Knowing his visitors were due and realising they might not take readily to a change of contact for their expected meeting, Crossman made preparations. He stuffed a gun in his waistband and had another weapon sitting in an open lower desk drawer, hidden from view.

His three visitors were all dressed in highly coloured tops, scruffy jeans and jackets that looked past their best, but was in keeping with others in the area where they operated. They all wore chains around their necks and had several pieces of flashy jewellery on their fingers and wrists. The East end of London was their patch and they needed to blend in with the locals. Mo was big at over six foot tall, with black wiry hair tied in a ponytail down his back and a bushy beard to match. His hands were large and he clenched his fist and banged it on the desk.

'I don't expect to be kept waiting,' he snarled.

'Why don't you sit down,' suggested Crossman, pointing to a chair in front of the desk; replaced after Mike Randle had demolished the original one over Crusher's head.

Mo kicked the chair aside. 'I didn't come here to sit down. I want the stuff I was promised by Phadkar. There's been enough delay already. My clients are getting restless, and so am I.'

'You'll get your stuff, but there have been some changes around here. I'm Jake Crossman and I'm in charge now.'

'I know who you are. I've seen you here before, but Phadkar's the man in charge. Where's is he?'

'He's gone up in the world, or perhaps I should say he's gone down. I'm not sure which.'

A frown crossed Mo's brow. He did not understand the sarcastic comment.

Crossman added, 'He's dead, and so is his twin brother, shot by some female while he was on a fishing trip.'

'A fishing trip?' queried Mo.

'Yeah, fishing for lost goods; the drugs. Well I've got them now and I've taken over the business. I'm the new boss around here, so if you want your stuff you'll have to deal with me in future.'

'Okay. So, where's the stuff?'

'Show me the money first.'

Turning to look at his men by the door, Mo nodded. One man stepped forward and dumped the attaché case on the desk and unlocked it. Mo flipped back the lid and spun the case round to reveal stacks of £50 notes crammed in tightly.

'£250,000 as agreed.'

A surprise look crossed the new bosses face. 'I understood this package is worth twice that amount.'

'My deal was for a quarter-of-a-million pounds,' assured Mo.

Crossman looked at him and said nothing. He picked up the telephone. 'Angie, get in here.'

Angie pushed her way through the doorway, forcing a smile at the three men in the office. She had seen them all before and new her old boss was careful not to upset them. They were good clients, but turned nasty very quickly when things did not go as planned.

'Yes, Mr Crossman,' she politely asked stepping up to the desk.

'Do you know what the arrangements were that the late Mr Phadkar had with these gentlemen about the payment for their goods?'

'Yes, I do,' she replied glancing at Mo with slight trepidation in her eyes. She did not want to anger him.

'Please explain, so we all know what that arrangement is.'

'Half of the payment would be brought into the office and the … items would be inspected. If that was okay, he … that is Mo, will take the items out to their car, where they will do some sort of test on them. If all is satisfactory you will receive the second half of the payment and they will leave with their purchase.'

'Thank you, Angie. That will be all.'

Looking warily at the men Angie slipped from the room, glad to leave them behind. With the unexpected new arrangement the tension was high, and filled the room like a heavy mist hanging in the air. Mo's men were armed and would not hesitate to use their guns if a double cross looked likely. Crossman knew this as well.

The door closed and a smile crossed Mo's face. 'I thought you knew about getting the second half when we get out to the car and do the test.'

'Is that so? Well, I do now. Right, so we all know where we stand, don't we?'

'Where's the stuff?' Mo demanded.

Sliding open the top desk drawer, Crossman pulled the package out and laid it on the desk. Mo unwrapped it revealing ten plastic bags bulging with white powder.

'One of them has been opened.'

'Merely to make sure it is of the highest quality for you and your customers, Mo,' bluffed Crossman. 'I assure you the quantity is correct.'

Mo looked unconvinced. He opened one of the other packages, licked his finger and tasted a small sample. He nodded in approval. 'It seems okay. I'll know for sure after we've done the tests and weighed it.'

He closed the package, tipped the money out of the attaché case on to the desk, replaced it with the drugs and headed for the door. Crossman grabbed the money, shoved it into the desk drawer and locked it.

Pocketing the keys he hurried from his office, entered the general office and quickly spoke to Angie. 'Find Lefty and tell him he's to secretly take photographs of all Mo's men as they test the drugs, and afterwards follow them back to his place. I want some evidence in case he gets awkward and I also want to know where he hides out.'

Angie nodded and Crossman hurried out through the rear entrance. In the yard were two vehicles. Mo opened the boot lid of his car to mask their actions from anyone who passed by the rear entrance and opened the package. His two guards watched to make sure they were not disturbed as an oriental looking man stepped forward and produced a small wooden rack holding ten test tubes. He added a liquid to them and sprinkled a small amount of the drug from each package into each phial before vigorously shaking each one in turn. When this was done he held the rack up to the light and inspected the colour. He nodded his approval and tipped the test tube contents on to the ground before pulling out a set of scales and weighing each package. The weights were satisfactory and he signalled to Mo that everything was correct.

'My man says it's all okay,' he announced, handing Crossman an attaché case containing the second half of the payment.

He thumbed through a few of the stacks of notes. 'That all seems to be in order,' he said.

'When do I get the next shipment?' Mo asked. 'This one is very late and I will need more of the stuff very soon.'

'I'm not sure at the moment. I'm setting things up right now. I'll let you know as soon as the arrangements are made. I'll probably ring you some time next week.'

With a scowl on his face and without replying, Mo and his men climbed into their cars and drove away.

'The longer you wait, the more eager you'll be to get the stuff and pay the price, and the next batch will cost you even more,' Crossman said to himself, watching their vehicles depart. Lefty jumped into the nightclub's Mercedes car. He looked at Crossman who nodded and watched him follow Mo's vehicles.

In their car Mo looked at his men. 'We will have to keep an eye on that new boss Mr Jake Crossman. I don't trust him like I did the Phadkar twins. It's very strange they should both die at the same time. It smells fishy to me. Crossman looks like a greedy man and may try to push the price up. If he does we will have to kill him, after we've found out how he imports the stuff. I'd like to cut him out of the loop, then there'll be a lot more profit in it for us.'

The men all nodded. 'This batch will satisfy our dealer network for a while,' one man suggested, 'but we'll need more of the stuff quite quickly if we're to keep everyone happy.'

'I know,' said Mo. 'I'll give Crossman one week to come up with a new delivery date before we take action.'

Today had been a good one for Jake Crossman. He had got rid of his old boss, taken over at the nightclub and received £500,000 for the drugs that Phadkar had organised and paid for. He knew Phadkar had used Angie to contact the supplier to obtain the heroin and also knew he could slip easily into assuming the role of being the boss. There was a lot of money to be made at this game, but he had to be careful. The police would be on the lookout now they suspected the nightclub of dealing in drugs and they were also looking for the men who had tried to kill Mike Randle. But, Crossman's wish was to be very rich very quickly, and control of the nightclub and drug dealings would enable his wish to come true.

Chapter Eighteen

SMJ Boatyard

With Mike not around because of his confinement in hospital, Suzie was certain she would receive a telephone call from Jeremy Pendleton and probably quite soon. It was a bright Monday morning. The good weather continued with the sun rising in an almost clear blue sky with a few cotton wool clouds drifting lazily across the heavens. Everyone was keeping their fingers crossed that the weather they were enjoying would continue. Mike was not one of them. He was spending his third day in Guildford General Hospital recovering from the trauma of his near-fatal encounter with Jake Crossman's Mercedes. The good weather did not enthral him a great deal, other than it gave the private room where he was recuperating a bright outlook blessed by the sun's warm rays cascading through the window. A damp, dismay rain clouded sky would only add to the dejected feelings he felt, coupled with the discomfort he was obliged to endure, because of a man he was unable to track down and deal with – for the time being.

Suzie was unaccustomed to sleeping in a large empty water bed on her own as comfortable as it was and found she tossed and turned giving her nights that were restless. After her early morning jog along the nearby beach, she drove to the boatyard and attended to business matters in the mornings and kept the afternoon free of appointments in order to visit Mike.

The telephone on her desk rang.

'Good morning, Suzie. And how are you this bright sunny day,' asked Jeremy Pendleton, his smooth telephone voice oozing the charm he possessed.

'Fine, thank you, Jeremy,' Suzie replied, congratulating herself that she had correctly anticipated his telephone call would arrive quite soon. She guessed what was coming next.

'I hear Mike has had rather a nasty accident and will be out of the picture for quite a while.'

'Yes, that is correct. Bad news travels fast it seems.'

'I still have a lot of contacts in the newspaper industry and they pass on any news to me that's interesting.'

'I see. And is news about Mike's accident interesting?'

'Any news that's connected with you is interesting to me.'

'Still watching me carefully then?'

'I like watching you, Suzie.'

'So it seems. Watching is one thing – touching is another.'

'I'll try to remember that in future.'

Suzie smiled to herself.

'But seriously, how is Mike?' he asked.

'He is in hospital it's true, but it wasn't an accident. Someone tried to kill him.'

'Really? I was told there was speculation that it was deliberate, but I couldn't believe it. Not Giles Harman seeking his revenge for your outburst at him during the London meeting I hope.'

'No, not that rat, but a different one, and believe me it's true. They've tried twice.'

'Twice!'

'And I was shot at during a break-in at our house, we suspect by the same unsavoury group of people.'

'Goodness me! You do lead a dangerous life, Suzie. I didn't realise that boat building was such a perilous occupation.'

'It has it's moments.'

'It's not connected with your murky past, is it?'

'No, it isn't. And there's nothing murky about my past.'

'Even though you refuse to tell me much about it.'

'It's private, Jeremy. Though I imagine you have been able to find out a lot of what I refused to tell you, no doubt through your contacts in the newspaper industry.'

'Perhaps, some of it. Maybe one day you'll tell me yourself what it's like to abscond from an approved school in England to become a mercenary fighting in the African jungle?'

'Hmm, perhaps.'

'In the meantime, as you seem to be surrounded by ruffians, would you like a couple of bodyguards to look after you?'

'I don't think that will be necessary, thank you, Jeremy. I'm not surrounded by ruffians and as your newspaper enquiries have told you, I was once a mercenary so I know how to look after myself.'

'Are you sure? I'd be very happy to guard your body if you'd let me.'

'Jeremy,' Suzie said in a mock telling off tone of voice. 'I'm an engaged woman now, and just because Mike is temporarily incapacitated, don't think you can start taking advantage of the situation.'

'Okay, Suzie. You're a hard woman to get close to.'

'So, why did you telephone me?'

'Oh! I almost forgot. Alastaire would like to visit your boatyard to assess its suitability for his project. I told him your assets were the best.'

Suzie smiled at the remark. 'Did you now? And what assets were you referring to?'

'Well, the boatyard and yachts of course. Though I did happen to mention that you are a rather very lovely and generally quite agreeable lady, as well as managing a boatyard that produces excellent craft. After a trip on my yacht and seeing you at the London meeting he was in full agreement.'

'I see.'

'If you are successful in your negotiations, I'm sure Alastaire would be only too willing to let you have a small part in his project.'

'Would he now? Well, no thank you, Jeremy. As you know, he's already suggested something similar to Jenny and me at the meeting, which we both turned down.'

'That's a pity. Much of his filming will be done on a sun-kissed beach, on a Mediterranean island with many scantily clad women in attendance. I'm sure you'd fit in a treat in your bikini and show many of them up.'

'Flattery will not get you anywhere with me, Jeremy,' Suzie stated, though she secretly enjoyed his continual complements while fending off his constant efforts to draw her into his charming web.

'Still, you can't blame a chap for trying.'

With a smile playing on the edge of her lips, Suzie remarked, 'I don't. Just be ready for a disappointment.'

'So, will you let Alastaire and me look over your assets?' he asked, tongue in cheek.

'I've already discussed the matter with Mike and the other directors, Jim and Jenny Sterling. You and Alastaire Bignor may visit SMJ Boatyard Ltd to discuss his project,' Suzie carefully worded.

'Good. When would be convenient?'

'I visit Mike at the hospital each afternoon, so it will have to be a morning if you would like me to be present.'

'Oh, I do. It wouldn't be the same without you. Shall we say tomorrow morning?'

Flipping the pages over in her diary, Suzie said, 'Tomorrow's a bit difficult, would Wednesday be suitable?'

'Wednesday's fine.'

'Say, around ten o'clock?'

'Ten o'clock it is. I look forward to seeing you then. Goodbye, Suzie.'

'Goodbye, Jeremy.'

Replacing the receiver, Suzie smiled at Jeremy Pendleton's persistent manner to remain as friendly with her as possible, while taking every opportunity to flatter and impress her. Having tasted the fruits of her enticing sexual expertise once, he craved more of the same and would not pass any opportunity to fulfil his dream, however remote the possibility remained, though as she was engaged to a man like Mike Randle, he knew he had to tread carefully not to upset either of them again.

*   *   *

Later that afternoon at 'The Rosy Cheeks Nightclub' in London, which was now firmly in the grasp of Jake Crossman, the new boss looked forward to a profitable time ahead. However Mo, the local drug dealer with whom he did business, was unhappy about his enforced change of supplier. Furthermore, he was considering cutting Crossman out of the dealings if time showed that events were not going to run as smoothly as they had previously done with the Phadkar twins, providing he could find an alternative means of supply.

In his office at the nightclub, Crossman, eager to line his pockets with easy money as quickly as possible, wanted to organise the next shipment of drugs quickly. He grabbed the telephone. 'Angie, get on to our supplier in South America and check when the next delivery is due,' he instructed. 'And check the price for me as well, will you?'

'Yes, Mr Crossman, but a shipment is not yet due for another six weeks.'

'I realise that, but I want to bring the delivery date forward if possible. Mo's bleating about the last shipment being late and he wants to receive another one as quickly as he can. It seems he's desperate, which is good news for us.'

'Good news for you, perhaps,' thought Angie.

'Ask them if they can hurry things along a bit, and don't say anything about the change in management to this office. I don't want to frighten them away. As far as they are concerned, everything is the same apart from us requesting an earlier delivery.'

'Yes, Mr Crossman.'

Phadkar had entrusted Angie with the job of ringing the supplier to confirm the arrangements, so she was familiar with the setup and her voice was known to them. As instructed, she said nothing about the new boss but simply enquired whether an earlier delivery could be made.

After the call she stepped into Crossman's office and explained, 'The earliest they can make the next drop is in three weeks time.'

He looked up from his desk. 'That's good. And the price?'

'The price is the same at $500,000 in cash.'

'Good. Tell them to make the early delivery in the usual way.'

'We'll need a motor yacht to collect the goods. Mr Phadkar was searching for one to purchase.'

'Not sensible when we can hire one. They cost a lot of money to buy and to keep, and they have to be registered. If it was spotted it would lead the police to us. No, it's best to hire one – much less of a problem. See to it,' Crossman demanded.

'Would you like me to ring Mo and give him the delivery date?'

'No. I'll do that in a couple of day's time. I want him to sweat a little. The longer he has to wait, the more cooperative he's likely to be.'

'I wouldn't bet on that. Mo doesn't look like the sort of bloke who's got where he is by being cooperative.'

'That's my concern. You sort out the ordering from our South American friends and the hiring of that boat.'

'I'll make a few enquiries, but I can't hire the boat until we get a firm date for the delivery.'

'Well, just get on with it,' Crossman said, waving his hand to send Angie from the room.

Angie pursed her lips in annoyance at the way she was being treated by her new boss. Mr Phadkar was much more pleasant to her. She nodded her compliance to the orders and left. Crossman picked up the telephone as the door closed, to contact Mo.

'I hope you've got good news for me,' stated Mo.

'Not exactly. I've been on to my supplier and they're not sure when they can make the next delivery. It seems things are a bit difficult at the moment.'

'What do you mean, a bit difficult?'

'They wouldn't elaborate, but let me assure you that I am doing everything I can to have the goods shipped here at the absolute earliest opportunity.'

'You wouldn't be stringing me along, would you?'

'Of course not,' said Crossman, with an elaborate gesture of innocence in his voice. 'I want the business as much as you do. I'll ring again when I've got more news. It should only be a few days.'

Crossman replaced the receiver and smiled. 'I'll get you the goods, but on my terms and at my price.'

Mo screwed up his face and scowled. 'I'm sure he's leading me on. We may have to take care of Mr Jake Crossman, he'd better come through with the goods and soon.'

Chapter Nineteen

The Boatyard Visit

Wednesday morning dawned with the good weather continuing and the sun again rose in an almost clear blue sky, with a gentle breeze blowing to counter the warmth penetrating the few clouds that lazily drifted across the heavens. It was a perfect morning for Alastaire Bignor and Jeremy Pendleton to inspect SMJ Boatyard's location and assets.

They arrived in a Rolls Royce driven by Pendleton's chauffer Henry, and parked next to Jim Sterling's Rolls Royce and alongside Mike and Suzie's Aston Martin. Both cars deliberately parked next to each other to counter any one-upmanship that Pendleton might attempt. He was adept at using his wealth to impress and influence people, a characteristic that Suzie was well aware of. Two could play at that game, and she wanted to make sure they were able to match him that day.

Jim, Jenny and Suzie stepped from the 1930's office block into the sun drenched yard to greet their visitors as Pendleton's chauffeur opened their car door. Suzie wore a light, summary trouser suit in pale green, a colour to match her eyes. She was expecting to show the men around and may have to clamber in and out of several of the yards vessels. She knew that wearing trousers would be more appropriate, especially with Jeremy Pendleton nearby. Not that she worried about hiding her long, shapely legs, she knew they were attractive and greatly admired, but this was not the right time or place to show them off. This was a business meeting and with Mike absent she wanted to make sure it stayed that way.

'Good morning, Suzie,' Pendleton said, grabbing her hand and planting his usual kiss on the back. 'And Jenny,' he added, repeating the action. 'Good to see you both again. And Jim,' shaking his hand vigorously, 'nice to see you again as well.' Both men had a strong grip.

Suzie smiled at Bignor, greetings and an introduction to Jim were exchanged.

'Good morning, Henry,' said Suzie, deliberately including the chauffeur.

'Good morning, Miss,' he replied, touching his cap.

She had previously met Henry when he ignored Jeremy Pendleton's instructions and gave assistance to her and Mike. It was a gesture he could have been in trouble with his boss for if Pendleton had proof that Henry had interfered with his plans. It was an unselfish act which Mike and Suzie greatly appreciated and helped them to avoid a difficult and potentially embarrassing situation.

Bignor, dressed in a purple shirt with a bright red cravat at his neck, scanned the boatyard and workshops with a camera lens pressed to his eye. 'You're right about this location, Jeremy, this is very good so far.'

'I knew you would be impressed with this location, Alastaire. It's perfect for your project.'

'This is a lovely entrance, coming through the archway and curving into the open yard,' he maintained, sweeping his arm round to indicate the movement. 'This would look very impressive if filmed correctly. And of course, I know how to get the best out of any location I film,' he boasted.

'Perhaps Miss Drake would kindly agree to show us around the boatyard,' suggested Pendleton.

'Jeremy is up to his old tricks again,' thought Suzie. She looked at Jenny and Jim.

Jim remarked, 'I have a potential client to visit shortly.'

'And I've got work in the office to do, following up on the equipment we've ordered for *Quester* to make sure we receive it in time,' said Jenny, with a slight grin on her face, aware she was leaving Suzie to continue her bantering exchanges with Pendleton.

'Well, it looks as if we've got you all to ourselves,' he suggested.

'Not quite, Jeremy' countered Suzie. 'George is looking after the workshops until our foreman Reg returns. It's his responsibility to accompany any visitors around the workplace. Health and safety rules you understand, Jeremy.'

'Yes, of course. It wouldn't do for us to be hurt in your boatyard. You've had enough of your people getting injured lately,' Pendleton stated, slightly annoyed that his efforts to get Suzie alone to accompany them seemed to be in vain.

His remark brought an icy stare from her.

A man wearing a bright yellow safety hat approached them.

They were introduced to George, a cheerful looking, slightly overweight man in his late forties with thinning hair and a dark complexion, due to the nature of his outdoor job. A job at which he had been employed most of his life.

'Your safety hats, gentlemen,' offered George, who also passed one to Suzie.

The two men donned their hats, as did Suzie. 'Follow me gentlemen,' she said.

George trailed along behind them and left his boss to do all the talking and explain what projects they were working on. Suzie showed them several vessels that were being refurbished or updated. Some of these were the yachts that were damaged by the intruders and were now being repaired, after the insurance agent, Mr Groombridge, had again made an examination of the damage.

Finally they came to the largest and most luxurious motor yacht in the yard. The group climbed aboard *Quester II*, using a specially prepared set of steps instead of the ladder the workmen used. The yacht was in a vastly improved state from the wrecked craft that was returned to them by the police but still had much work to complete before she was ready to take to the water again.

'This is the luxury yacht we are offering for the filming. As you gentlemen can see, this will be a fine vessel once again when all the work has been completed,' maintained Suzie.

'Is this a new vessel you are building?' asked Bignor.

'No. This yacht was hired out by us to clients and unfortunately it transpired that she was used by pirates to smuggle drugs.'

'How exciting,' said Bignor.

'Not for us. The inside was damaged beyond repair, which is why we are rebuilding her,' said Suzie, deliberately omitting to reveal that three men were murdered aboard the vessel. 'Unfortunately she won't be ready it time for the customers who'd booked it for their holiday, but she should be finished quite soon and will be available for your project if she matches your requirements.'

'You've had to disappoint your customers then?' Pendleton asked.

'No, we try not to disappoint them. They've agreed to use a smaller craft that we've made ready and we have offered them a full refund. They were very happy to receive a free holiday, even if it was aboard a vessel that is slightly more cramped than the one they'd originally booked.'

'That was very generous of you.'

'It keeps our customers happy, Jeremy. Hopefully they will tell their friends and return many times to us in the future for their boating holidays.'

'Bravo, Miss Drake. That was a very sound move and you are to be congratulated for having such good business sense,' asserted Bignor.

Suzie smiled, 'Thank you. Would you gentlemen please follow me.'

The group followed Suzie below deck, and surveyed the lounge, galley and cabins.

'This is an excellent boat,' enthused Bignor.

'This is a luxury motor yacht,' corrected Suzie. 'Or at least it will be once we've finished refurbishing her.'

'Yes, quite.'

'She is sixty foot long, has three double bedrooms, two en-suite, a lounge/saloon, a galley and a laundry, and with twin 600 HP diesel motors will cruise at around seventeen knots.'

'Would it be possible to make a few alterations, as you are working on her anyway?'

'Possibly, Mr Bignor. It depends on what sort of alterations you are thinking of.'

'If certain areas could be widened slightly to accommodate the cameras, lighting and sound equipment, it would be a great help. Also, it would be useful if a ramp could be fashioned down the steps to below deck for us to wheel the equipment in. It is quite heavy.'

Suzie nodded. 'What areas are you thinking of?'

'The passageway leading to the bedrooms is a little cramped for our equipment and the doorways are slightly narrow.'

'The doors are a standard width and would look odd if they were widened, but the passageway could be made wider. How much extra width are you thinking of?'

Bignor took out a tape measure and stretched it across the passageway between wooden uprights. 'Not a lot wider. Perhaps nine or ten inches, say 250 millimetres. I know it's only a small amount, but it would make a big difference.'

Looking towards George, Suzie asked, 'What do you think, George? Can they be widened, and easily?'

'They can certainly be widened, Miss. Making a ramp to fit on the steps is no bother. Our carpenter can do that. Widening the passageway is a bit more tricky. It'll make the bedrooms a little smaller, but they're all a good size and there's still plenty of room in them. This framework will need to be replaced,' he said, slapping the cabin upright.

'How long would it take?' asked Suzie.

'I reckon it's about an extra three to four days work, Miss.'

'That's manageable.'

'Good,' stated Bignor. 'If that's acceptable to you, and if we can agree the financial details, I think we may have found what we are looking for. Don't you agree, Jeremy?' he asked, turning to face him.

'I most certainly do. I always though this was the most suitable boatyard.'

'Are you not looking at other yards?' Suzie asked.

'Not if we can settle arrangements here. Jeremy is quite right, this yard is perfect for my requirements. I don't need to waste time looking any further. Your staff can carry on working while we film. I want everything to look as authentic as possible.'

There were smiles all round and after a look at the rest of the yard while he checked camera angles and made notes, Alastaire Bignor and Jeremy Pendleton said their farewells.

'Thank you for a very enjoyable morning, Miss Drake,' Bignor said as they shook hands. 'My financial director will be in touch with you about the arrangements later today. I'd like to get things finalised as quickly as possible.'

'Thank you, Suzie,' Pendleton added, planting a farewell kiss on her hand. 'I'm pleased that Alastaire agrees your assets are the best.'

Suzie pursed her lips to try avoiding a smile, but did not succeed. 'Thank you, Jeremy. I always knew that my assets were the best.'

It was Pendleton's turn to smile. 'And with the prospect of both our yachts taking part in this venture, I hope we will be able to forge closer ties and forget about any little problems that have occurred in the past between us.'

'I'm not sure Mike would agree with that sentiment, but we'll see how things progress.'

With a cheerful look on his face, Pendleton was happy the morning had brought him good news and all he could hope for at that moment. He may soon be sharing a seaborne venture with Suzie. The future was looking brighter again.

Chapter Twenty

Nightclub Chaos

On Wednesday afternoon, Jake Crossman thumbed through the photographs Lefty had taken of Mo and his gang testing the drugs and stuffed them in a folder along with Mo's basement flat address. The photographs were taken a hidden camera, and the indifferent quality was reflected in the result. But they were clear enough for anyone to recognise the men who were testing the drugs and were good enough for Crossman's needs should they be required.

Mo and his men were busy selling and distributing the drugs they purchased from Crossman and the supply was diminishing fast. Mo wanted a fresh supply and soon, but was kept waiting for news of the next drugs delivery date for several days by Crossman. He decided the time was now right to inform Mo about the news … both good and bad. He punched the buttons on his telephone and was greeted with a grunt when the call was answered by one of Mo's gang. After establishing who the caller was, Mo came on the line.

'What news have you got for me this time, Crossman? It had better be good,' he scowled.

'It is good news this time, Mo. I can get you the next shipment early. In just under three week's time,' announced Crossman, in a pleasant tone as if it was an enormous favour he was doing for him.

'Okay, that's good.'

'The bad news is … the price has gone up.'

'Gone up! Why? By how much?'

'Fifty percent extra. The price is now £1.5m for the same quantity.'

'£1.5m! You've got to be kidding me, man. I can't afford a hike like that. How am I supposed to make a profit when you're bumping up the price like that?'

'It's not my fault, Mo. It's no good blaming me. It's the supplier who's increased his price,' Crossman lied. 'I told you he was having problems. I tried to argue with him about it, but he's adamant that is the price if we want the goods. He said they are much in demand and he could easily sell the stuff ten times over. It sells on the streets for about £70 a gram he tells me.'

'That's what he tells you. Who is this supplier? I'll talk to him,' suggested Mo, hoping that Crossman would divulge his contact's identity.

'You can't seriously expect me to tell you that Mo, surely? You are not known to them, so they wouldn't talk to you anyway.'

'Let me try.'

'No chance! If you managed to contact my supplier direct, you'd cut me out of the deal and I'd lose the little profit I make.'

'Little profit is it?'

'Just ten percent for my troubles and as I'm sure you know the police have been very active lately and visited our nightclub in the search for your drugs. Our solicitor has been in great demand. I need my ten percent to cover his fees.'

'And I'm supposed to believe that, am I?'

'Anyway, you could raise the price to your customers. I'm sure they'll be happy to pay.'

'Many of them have a problem paying me as it is.'

'That's because you charge too much for such a small amount and make a big profit by selling it to them.'

'I take a heavy risk selling it on the street and I too have to be very wary of the police. It also costs me a bundle of money for solicitor's fees to get my men bailed out if they get caught.'

'That's the nature of the business, ol' son,' stated Crossman. 'I've got plenty of other customers who I can sell the stuff to if the price is too high for you. So what's it going to be? Do you want it or not?'

'I'll think about it, ol' man,' retorted Mo.

'Don't take too long. I'll expect to hear from you in the next day or two at the most, or I'll make arrangements to sell the stuff elsewhere.'

Crossman put down the telephone and a smile played on his lips. He knew Mo was desperate for the consignment and was not able to get the quantity he needed anywhere else in a hurry. He had little choice if he wanted to continue making a profit and not lose his customers. There were other dealers who were only too ready to poach his clients.

In his basement office, located in a run-down area of East London close to the River Thames, Mo slammed the telephone down and scowled to his men, 'That bastard Crossman's put the price up by fifty percent.'

The men gasped at the news. They had all guessed Crossman was likely to hike up the cost, but fifty percent was much higher than any of them had anticipated.

'He says he can sell the stuff elsewhere if we don't pay. I'm not sure he's got another buyer but I can't take the risk. I knew he was bad news. It wouldn't surprise me if he got rid of the Phadkars so he could take the business over. The man's ruthless. He's very greedy and we will have to watch him carefully.'

'Do you want me to take care of him, boss?' offered Deven, a heavy-set overweight gang member. Deven's round face and chubby cheeks displayed a small chin, which was hidden by a black scruffy beard. His reputation of hurting people when they were unable to pay for the drugs had made him a man to be feared in the district.

'No, not yet anyway. I need to find out who his supplier is first, or we'll have to find a new contact. The drug squad has been active lately so it could take time and that would lose us customers and profit.'

'What then? You're not going to pay that rat, are you?'

'Not if I can help it. Crossman said he wants to hear from me soon. He'll hear from me soon all right, sooner than he bargained for. We'll visit his nightclub later tonight and mess it up a bit, that'll teach him to try and rip us off. Perhaps he'll then see we are not the easy pushovers he thinks we are. He assumes that because we need the stuff urgently, he can push us around and dictate his terms and we'll have no choice but to roll over and agree to them. He's in for a surprise.'

'What happens if he still won't play ball?'

'Then we have to step up the treatment and dish him out more trouble than he needs. He told me the police recently searched his nightclub looking for drugs. He won't want to attract more attention by getting them involved with his problems. We'll just shake him up a little to start with.'

'Good. When do we do it?'

'We'll meet back here at 3 a.m. That's when the nightclub shuts. It should be nice and quiet by the time we arrive. Bring a sledgehammer or something heavy to do damage with.'

*   *   *

At the appointed hour, Mo and four of his men met at his basement flat and bundled into their car. Their 4x4 Land Rover sped to the nightclub through London streets free from the nose to tail traffic jams that slowly clawed the way to their destinations throughout the working day. Parking near the rear entrance they saw lights still showing from the nightclub.

'We'll wait for a bit,' stated Mo. 'Most of the staff will be leaving shortly and the nightclub should be empty quite soon.'

'Do they have a night guard?' asked one man.

'I don't know. If they do we will have to take care of him, but no killing. We're here to mess up the place and teach Crossman a lesson, not to start a murder hunt. Is that clear?'

Grunts of agreement issued from the other men.

It was not long before the rear door opened allowing the striptease dancers and bar staff to emerge, their work done for the night. Lights from inside the nightclub dimmed and the rear door was slammed shut and locked amid calls of goodnight and arm waving. The roar of their cars disturbed the quiet night air as the staff departed.

'Right. It's nearly time to begin the fun,' announced Mo, watching the last of the women driven away in her boyfriend's car. 'We'll give them a few more minutes to make sure everyone has gone, then we'll go in.'

Approaching the rear entrance, Mo and his men crept from their vehicle while one man extinguished the only lamp that gave any light to the area, situated above the door. The moon shone brightly clothing the men in a grey half-light. The occasional car motored by in the distance as Deven, armed with a crowbar, prized the door open allowing the men to sneak into the nightclub.

They passed along the corridor outside the offices and entered the entertainment lounge bathed in semi-darkness, which was lit by a few safety lights dotted around the room. A small strip light under the hanging spirit bottles in front of a mirror at the back of the bar offered a further ray of light to the room. The aroma of stale cigarette smoke and booze hung in the air. The dimly lit room was cloaked in an eerie silence with the semicircular stage devoid of any dancers to bring it to life. Wall mounted speakers sat silently waiting for the show to begin again the following night, before blasting out their loud music for the girls to dance their enticing act to. Unwashed ash trays and a few bottles and glasses along with an assortment of rubbish littered the bar where most of the clearing up was done later in the morning. This allowed the tired staff to get home and flop into their beds by 4 a.m.

Mo's men, wielding their hammers and hatchets, started to smash everything in sight, breaking tables and chairs, glasses, bottles and the mirror in the bar. The commotion was heard by Angie in the general office, who had been cashing up the day's takings. She flung open the door to investigate.

'What the hell do you lot think you're doing?' she asked, looking in horror at the damage being wrought.

'We're gonna teach Crossman a lesson in what happens when he tries to rip us off,' declared one man, grabbing Angie by the hair.

She screamed.

'Let go of me you bastard,' she spat, punching him in the face and struggling to free herself.

Mo stepped forward. 'I've seen you here many times when I come to pick up the stuff, so I know you've worked here for the Phadkar twins for quite a long time. You must know who the drugs supplier is. Talk, or I'll let my boys go to work on you.'

'I only help out with the general running of the office, I don't know anything about the ordering of the drugs,' stated Angie.

'I don't believe you. You knew exactly what happened about the testing and payment arrangements. Make her talk,' he instructed.

Angie, shouting and screaming, was dragged by her hair back into the general office. The thug grabbed the front of her dress to tear it off, and yelled out as Angie sunk her teeth into his fist.

'Bitch,' he swore, smashing a fist into her face and tearing her dress wide open.

The force propelled her to the floor where she crashed her head on the desk and slumped to the carpet. He grabbed her and was dragging her to her feet when Crusher appeared at the door. He had been sleeping off a hangover in one of the upstairs rooms and came down to investigate the noise.

Pushing Mo aside he rushed at his man. 'You leave my Angie alone you bastard,' he yelled.

Turning to see where the voice came from, the thug was not quick enough to avoid the charging fist that smashed into his jaw, breaking it and sending him careering into the desk. Before he could regain his senses, Crusher was upon him and slammed a fist into his midriff, cracking several of his ribs.

To prevent his man from being killed, Mo rushed forward and jumped on to Crusher's back to drag him away and was thrown aside by the increased strength that Angie's protector had generated through his anger. He kicked out at Mo and caught him a hefty blow to the midriff, winding him. The noise attracted Deven, who appeared at the doorway and saw the fight taking place with Mo and his man both floored by the angry Crusher.

He drew a gun and aimed it at Crusher as Angie yelled out, 'No!'

Deven pulled the trigger and the bullet hit Crusher in the small of his back. Angie screamed out loud as he dropped to his knees and Crusher fell face down on the floor, blood colouring his shirt a crimson red.

Deven prepared to fire again as Mo got to his feet and held up a hand. He shouted at him, 'Stop! I told you we didn't come here to kill anyone, idiot.'

'I thought he was going to kill you,' Deven stated.

Angie crawled across to Crusher and cradled his head against her bosoms. 'Crusher, speak to me.'

He opened his eyes and smiled, 'You do care for me then?'

Mo looked at them. 'You don't say nothing to anyone,' he pointed, wagging a finger at Angie to emphasise his words, 'or we'll be back to dish out the same to you,' he growled.

He dashed from the room waving and shouting, 'C'mon you two, let's go.'

All of Mo's men ran from the building. Jumping back into their car they sped away leaving the nightclub badly smashed up and a distraught Angie holding on to Crusher. She dialled 999 and asked for the ambulance. When they were told it was to attend a man with a gunshot wound, the police were automatically contacted. The ambulance and police arrived ten minutes later to find a battered and crying Angie sitting on the office floor cradling the bloodstained body of Crusher.

Chapter Twenty-One

Aftermath

With its lock smashed by the intruders, the rear door to 'The Rosy Cheeks Nightclub' was flung open and crashed back on its hinges as Jake Crossman strode in. He dashed into the lounge, surveyed the damage and cursed out loud. Mo and his men had not remained in the nightclub for very long, but it had been sufficient time for them to smash almost everything in the bar and lounge area. Few tables and chairs remained undamaged, the rest were now only good enough for firewood. Smashed bottles and glasses littered the floor.

An hour earlier, after asking for the manger's address from Angie before she was taken to hospital for a check-up, the local police had knocked on the door of Crossman's flat and informed him of the break-in at the nightclub.

It was 7 a.m. on Thursday morning, the first day of June, and the month had not begun well. DI Colin Brooke was informed of the break-in because of his interest in the nightclub as a distributor of drugs and he came straight over to take charge of the incident, asking DCs John Green and Ray Teal to join him at the scene.

Brooke stepped forward to speak to Crossman. 'I understand you are now in charge here, Mr Crossman?' he began.

'Yes, that's right,' Crossman replied. 'I'm the new manager, come into my office.'

The two men entered his office, untouched by Mo's men. Crossman wearily sat down at his desk. 'What a mess! I trust you will catch the villains who've smashed up this place?' Crossman asked, more in anger at the damage rather than Crusher's demise.

'What happened to Mr Phadkar?' asked Brooke.

'He returned to Pakistan when he found out that his twin brother had been shot dead by some gun-happy woman.'

'I see. I've not seen you here at the nightclub before.'

'No. I've had a lot of business to take care of. I've been out of the district much of the time.'

'Anything to do with buying or selling drugs?'

'Certainly not. This is a reputable establishment – a private nightclub that caters for the discerning gentleman who likes to have a drink while watching attractive ladies dance for them. We don't deal in drugs. The police searched the place last week and nothing was found.'

'I know, I was here.'

'Then why did you ask the question?'

Brooke ignored the comment. 'And how is it that you are now running this nightclub? Mr Phadkar told us you were not employed here any more.'

'We had a temporary disagreement but that was sorted out. I was the manager here, so Mr Phadkar left me to run the nightclub until he returns. You seem to be more interested in me, instead of finding out who smashed up the place and killed my employee.'

'I'm just getting a complete picture of what goes on here, Mr Crossman. The twin brother of Mr Phadkar was shot when he was caught burgling a house. What do you know about that?'

'Nothing. As I said, I was not here at the time.'

'So, you haven't visited Guildford General Hospital recently?'

'No. Why on earth should I?'

'Our witness says you are the intruder who visited a private room in an attempt to kill Mr Mike Randle, the owner of that burgled house.'

'I look after the nightclub. I don't go around shooting people. The local police have already asked me about that and are satisfied with my answers.'

'I didn't say the attempt was to shoot someone.'

Crossman bluffed. 'I … was told by the police that a gun was used when they questioned me. Shooting was responsible for Mr Phadkar's death and Crusher was shot here in the nightclub so guns seem to be the weapon that most people use, but not me.'

'So you're sticking to breaking and entering and drilling open people's safes, are you?'

'What safe?'

'The one at SMJ Boatyard, where you were caught on camera.'

'It wasn't me that drilled open the safe.'

'The recording shows you taking the drill from the boot of the car.'

'I simply collected it for someone else.'

'Hmm,' breathed Brooke, knowing Crossman was lying but also knowing he was unable to prove it. 'Would you agree to standing in an identity line-up?' he asked, adding as much pressure as he could.

A worried look came over Crossman face. 'Err ... it's not that I object ...'

'But?'

'But, I've already told you that I've talked to the local police and I'm a busy man. I've only just got back. With all this clearing up to be sorted out, and trying to get the nightclub up and running quickly so we don't lose too much business, I'm afraid it's not convenient.'

'Some other time perhaps?' pressed Brooke.

'Perhaps, but I doubt it.'

The rear door to the nightclub banged shut and Angie appeared at the office doorway in a torn dress. She was badly bruised and had a swollen lip and a black eye, but no broken bones. The hospital doctor allowed her to leave provided she went home and got some rest.

Brooke turned to approach her. 'You're Angie, who works in the general office, aren't you?'

'Yes, that's right.'

'I was told you were quite badly beaten.'

Angie nodded. The glamorous look she possessed was gone, replaced by a look of sadness and bruising with eye makeup that had smeared because of her tears.

'And you were here when the man known as Crusher was shot?'

'Yes,' she replied in a quiet, distressed tone of voice. 'He was trying to protect me.'

'From who?'

'From the men who broke in. They wanted to know the combination to the safe and thought I could tell them. When I told them I didn't know what it was, they started hitting me.'

'Why did they think you knew what the combination was?' Brooke pressed.

'I don't know. Perhaps because I work here.'

'Can you identify the men?'

'No. They all wore stocking masks.'

'How many of them were there?'

'About 6 or 8. I was too busy trying to defend myself to really notice.'

'Okay. Thank you. I'll speak to you both again later,' advised Brooke, returning to the bar area.

He was approached by DCs Teal and Green.

'Did you find anything useful in here?' he asked them.

'Nah. Everything here's been smashed to bits,' stated Green. 'We've got no chance of finding any fingerprints.'

'The general office is the only other room to be damaged,' said Teal. 'That's where Crusher was shot dead. There's blood on the carpet.'

'Yes, that's curious. Angie told me they wanted to know the combination of the safe, yet Crossman's room is untouched and that's where the safe is located. If I remember rightly, Phadkar opened it with a key, it's not a combination lock. The gang doesn't seem to have even searched for it, they've simply smashed the place up.'

'Do you think she's lying?' asked Green.

'Yes, I think so. I've got a feeling that drugs are mixed up in this somehow. Maybe that's why she's reluctant to tell the truth.'

'Perhaps they threatened to come back and shoot her as well,' Teal postulated.

'After seeing Crusher shot dead she's likely to be pretty scared, especially if it was a revenge killing to teach someone a lesson. That would also explain why so much damage was done,' Green added.

'Whatever the reason, we'll have to keep a constant eye on this place over the next few days. I want you two admirable policemen to organise that between yourselves.'

Both the policemen's faces dropped. 'Do we have to?' complained Teal. 'We'd hoped by now to have finished with menial tasks like surveillance. I get fed up with doing nothing but standing around all day waiting for something or someone to appear.'

Brooke stared at his two men's gloomy faces. 'It's an important job but, I'll try to find someone else to take over.'

Smiles returned to their faces.

'But you two will have to do it until I can get agreement from HQ for the manpower.'

The two men looked at each other. 'Okay.' They agreed.

Meanwhile in his office, Crossman was grilling Angie about what really happened that morning. 'Close the door,' he told her, 'and tell me what actually went on here this morning.'

'It was Mo and his men. They smashed the place up because he said you are trying to rip him off and he wanted to teach you a lesson. When he found me here he tried to force me to tell him who your drug supplier is.'

'You didn't tell him, did you?' asked an anxious Crossman.

'No. I told him I didn't know. He threatened to come back and shoot me if I told anyone it was him and his gang.'

Crossman face contorted with anger. He banged his fist on the desk. 'Right! I'll show that creep he can't mess with me and get away with it.'

'I'd like to go home now,' said Angie. 'The hospital doctor said I should get some rest. I've got a splitting headache and I haven't had any sleep yet.'

'Okay, Angie. You take a day or so off to let your face get better. It'll take a while to get this place cleaned up and it doesn't help the nightclub for the customers to see a staff member looking all beaten up.'

'Thanks,' Angie said sarcastically. 'It's good to know you care about me. At least I know that Crusher did.'

Crossman ignored her jibe. 'Do one thing for me first. See if you can rustle up some help to clear the place up. I'll order some replacement furniture and a rug to cover up the stains on the carpet in the general office until I can get it replaced.'

'I'll ring the bar staff and the girls and ask them to come in early. I'm sure they'll all agree to help considering what's happened. The place won't seem the same without Crusher. He was a big kid really.'

'Yes. Good. I want to get things straight and open tonight as if nothing has happened,' Crossman stated, ignoring Angie's lament at Crusher's death.

'I'll ask barman Andy to order more drink and glasses,' she said.

Angie left the room and after making her telephone calls went home. Crossman switched on his computer to search for the email that Phadkar had sent to the hit man with details of the contract on Suzie and her black friend. His luck was in, he had received an email in reply from the man to say his present contract was finished and he was now in a position to take care of this new problem. Crossman answered the email with a request to modify the set of instructions. It was time for him to use the contact and make changes to the brief.

Chapter Twenty-Two

All Aboard

Friday dawned. A week had elapsed since Mike's motorcycle accident and he was beginning to make progress. The trauma of the event was fading with each day that passed and he was coming to terms with the injuries he received. Mike was anxious to get fit enough to find those who had inflicted such a traumatic event on him and exact what he considered to be a justifiable punishment for the pain and suffering it was causing him, as well as the damage done to his beloved Triumph Bonneville motorbike *Bonnie.*

The plaster on his left arm was cut down to below the elbow enabling Mike to have more movement and to be able to feed himself. His leg was out of traction and covered in a plaster cast. After speaking the previous day with the surgeon, Mr Craig, an almost baldheaded man with warm hands and a pleasant smile who carried out the operation, Suzie visited Mike with some good news.

'How are you feeling today,' Suzie asked giving him a kiss.

'Okay, considering I'm a cripple.'

'Don't be silly. You're not a cripple and you'll be back on your feet before you know it.'

'And running the London Marathon I suppose,' he moaned.

'Not for the first few weeks, you'll have to stick to ballroom dancing.'

Mike smiled. 'I'm sorry. It's just that I want to get out of here and get my hands on the bastards who put me here and smashed up my favourite motorcycle. How is *Bonnie?*'

'*Bonnie's* a bit of a wreck. It'll take you a long while and a lot of hard work to restore her to her former glory,' stated Suzie.

She was hiding the fact she had been on the internet and located another Jubilee Triumph Bonneville motorbike for sale. She knew Mike loved his motorbike and wanted to repair his original one but it was smashed beyond repair. She kept her purchase of a new bike as a surprise for him when he was well enough to leave the hospital.

'I'm surprised the bike is repairable after what we went through.'

'I'm sure you will be riding your motorbike again in the very near future,' she encouraged.

'I hope you're right.'

'And speaking of getting your own back, Colin Brooke visited me earlier today and told me that 'The Rosy Cheeks Nightclub' had a break-in yesterday morning. The place was smashed up quite badly and there was a shooting.'

'Anyone hurt?'

'Apparently, a guard named Crusher was shot dead.'

'Crusher! He's the bloke who beat up Reg so I'm not going to shed any tears over him.'

'DI Maidley returned the DVD taken by our security cameras, so I watched it. I saw Crusher on the recording beating up poor Reg. He's also one of the men who burgled our house. I caught a brief glimpse of him coming down the stairs as he shot at Jenny and me through the doorway.'

'He's one person I won't have to worry about then. I wonder what the nightclub break-in was all about.'

'Colin thinks it's connected to the drug smuggling he's certain goes on there.'

'I reckon he's probably right.'

'He told me a man named Jake Crossman is the new boss of the nightclub. He too was on the security DVD. I recognised him from the photos taken from the DVD that Colin showed me. It was the same man who came into this room to shoot you.'

'Really? Is he going to arrest him for that?'

'Crossman has witnesses to swear he was with them at the time, so Colin can't do anything about that except keep a close eye on him. He was arrested for breaking into our yard, but his solicitor soon got him bailed out.'

'At least we're now sure who it was. I'm not restricted by the law in the same way that policemen like Colin is. When I'm fit again, my time will come. Crossman's not going to get away with nearly killing me and smashing up my motorbike. I'll see to that.'

'You may have to wait for a while before you go searching for more trouble.'

'I can wait. It's a good incentive to get me back on my feet again.'

'When you do get back on your feet you'll have to start by getting around using gutter crutches.'

'Gutter crutches?'

'Yes. They're crutches especially designed for people who have their wrists in plaster. It'll be a couple of weeks before you're well enough to use them, Mr Craig told me, but I've got some good news for you. He says you can go home next week, if there's someone to look after you for the first couple of weeks.'

'That's great! While it's nice to have a private room it's a bit lonely and it must be costing a lot.'

'£350 a day.'

'What! That's daylight robbery! Get me out of here today.'

'Don't be silly. Our insurance is paying for it.'

'Thank goodness for that.'

'I made a few enquiries and hired a nurse for a couple of weeks to attend to your every need while you're recuperating at home.'

'That's great. Thank you, luv. You think of everything. Is she pretty?'

'I don't think you could exactly call him pretty.'

'Him! You mean you've hire a male nurse? You rotten sod.'

'With your roving hands and eyes it seemed a sensible thing to do. I've heard rumours you've been trying to grope the pretty nurses here now that one of your hands is free.'

'That's a rotten lie. I've simply not got used to handling things with these plaster casts on.'

Suzie smiled at Mike's ridiculous excuse. Mike looked at her attractive face and couldn't help smiling along with her. Mr Craig, in his clean white overall with stethoscope dangling around his neck, stepped into the room at that moment.

'I'm glad to see you are recovering so quickly. Laughter is a great medicine. At this rate you'll be on your feet in no time.'

'How long before the plaster casts are removed?' asked Mike.

'It will be about eight to ten weeks. In the meantime you will have to get around on crutches for a few weeks. Broken bones take time to heal.'

'And what about the plate in Mike's wrist,' asked Suzie. 'Will it stay in?'

'No. We will remove that in about a year's time. It's a simple operation and you will only need to be in hospital for a day or so.'

Mike blew out a lungful of air.

'Don't worry,' Mr Craig said, tapping Mike on the shoulder, 'I've seen men die with lesser injuries than you've received. One bad crack on the head during that accident and you could have easily ended up dead.'

'I guess I'm quite lucky, really,' Mike said, grabbing Suzie's hand and holding on to it.

'I would say so. I'll be back to see you again later,' the surgeon said, departing.

'The repairs to *Quester* are going well,' Suzie told Mike.

'That's good. When will she be ready to sail?'

'About the end of next week. Our holidaymakers arrived this morning to collect the other motor yacht. They seemed quite pleased with her.'

'Good. Let's hope they aren't smugglers as well.'

'Don't be silly, of course they're not. They're a group of youngsters out for a good time.'

'Where did they get the money from to hire a luxury yacht like *Quester* then?'

'One of them is the son of that politician in the government who's in charge of the taxes.'

'Charles Dixon, the Chancellor of the Exchequer?'

'That's him.'

'If I'd known that, I wouldn't have let that money grabbing bugger's son have the yacht for free. His dad earns a fabulous wage and he charges us and our business a fortune in taxes, and I bet he's one of the buggers who claim everything on expenses. He's probably even claiming the hire costs for his son's trip. He's making a fortune out of us.'

'Don't worry about it. And since you've mentioned a fortune, reminds me that we reached an agreement with Bignor about using our yard and yacht for his filming.'

'That's good news.'

'Yes, our accountant has finally reached agreement with the financial backers of Panache TV Productions Incorporated, Alastaire Bignor's production company.'

'I thought Jeremy Pendleton was the financial backer.'

'I gather he has put some money into the scheme, but is not the only backer.'

'Hedging his bets eh? So, have we got a good deal?'

'I wouldn't go so far as to say that, but it does mean *Quester* will be earning us money again and we'll be able to give her an extended test to the Mediterranean Sea to make sure she's in tiptop working order. Jenny and I will be going along with Bignor and his crew to keep an eye on things.'

'Lucky you. I hope you aren't going to sunbathe in your usual skimpy attire.'

'Don't worry. I shan't be sunbathing topless if Jeremy Pendleton's within viewing distance. That would be tempting fate far too much.'

'So, he's going along as well?'

'Yes, of course. He also wants to keep an eye on his yacht *Julia* and probably the scantily clad females Alastaire Bignor is using in his production.'

'Lucky him. When is this trip scheduled for and who's looking after the business while you and Jenny are away? Only Jim?'

'Jim and Reg, helped by George, will be looking after the business. Reg returned yesterday to work a couple of days this week to see how he getting along and says he will return full time next week. I think he misses the place.'

'Yes, the boatyard does seem to be his life.'

'Bignor wants to do some filming in the boatyard during next week and set sail for the Mediterranean Sea on Friday.'

'I wish I could go with you,' lamented Mike.

Suzie thought. 'Why not?' she said. 'You should be out of here by then. Jenny and I will be your nurses instead.'

'That sounds a lot better than having a male nurse.'

'Perhaps sunning yourself in the Mediterranean will help you to get better. Bignor tells me he is heading for Ibiza via Gibraltar.'

'It might be difficult for me to get around the yacht on crutches.

'You'll be resting most of the time and anyway, the entrance steps will have a ramp for Bignor's film equipment that we can use for your wheelchair. And the gangway in *Quester* has been widened to accommodate Bignor's cameras, so it should make it a lot easier for you.'

'The ramp might be a bit too steep for a wheelchair.'

'If it is, you'll have to hobble down the steps instead.'

'How many bedrooms is Bignor intending to use?'

'He told me he will need to film in the lounge, the galley and only one bedroom, so that leaves an en-suite bedroom for us and one for Jenny. It's perfect!'

'It would be great if I could come along,' said Mike.

'I'll ask Mr Craig and see what he says,' suggested Suzie.

Mr Craig agreed it could help Mike to recuperate as long as he was careful and had someone to watch out for him. Suzie explained that she and Jenny would be there to keep an eye on him, for more than one reason, as scantily clad females were likely to be around on the yacht. With his cautionary word noted, he gave his approval for Mike to go on the voyage.

After a week in the hospital, Mike was looking forward the trip. The anticipation of not only getting out of hospital but also going on a cruise to the Mediterranean along with a bunch of lovely girls dressed in skimpy bikinis lifted his spirits. Going on the trip was the best medicine he could receive.

Chapter Twenty-Three

A Change Of Plan

In the dim light of his office at the nightclub, Jake Crossman checked the takings for the night. Angie was at home recovering from the bruises she had received from Mo's men when they tried to get information about the drugs supplier from her. After a frantic day's work to get the bar restocked and the tables, chairs and glasses replaced, business had been slow. Word had quickly circulated about the killing at the nightclub and it would take a while longer before all the members ventured back into the establishment. Many of those who came either did not know about the murder, or were curious to see where it had happened. The first night had been very quiet, which was repeated on this following Friday night usually one of the busiest nights of the week.

It was nearly 4 a.m. on Saturday morning and the night sky was about to see the first light of the day and lose its jet black cloak. Crossman was tired, it had been a trying couple of days and it was time he went back to his flat for some sleep. He slammed the cashbox lid shut and jammed it and the accounts book into the floor safe. He spun the dial and replaced the carpet.

Wearily he sat down at his desk, closed the drawers and turned his key in the lock. He put his hands on the desktop and was about to haul his wiry frame to his feet when he looked up and visibly jumped at seeing a dark figure standing inside the doorway.

'Who the hell are you, and how did you get in here? The nightclub is closed for the night and the doors are supposed to be locked.'

Standing in shadows with only the stocky outline to his five foot eight inch frame visible the man stated, 'Locked doors are not a problem for me,' in an accent that suggested he was of Russian origin.

'What do you want?' asked Crossman, fearful that Mo had sent another thug to the nightclub to kill him.

'Are you the boss?' the stranger enquired.

With a slight hesitation Crossman nodded. 'I am. What do you want at this early hour?' he asked, sitting down and quietly unlocking the centre draw in his desk where he kept a gun.

'I am Viktor Belanov. I understand you wish to change the arrangement we have made to pass on a surprise package to two ladies? Before you reach for that gun.'

Crossman pushed the drawer shut. 'Oh, right. It's you. You had me worried for a moment. We've had a bit of trouble at the nightclub, which is why I sent you that email the other day,' said Crossman, knowing that Phadkar had used only his initial and not his name when sending him the email, so the man was not aware of any changes at the nightclub.

'So I have heard. I gather one of your employees was killed.'

'That's right. He was shot dead by a nasty rival, which is why I want to change our arrangement – to avenge the death of my trusted man, who was also a good friend,' Crossman said, to give the impression this was the real reason why he wanted the change.

'Your voice sounds different to how I remember it on the telephone,' the man said, recalling the person he spoke to had a strong accent.

'Err, yes. That's because it was my business partner who called you. He's not here at the moment. We both agreed to hire your services.'

'I see. I have to be careful you understand?'

'Yes, of course. We too have to be cautious. Is it possible for me to change the deal with you to eliminate just one man instead of the two women at a reduced rate?' asked Crossman, hoping to retrieve some of the high cost Phadkar had paid to the hit man.

'I do not give refunds, but we can discuss changing the arrangement from a woman to a man if you so wish. Do you have an address on this new person? Is it close by?' Belanov asked, continuing to mask his face in the shadows.

'I do, and yes it's close by, here in London. I also have a photograph of him, taken by another of my employees who is also anxious to revenge the death of his good friend.'

'And what of the two women?'

'Will you change the arrangement to one man and one woman instead of two women for the same fee?' asked Crossman, not wishing to part with more money unless he had to.

'Which woman? There are two, and I have details of only one.'

'To replace the one we are less sure about. The one we do not have a name and address of - the black woman.'

'As I do not have to search for the man, as I would have for this women, then I can carry out your wishes for only a slight increase in the cost.'

'Slight increase! How slight?'

'Men sometimes cause more trouble than women, especially if they have guns. Shall we say a further $10,000?'

'As the women also have guns, how about making it $5,000. You've already been paid a lot of money.'

'I'll do it for $8,000, as you waited patiently for me to finish my previous contract.'

'Okay. It's a deal,' agreed Crossman, anxious to confirm the arrangements. 'I'd like you to deal with the man first. That problem is more important.'

'As you wish. You can have the payment transferred to my account in the same way as the last one.'

'Err ... you'll have to give me the details again. We destroyed the information for security reasons,' Crossman bluffed, unsure of what Phadkar had arranged.

Crossman had control of the doctored business finances but had not yet figured out how to get his hands on Phadkar's private bank accounts and the information he needed to pay the hit man.

'Give me the photograph and address,' Belanov stated, scribbling his bank name and account number on a piece of paper.

Searching his desk drawer, Crossman retrieved the photo taken by Lefty and drew rings around Deven and Mo, and wrote their address on the back. The man held his hand out and remained in the dark. Crossman approached and they exchanged the information.

'I've ringed Deven, the man you are to deal with in red. He is the one who killed my employee. The address of their headquarters is on the back. The other man ringed in blue is Mo, the gang leader. I would like you to give him a message from me after you have completed this part of your contract, and say 'an eye for an eye'. That should make him aware of why his murderous man was killed and convince him he cannot come in here to smash the place up and kill my employee and get away with it. Is that all clear?'

The man took the photograph and glanced at it, 'Da. You have a gun for me, as requested?'

'Yes,' said Crossman, slipping on a glove to take a Yarygin PYa pistol and silencer from his desk drawer and hand them to Belanov. 'It's clean,' he remarked. 'We had a job to get this model. I hope it's okay.'

'It is good,' the hit man said, checking the weapon. 'I see you are cautious about handling this weapon.'

'Yes. I try to keep my fingerprints away from any gun I handle. When do you expect to complete this part of the contract?' asked Crossman.

'In a few days, after I have had time to look over their place. They are men with guns and will use them, as you have found out, so I need to be careful and sure of my position when I go in.'

'Of course. There may be other members of the gang at this address as well and they are all viscous, so I would be careful.'

'I am always careful. That is how I stay in business.'

'I'll transfer your money now,' said Crossman, looking at the man's note, all written in block capitals.

He opened his laptop and pressed the 'on' button. The machine beeped and whirred into life. Crossman accessed the bank website. He entered the account number and the amount and pressed the button to send. This amount of money would hardly be noticed by him now he had been able to collect the last drug payment from Mo. It pleased him to think that Mo's own money would be paying for a hit man to exact his revenge.

'That's done,' Crossman said looking up. The stranger was nowhere to be seen. 'Hello. Are you still there?' he asked. Only silence greeted him. 'I'm sure he'll check to make sure the money was transferred okay,' he muttered to himself.

Switching the lamp on his desk off, Crossman locked the office door behind him. Yawning he left the nightclub, climbed into his Mercedes and set off for his flat. He was happy in the knowledge that Deven would pay for killing Crusher and more importantly, Mo would know he could not intimidate him and would have to pay the high price if he wanted to receive the drugs. With no other supplier around and Mo's customers expecting their fixes, he had little choice but to agree. Crossman was already thinking about the vast payment he would receive and anticipating he would soon be a very rich man.

Chapter Twenty-Four

Payback

The hit man Viktor Belanov spent several days surveying the run-down apartment block, where Mo had his headquarters in the basement, in his objective to fulfil the first part of his contract with Jake Crossman. Like many in his profession, he was an ex-employee of the Russian security service and was now using the talents they taught him to fashion himself a more lucrative way of life. This existence was somewhat nomadic and lonely. He travelled wherever a suitable job was offered and stayed as inconspicuous and faceless as possible in order to continue his work unhindered. This inevitably meant having few friends and mistrusting almost everyone he came in contact with, including other men in his profession – they all killed for the financial rewards it brought and it was every man for himself. It was a profitable but lonely life.

Belanov's surveillance had established that four men regularly stayed in the basement flat all night including Deven, the man he was after. The Russian knew that in order to get to him he would probably have to kill more than one man. Which of them were armed, apart from Deven, he could not tell.

'I will assume all of them carry guns,' he told himself. 'That way I cannot be surprised.'

He noted that none of them look as if they were well off yet many people visited the flat every day, so they must be selling something. Almost certainly drugs he thought, looking at some of the faces with heavy eyes surrounded by black circles who came and went from the flat at all hours of the day and night. Belanov assessed it would be difficult to find a time when his target was on his own and calculated he would have to go in early in the morning, when the occupants are likely to be asleep or at least tired.

It was Tuesday, and Belanov decided he could learn no more from watching the apartment and this was the night he would make his move. He spent the evening in a quiet café several miles away from the apartment block, knowing it was not sensible to wait nearby on the eve of a hit. The police would question people in the close vicinity of the flat hoping for a witness. That was providing they were informed of the attack, which the Russian doubted having assessed what trade they were dealing in. A close police investigation is something they would want to avoid at all costs, but may not be possible. However, it was still sensible to take every precaution. Taking great care was essential for a man in his profession to both staying alive and remaining one jump ahead of the authorities.

The café he chose was situated in a quiet side street and closed at midnight. While he waited at a table in a corner, Belanov slowly drank two black coffees. As midnight approached and the customers began to depart, he used the washroom before leaving a small tip for the waitress, ensuring he did nothing out of the ordinary to attract attention to himself and give someone a good reason to remember him. Belanov wore jeans and a loose fitting casual top to hide the bulge under his left armpit where his gun was holstered.

Turning up his collar, Belanov set out on the three miles walk to Mo's apartment block through streets that were brightly lit by the never-ending rows of shops, their front windows a blaze of lights to encourage passers-by to window shop. The roads still held much traffic and the pavements thronged with late night visitors in this part of town where shopping and tourism were the main attraction, despite the light rain that began to fall. The shops all gradually disappeared as the hit man neared his destination, replaced by plush residences that turned into grimy office blocks and eventually to high rise apartments.

The exercise was good for him, staying fit was an important part of the routine in his profession in case of problems and the cool spatter of rain was a welcome refreshment on his face. An escape route, by either car or on foot was carefully planned, as sometimes an unexpected problem would arise and the ability to make a hasty getaway and cover a good distance was a requirement only an amateur would ignore. Belanov was not an amateur, he was a professional, and had been well taught by his Russian tutors.

For part of his plan the hit man needed to steal a car and park it a few streets away to make good his escape afterwards. Older cars had less sophisticated alarm systems, and a ten-year-old VW Golf caught his attention. It was parked in a back street less than 500 yards from his target's apartment and was an ideal vehicle. It had no alarm and was easy for Belanov to break into and hot wire. Satisfied the Golf was ready for his escape he closed the door and made a mental note of its location. He wandered to a dark doorway across the far side of the street from the entrance to Mo's apartment block where he could watch and wait.

The street was deserted of people, but was crammed full with rows of cars parked on both sides of the road. Lighting was by the well spaced out columns of fluorescent street lamps giving out their orange glow and left much of the street in semidarkness along this stretch of 1950s high rise blocks. The sky above was black and the light rain fell persistently, mirroring the gloom of the task he was hired to carry out. Belanov was professional about every job he took on, but he still had a feeling of anticipation and of slight trepidation, which rose in his body each time he reached the business end of his contract.

Belanov looked at his watch. It was 1.30 a.m. – another hour or more to wait and watch until he was ready to make his move. During the next ninety minutes, nobody descended the grey, concrete steps down to the basement apartment where his target resided.

'It looks like a quiet night for Mo and his boys,' thought the Russian. 'Well that is all about to change.'

Checking the clip and screwing the silencer on to his pistol, he was about to move when a man appeared at the top of the steps from the basement apartment and looked up and down the street.

'What a stroke of luck,' Belanov murmured. 'My victim has just emerged from his hideout.'

He steadied himself against the side wall of the doorway and was about to pull the trigger when a taxi motored past spoiling his aim. It splashed its way along the road and disappeared around the corner.

'Blast!' Belanov cursed.

Before he could settle back and take further aim, Deven started his way back down to the basement. Taking a quick glance for more traffic, Belanov darted across the road to the railings at the top of the steps. He looked over them in time to see the door to Mo's apartment bang shut.

He had previously checked out what he could of the premises by slipping down to the door and pretending he had made a mistake and called at the wrong address, after following an unkempt young man to

153

the door and hiding behind him. His ruse had provided him with some information about the apartment when the door was opened, including a look at the locks and the knowledge that Mo was careful enough to fit a spy hole and grill to the door in order to see and talk to any caller before letting them in to do business. Entering the apartment was a tricky problem, but knowing they dealt in drugs gave him an excuse to call there as if he was in need of a fix and wanted to buy some. This he would chance doing if no other way of entering the premises revealed itself.

Returning to his hiding place in the doorway, the Russian patiently waited for a while before deciding it was time to make his move and try his trickery to gain entrance to the flat. Suddenly a young girl wearing a scruffy plastic mackintosh stopped by the railings. She took a furtive look up and down the street before descended the steps to the basement apartment.

This was the opportunity that Belanov had been hoping for. Hurrying across the road, he reached the top of the steps as the girl, hands in pockets and her shoulders hunched, spoke to the guard through the grill. The lock was snapped back and the door opened. Taking the damp, slippery twelve steps three at a time, Belanov reached the door as it was about to close. He put his shoulder to it and barged the door open, knocking the guard to the floor. The hit man put an arm around the girl's face and held a hand over her mouth to keep her from yelling out.

The guard yanked a gun from his waistband, but was slow to react as the Russian's silenced gun spat twice, slamming two bullets into his body. His face contorted, he rolled back and slumped to the floor. The girl fainted at the sight before her and Belanov lowered her to the well-worn mat that ran the length of the passageway.

The hit man stepped over them and tiptoed along the dim grimy passageway, lit by a single low wattage bare lamp that hung from the ceiling. Muffled voices came from the far end behind a door. Hugging the nearside wall, Belanov moved forwards until he reached a door on either side of the passageway. He kept a wary eye on the door at the far end and stopped by the first door, slowly twisting the handle and pushing it open. He saw and smelled immediately that it was a grimy bathroom and was empty. Closing the door, Belanov moved to the opposite side and gently opened the door there. It swung back to reveal a man sleeping on a bed with his back towards him, making identification difficult. The room was in darkness, lit only by reflected light from the passageway. The man was not bulky enough to be Deven, but could be Mo, the man he was instructed to give a message to but not to kill.

A gun lay on his bedside cabinet. Taking two quiet steps into the room, the Russian picked up the gun with his left hand while keeping his pistol in his right hand trained on the man in case he awoke or was feigning sleep. He slipped back out of the room and quietly closed the door stuffing the gun in his waistband.

Drifting along to the end door, voices from within the room became clearer.

'It's your deal,' he heard one man say.

'Where's Harry, he should be back by now?' another asked.

'I'll see what's happened to him,' the man replied.

A look of shock crossed his face when he opened the door and Belanov shoved his way in, knocking him backwards into the card table and tipping both of them over.

Deven sharply rose to his feet as the card table and his companion crashed to the floor.

The hit man pointed his gun at him. 'You're the man that I want,' he growled. Belanov detected movement behind him too late, and felt a gun barrel touch the small of his back. A big smile crossed Deven's face.

'I thought I heard someone come into my room,' said Mo. 'Leaving Harry's gun by his body in the hallway was careless of you. What are you doing here and who sent you?' he asked, putting a hand on Belanov's gun, held vertically in his right hand.

The hit man did not know if the gun he had grabbed from Mo's room, which was still in his waistband and hidden from view, was loaded and ready to fire, but his situation was desperate, and in his profession he was constantly faced with taking risks.

Belanov grabbed the gun, half turned, swung his left arm across his body and pointed it behind him as he pulled the trigger. The gun fired and the bullet ripped through Mo's leg. He screamed out loud, dropped his gun and released his grip on the hit man's weapon. Deven reacted to the danger and went for the gun in his waistband. The hit man turned to face him and both men fired at the same instance.

Deven was slammed backwards as the bullet hit him in the forehead and his life came to an abrupt end. At that same instant, his bullet struck Belanov in the chest, propelling him through the doorway into the passageway and knocking him to the floor alongside Mo. Seeing the intruder shot, but still alive, Deven's accomplice snatched out his gun and died as the hit man recovered quickly and fired two more shots from each of the guns as he lay on the floor.

Belanov got to his feet and turned to Mo, who was nursing his injured leg. He kicked his gun away as he stretched out a hand to grab it.

'Why ain't you dead?' Mo asked.

Opening his shirt, the Russian revealed his bullet proof vest.

Mo nodded. 'I should have guessed. You're a professional. So, what's next? Are you going to kill me too?'

'No. I was hired to kill your man Deven only. I have a message for you. An eye for an eye. Do you understand?'

Mo thought for a moment. 'Yeah, I understand,' he stated.

'Good.'

Backing out down the passageway, Belanov stepped over the girl, who was moaning as she began to rouse from her fainting spell. He climbed the steps, dropped both guns into a rubbish bin clamped to a lamp post and staggered back to the VW car as the girl's screams shrilled into the damp night air.

With a hand around his waist, Belanov cradled the bruise to his ribs and mumbled to himself, 'That hurt. It was a good job he did not shoot at my head.' He fingered a painful spot on his chest. 'I might have a cracked rib. I had better get it looked at. The health service here is good. They will fix me up.'

Dumping his frame into the getaway car, Belanov grunted at the pain that shot through him and he drove slowly back to his London hotel. He booked out and moved on – always a sensible thing to do after a hit. Abandoning the VW, Belanov collected his hire car and began the long drive to Brighton in Sussex. He drove the fifty-mile journey keeping to the speed limits. Leaving London, he motored on to the M23 and kept his speed to 65 mph, careful not to attract any attention from the police. The trip took him an uncomfortable two hours, and he was pleased to see the sign welcoming visitors to Brighton.

Once there he booked into 'The Carrington Hotel', a hotel he had already checked over and found to be suitable. He registered as a Bulgarian business man, and was grateful to swallow some pain killers and dump his frame on to a bed. It allowed him to get some respite from the ache that persisted from his injured ribs.

Later that morning after a fitful sleep and still suffering the pain, he drove to 'The Royal County Sussex Hospital'. There he entered the Accident and Emergency department and was seen by a student doctor, who was dressed in a white overall and had the obligatory stethoscope hanging around his neck. After examining Belanov, he sent him to have an X-ray.

'The X-ray shows you have a broken rib,' said the doctor, taking a second look at the bruised area. 'It looks to be a pinpoint break with no other break or bruising around it. How did it happen?'

'I fell and hit the corner of a table,' Belanov said.

'I see. That would explain it. The nurse will put a support strapping around your chest to protect it. That's all we can do. The break will heal itself. I'll give you some pain killers to take for a few days until it settles down and stops hurting.'

'Thank you, doctor.'

'Try not to fall over or knock it again and get some rest. That's the best medicine.'

'I will.'

Belanov left the hospital and returned to his hotel. 'Checking out Miss Drake and her house will have to wait for a few days,' he told himself. 'There is no immediate hurry to complete the contract so I will take a little time off to rest like the doctor suggested.'

Unknown to Mike and Suzie, the contract Khurram Phadkar had organised to kill the two women to revenge the death of his twin brother, was delayed thanks to the bullet of Mo's strong-arm man Deven, who's body now lay in the morgue.

Mo tried to hush the whole shooting up but though his leg wound was not serious, because the bullet had gone right through and missed the bone, it still bled a lot and he needed hospital attention. The doctor reported it to the police when he recognised it as a bullet wound, even though Mo had tried hard to convince him otherwise. This, coupled with the screaming young girl who fled from his flat and ran to the police station in a petrified state, had prevented any cover up of the attack being possible. Mo told them it was a gangland attack by masked men he could not identify, while silently cursing Jake Crossman for hiring a professional hit man. It was an act he would not forgive or forget.

Chapter Twenty-Five

The Yachting Trip

Two weeks after his admission to hospital, Mike was well enough to leave on a supervised yachting trip with Suzie and Jenny acting as nurses for him. They were heading for the sunny climate of the Mediterranean Sea along with Alastaire Bignor, his film crew and stars. The day had finally arrived for the newly refurbished motorsailer yacht *Quester II* to be relaunched. Bignor's modifications had been incorporated, and the galley equipment eventually arrived with less than forty-eight hours before the start of the journey and was hurriedly fitted.

Alastaire Bignor and his team had filmed several scenes at SMJ Boatyard on the previous few days, and badly interrupted the boatyard's schedule with his fussing and insistence on getting things right – no matter how many takes he had to film. Now with his camera crew and the stars of his production, he wanted to move the filming to outside shots on the high seas and the more exotic sun-drenched location of the island of Ibiza.

The plaster on Mike's right arm was cut down to below the elbow to enable him to have good movement of both arms. He was wheeled out of hospital by Suzie and Jenny into the specially adapted MPV with a wheelchair lifting platform. They motored to their boatyard on the River Hamble to begin the five day trip to the Mediterranean. Suzie accompanied Mike in his motorised wheelchair into the yard. Reg had returned to the yard and was working full time and the two men were pleased to see each other.

'How are you Reg?' Mike asked. 'Sorry, but it's a bit difficult for me to shake hands.'

'I'm fine, Mr Randle, a lot better than you by the looks of it,' he replied, shaking his head at the sight of Mike's wrists and leg in plaster.

'At least I'm going to get a holiday cruise out of all this mess,' he joked.

'George and me will look after things in the yard, and Mr Sterling and the girls will look after the offices. You have a relaxing time and get well, and don't worry about a thing.'

'Thanks, Reg.'

'We'll keep in touch through the yacht's radio, or else by mobile phone,' Suzie said. 'Jim's got my number in case you need to contact us about anything.'

'I'm sure we'll manage okay, Miss. If there are any problems Mr Sterling knows what to do.'

The whole workforce were called out of the office and workshops, and stood alongside *Quester II* on the jetty with Suzie, Mike, Jenny and Jim to celebrate the re-launch with a glass of Champagne. They were joined by Jeremy Pendleton, Alastaire Bignor and his cast and crew.

'You men and women have worked hard to bring this luxury yacht back to her former glorious condition in record time. Thank you all very much,' declared Jim, raising his glass.

'And may she bring pleasure to all who sail in her,' added Suzie.

The assembled group raised their glasses and drank a toast to the newly refurbished yacht. Suzie helped Mike up the ramp to board *Quester II* assisted by George. Jeremy Pendleton's yacht *Julia* was berthed alongside. Both vessels were loaded with the camera crews and their equipment, along with provisions and spare fuel for the trip. *Quester II* was loaded with her food and drinks from the local supermarket, but two 'Harrods' delivery vans brought the provisions for *Julia*. Pendleton had no intentions of eating and drinking anything that was not up to his usual standards, even when sailing on the high seas.

The productions stars, support actors and a bevy of attractive women all boarded Pendleton's yacht, a 100 foot long vessel with accommodation for fifteen people. The yacht was larger and more luxurious than *Quester II*, which was much to the chagrin of Mike who watched the procession boarding her, dashing his hopes to become better acquainted with some of the glamorous women. Only one older executive woman, the camera crew and the male star who used *Quester II* as his yacht in the show, came aboard.

'That's put paid to your little chat up ideas,' suggested Suzie, watching the young giggling women boarding *Julia*.

'I don't know what you mean,' defended Mike.

'I'm sure being in a wheelchair wouldn't dampen your ardour. You'll have to put up with me and Jenny and a couple of the camera crew.'

Mike was wheeled down the ramp into the lounge and shortly afterwards both vessels set sail for San Antonio de Portmany in Ibiza via Gibraltar. Casting off, the yachts sailed down the Hamble River past the Isle of Wight and out into the English Channel on their southern route towards the Mediterranean Sea.

During the voyage, filming took place on both yachts with a few of the glamorous women transferring to *Quester II* for some scenes, so Mike had a chance to chat to some of them after all.

With both wrists and one leg in plaster, getting around using gutter crutches was difficult enough on dry land, but possible. On a yacht, tossed by rolling waves and the occasional sea swell causing the vessel to rise and fall dramatically, it was impossible. Being confined to a wheelchair made him the focus of attention and he enjoyed telling the women about the dramatic 110 mph. chase on his motorbike and his subsequent accident. It was a tale he embellished with more death defying climaxes each time the story was related.

Suzie looked on with a smile at his efforts to impress the attractive bevy of women, knowing that while he was in a wheelchair doing anything other than talking was virtually impossible, especially with her keeping an eye on him.

Following one such story telling, when the yachts came alongside each other and the women returned to *Julia*, Mike remarked to Suzie, 'They're a lovely bunch of girls.'

'And if I wasn't here to keep an eye on you, you'd be up to your old tricks again.'

'How could you possibly think that with me in this condition?' he pleaded, raising his plastered arms.

'I'm sure you'd find a way, lover boy!'

'Did you notice how the girl named Rachel bears a remarkable resemblance to you?' Mike asked, changing the subject.

'I did. I also heard that Jeremy has found her attractive and has taken her under his wing, so to speak.'

'Do you think that's because he still fancies you and is attracted to her as a sort of substitute?'

'Possibly. Why don't you ask him?'

'No, thanks. I've spent enough time worrying about him chasing after you without stirring things up. I still haven't forgotten about the rotten trick he tried to play on us in Cannes in an attempt to break us up.'

'Forget about that. It didn't happen then and it won't happen now – I promise you,' said Suzie, giving Mike a kiss.

The look that passed between them assured both of them about the strength of the bond that existed in their partnership, even though Mike liked to think of himself as a Valentino that women could not resist.

Filming continued on both yachts for the first three days until they docked in Gibraltar. Bignor took the opportunity to secure some footage on the rock for possible inclusion either now or later in his expected series. He did however lose some equipment when monkeys grabbed a microphone boom and ran off with the wind cover, much to the amusement of the actors and technicians though not to Bignor who scowled at the interruption.

Mike and Suzie, who had to make way for some filming aboard *Quester II*, went ashore. Jenny stayed to watch the filming, though Bignor seemed unhappy about her presence and told her to keep out of the way – in a manner she though of as rather rude. She half thought about reminding him she was a co-owner of the yacht but decided it was not worth upsetting him and kept silent for the moment.

Mike was carefully wheeled ashore. 'I wasn't able to take a look around Gibraltar when Reg and I were here doing the repairs to Pendleton's yacht,' he stated. 'We were too busy and in too much of a rush I seem to remember.'

'Then let's see if we can rectify that,' suggested Suzie, while your wheelchair battery is on charge. You should have made sure it was plugged in last night. It's a jolly good job we brought this other one as a standby or you'd be well and truly stuck.'

'I'm Sorry. I'll try not to forget in future,' Mike said, with a 'please don't be angry with me' look on his face.

Suzie acknowledged his apology and could not resist the hurt look on his face, which she knew he used to his advantage. She pushed Mike's wheelchair the fifteen minutes journey into Main Street on a warm day under a sunny sky.

'Look, an English pub,' pointed Mike. 'Let's go in for a drink.'

'Okay. I could do with a rest. Pushing you around in this wheelchair with this hot sun beating down on me is no joke.'

'I though all that jogging you do in the mornings was supposed to keep you fit,' teased Mike.

'It does, otherwise I'd have given up halfway here.'

Outside the pub, Suzie sat at a wooden trestle table with Mike alongside in his wheelchair. He ordered a bitter shandy and Suzie drank a dry Martini and lemonade with ice. They ordered a light lunch of a plain omelette and a salad, and basked in the warm sun as they relaxed and watched the tourists wandering by, most of them below the age of thirty.

'That was very refreshing,' Suzie remarked, finishing her meal and placing her glass on the table.

Mike downed his last drop of shandy, 'One for the road?' he asked.

'Not for me, and you should think twice about consuming too much alcohol while you're taking those pain killer tablets. And I'm not sure how well you'd manage in a public loo if you needed one.'

Mike gasped, 'That's true. Good point. I'll wait until we get back to *Quester* before I have another drink.'

They left the pub and after a look in the shop windows up and down the crowded main shopping street, Suzie pushed Mike back to the yacht.

That evening Bignor took some night shots in the town and on the rock before joining Pendleton and the cast and crew having a party on his yacht, which he was also filming. Mike and Suzie declined the invitation to attend. Being confined to a wheelchair most of the day was frustrating enough for Mike without having to watch everyone else dancing and enjoying themselves.

'Do you mind if I go to Jeremy's party?' asked Jenny. 'He did invite me, and I might even get my face into one of the scenes Bignor's shooting for his production.'

'No, of course not,' replied Suzie. 'You go ahead and enjoy yourself, but be wary of Jeremy, he's very charming and very persuasive when he wants to be.'

'I'm married, so he won't be interested in me.'

'Believe you me, that's never stopped him before, and won't stop him now.'

'He's more interested in his new girlfriend, Rachel,' suggested Jenny.

'Perhaps, but stay on your guard just the same. He's always looking for a new female to conquer.'

'Okay, I will. I'll see you later.'

Jenny, looking very attractive in a white figure hugging T-shirt and white trousers that contrasted to her dark skin, departed to join the party. Jeremy Pendleton's parties had gained the reputation of providing guests with free flowing drinks and lavish food, coupled with noisy music and ending with many of the guests adjourning to the bedrooms in pairs, including Pendleton if he could attract the attention of a different woman.

Alone on *Quester II*, Mike and Suzie listened to the loud music and moved to their bedroom along the wider passageway, which was ideal for Mike in his wheelchair.

'Why don't you join Jenny?' said Mike. 'You've had the job of pushing me around all day and you deserve a break. I'm sure Jeremy will be delighted to see you, and Jenny might be glad of the company, or perhaps might need someone to rescue her from Pendleton's clutches.'

'And what are you going to do?'

'I'm a little tired and I need rest to get these broken bones mended, and I'm not very good at dancing at the moment.'

Suzie chuckled. 'You'll be dancing the cha-cha-cha in no time at all. Let's see what you *are* capable of,' she said, undressing Mike who had hobbled from his wheelchair and was sitting on the edge of the bed.

Pulling his shirt off over the plasters on his arm was tricky and had to be carefully judged. His shorts and underwear slipped off more easily. He laid back on the king-size bed and watched Suzie remove her chiffon top and bikini bottoms.

During the journey she had topped up her suntan by lazing on the upper deck topless when Bignor and his crew were not filming aboard the yacht. She and Mike both noticed Jeremy Pendleton eyeing her through his binoculars from *Julia* at each opportunity. A thin chiffon, almost see-through top was all she added for their trip into town.

Now, with the pair of them naked and in the privacy of their bedroom, Suzie straddled Mike and lent forward, brushing his face with her breasts. The plasters on Mike's wrists prevented him from petting her easily, but his lips were able to savour the taste of her breasts and his tongue caressed her nipples. His lips teased them as he sucked gently, first one, then the other, making them hard and erect, pleasuring both of them.

The effect on Mike was soon evident as he became hard and bold, eager for the satisfying pleasure of penetration, which Suzie made him wait for. She was in total command of their actions and after stimulating him by brushing herself against his face, she finally obliged him with his pleasure as she slowly impaled herself on his erect member.

'Oh, God! That's good,' Mike pronounced, the position affording him to slip easily and deeply into her.

Suzie bent forward and they shared a passionate kiss, their tongues caressing each other and exploring the insides of their mouths. Their bodies remained locked together in stillness. Despite the absence of movement the excitement gradually increased in both of them. The years of love making had not dampened the thrill of their union, and time had only served to strengthen the bond between them.

Mike began to wriggle as the heady desire to extract more pleasure from his penetration grew in him. Suzie consented to his desires by slowly pushing up then relaxing, allowing Mike a little movement within her. He desired a faster rhythm, but was helpless to obtain it. Suzie was in control and rested her weight on him, allowing Mike only a small amount of additional movement at a time. His yearning to gain more movement intensified the desire in him and hardened his member even more as Mike arched his back in an attempt to increase his penetration and gain more movement. Suzie was wise to that manoeuvre and countered it by rising and falling with him, causing Mike more frustration and a stronger desire to receive the extra pleasure that was tantalisingly just out of reach.

Finally, Suzie relented and let Mike thrust into her with all the speed he could muster. With only his fingers free, he grasped her smooth backside and squeezed Suzie's buttocks together to hold her still, a few inches above him. This made room for him to arch his back and thrust eagerly into her. Their breathing became faster as they neared their climaxes with both of them crying out with un-abandon when the final moments of glorious ecstasy arrived. Mike's body jerked as he ejaculated in several bursts with Suzie feeling the exploding movement within her.

'Aah! That was great!' announced Mike, relaxing his arched back and sinking into the bed. 'Don't ever stop giving me such a wonderful sexy time, Miss Drake.'

'I won't, as long as Miss Drake becomes Mrs Randle at some point in the not-too-distant future,' Suzie asserted, resting her weight on top of Mike and cuddling him.

'It will. I don't want to lose you. After all, you might take a fancy to Jeremy Pendleton and marry him for his money.'

'I might. He's got plenty of it, and more than just money to offer.'

'Now, now, don't remind me of the time you had with him.'

'I told you then, nothing's as good as being with you. And that has not changed.'

'I'm glad to hear it.'

They lay still for a while, basking in the glow of their sexual fulfilment and savouring the enjoyment of their union. Suzie was the first to move, lifting her body and extracting herself from Mike's diminishing member.

She gave him a kiss and brushed into place a lock of his hair that had fallen across his brow.

'You have a sleep and I'll be back a little later on,' Suzie said.

'Okay, luv. I'll see you when you return. Don't do anything I wouldn't do,' Mike said.

'Right. That doesn't leave me much in the way of restrictions.'

Mike smiled and closed his eyes.

Chapter Twenty-Six

The Party

While the two yachts were berthed in Gibraltar, Jeremy Pendleton organised a party aboard his yacht *Julia*. Mike and Suzie made love aboard *Quester II* before Mike took a rest and Suzie prepared to join Jenny at the party.

She had a quick shower in the en suit bathroom, dressed in her favourite canary yellow top and shorts and brushed her shoulder length black hair. Her smooth, clear bronzed skin was attractive enough without any makeup and a touch of lipstick was all she generally applied. Suzie stepped ashore, wandered along to Pendleton's yacht berthed alongside and joined the party.

'Suzie!' cried Pendleton as she stepped into the room. 'I'm glad you changed your mind and decided to join us. The cast and crew are enjoying the rest of the night off from filming. Alastaire took a few party shots earlier with his stars. Now that's all finished we're carrying on with the party.'

'So I see,' remarked Suzie, casting an eye around the voluminous lounge.

The room contained a bar, well stocked with alcohol as usual, and a table with a diverse supply of food to satisfy the taste of anyone. Couples danced to a six piece band sitting on a small dais and blaring out mainly up-tempo music.

'This was all needed for a couple of Alastaire's scenes, and there was no point in wasting it. Was there?' Pendleton asked.

'Of course not Jeremy, though you could probably have cut down on the quantities a little,' suggested Suzie.

He looked around the lounge at the vast amount of drink and food being consumed. 'Probably, but everyone seems to be enjoying themselves and I don't do things by halves.'

'So I've discovered. I see Jenny is enjoying herself dancing.'

'Yes. She's a very good dancer. Black people always seem to have a better sense of rhythm it seems to me. She's very attractive and has a wonderful figure.'

'I thought you might find her shapely bosom attractive.'

'Yes, it glides up and down with the tempo of the music adorably in that very tight T-shirt.'

'She's married.'

'Yes, I know.'

'She's happily married and is not looking for any flirtatious excitement.'

'What's that got to do with me admiring her assets? After all, I also admire yours.'

'And like I said, the rules are, looking's one thing, touching is another.'

'But what a boring world it would be if we all obeyed the rules. Don't you think, Suzie?'

'Perhaps.'

An attractive dark-haired female in her mid-twenties crossed the room to join them.

'Ah, Rachel. Let me introduce you to Suzie Drake. She and her partner ... sorry, fiancé, own the other yacht *Quester.*'

Suzie gave Pendleton a knowing look at the deliberate slip of the tongue he made.

'Yes, I saw you there when we were filming. Your fiancé's the good looking bloke who foiled a drugs gang but ended up with busted arms and a leg, isn't he?'

'That sounds like him,' agreed Suzie.

'Now you two are together, I can see the resemblance some people have spoken of,' said Pendleton.

'You mean it didn't occur to you before, Jeremy?' asked Suzie, in a voice that rang of disbelievement.

'Well, it had fleetingly crossed my mind.'

Suzie looked at this attractive woman Rachel. She certainly did have a remarkable resemblance to her, though she was clearly around ten years younger. 'Have you had many television or film parts, Rachel?' Suzie asked.

'No, none. This is my first chance at stardom. Mr Bignor did a search for actors and I was fortunate enough to get selected to audition just a few days ago. Everything's happened so quickly.'

'You were obviously good enough to get the part.'

'Yes, I suppose so,' Rachel said, not sounding too sure if her acting was the reason she was selected. 'The only thing I was not so happy about was having to strip naked for a love scene.'

'All productions have to include a love interest of some description,' concluded Pendleton. 'I'm sure it will be tastefully done by Alastaire.'

'I hope so,' she replied. 'I'm a bit shy really.'

'That reminds me,' said Pendleton, taking Suzie by the arm and walking her to a quiet corner of the lounge while leaving Rachel standing on her own. 'Suzie, as a great favour to me, and in recognition of the fact that I was instrumental in, not only helping you to get this filming contract, but also in greatly speeding up the return of your yacht *Quester* from the local police, would you consent to letting Alastaire use you in a few very small scenes in his production?'

'Why? He has a whole bevy of attractive women to film.'

'I know, but he was quite taken with your beauty and charm, as am I, and would like to include you in his production, and has asked me if I would try and persuade you to agree.'

Suzie guessed that Pendleton would ask for some sort of favour in return for his intervention to secure the early return of their yacht, but had not anticipated it being this. 'I'm not sure, Jeremy. How small a scene? Will it require me to speak? I'm not an actress you know. Don't you need to be in some sort of union before you can appear in a film?'

'I don't know all the details. Alastaire will have to give you the information about that. I think you may be required to say a few words, but not many. How about it, Suzie, just for me?'

She thought for a moment. 'I'll talk with Alastaire Bignor and Mike about it first, before I decide what to do.'

'Good, that's settled. How about a dance?' he asked, grabbing Suzie's hand when a slow smoochy number began. Pendleton led her to the dance floor, put a hand around her waist and pulled Suzie's body tightly up to his. 'This is the closest I've been able to get to you since that afternoon in Cannes,' he commented.

'Don't start getting any ideas, Jeremy. If Mike saw you trying anything on with me he'd probably have no hesitation in punching you on the nose.'

'He might find that slightly difficult with both of his arms in plaster.'

'I'm sure he'd find a way.'

'Hmm. I must not forget that he's a rough character.'

'He's not a rough character, he's a fighter and you're only this close because he's incapacitated at the moment and can't be here.'

'While I sympathise with his plight, I can't help thinking that every cloud has a silver lining.'

'Just don't go thinking you've struck gold because of it.'

'Now would I?' he answered, a smile beaming from his bronzed, handsome features.

When the music stopped, Suzie pulled herself away from his clutches. She wandered to the bar and ordered herself a dry Martini and lemonade. Pendleton followed her.

'We have champagne on ice if you'd prefer.'

'Thank you, Jeremy, but I'm quite satisfied with this,' Suzie replied, collecting her drink and thanking the barman.

Pendleton nodded to the barman, who had been given instructions about his requirements, and he poured a glass of champagne for his employer. Suzie looked across the room and saw Rachel was sitting on her own. She presumed that, as she was known to be with Pendleton at the moment, nobody else wanted to take the chance of aggravating him by taking too much interest in her.

'Your girlfriend looks a bit lonely,' Suzie commented. 'Why don't you dance with her?'

'Oh, she'll be all right.'

'You ought to dance with her. Nobody else is.'

'I'd rather dance with you.'

'Perhaps, but I'm not available, and I think it's time I returned to see how Mike is. Goodnight, Jeremy,' Suzie said, putting her half-drunk glass on the bar.

'Goodnight, Suzie. Sleep tight.'

Suzie waved goodnight to Jenny, who waved back as she continued dancing. She left Pendleton and the rest of his guests to carry on the partying, and returned to her bedroom aboard *Quester II* where Mike was asleep. She undressed and slipped into bed beside him. Mike stirred.

'Enjoy yourself?' he asked, turning over to face her.

'It was okay. Jeremy put a proposal to me.'

'Did he now? You're not going to marry him, are you?'

'Not that sort of proposal, silly. An interesting one though. I'll tell you about it in the morning.'

'Okay, luv. Goodnight.'

The music from the party in *Julia* continued, with a low thud to each beat as the band encouraged the party revellers to take to the dance floor. Suzie gave Mike a kiss and they settled down for the night.

Chapter Twenty-Seven

The Search Begins

The first phase of the Russian hit man's contract was now complete. Viktor Belanov had passed Crossman's message to Mo after he eliminated Deven, and was obliged to kill two other members of his gang to achieve it. Belanov ended up with a broken rib, care of the bullet Deven shot him with in their duel. His bulletproof vest had done its job and saved his life from the small slug of metal that would have rammed into his body. If Deven had aimed for his head, it would have been a much more deadly matter and he would almost certainly have died. Belanov was used to taking risks in his profession and his luck held with him suffering only a minor injury.

Through his contracts he had amassed a great deal of money, safely tucked away in a Swiss bank account. With this latest near miss, he began to think about retiring from his profession while he was still alive and had the opportunity.

Following a journey to Brighton in the early hours of Wednesday morning and a change of identity when he booked into a hotel using one of many fake passports he carried, Belanov decided to take a few days rest as the doctor at Brighton Hospital had suggested. A break, before continuing with the next phase of his contract to eliminate Suzie Drake, would give his ribs the chance to start mending and be less painful. Sunday night was a good time to watch her house. If a person was going out to a restaurant, a party or a show, it would usually be on a Friday or a Saturday evening. On Sunday nights, people were getting ready to return to work in the coming week, and this was the best time to watch for them. With a few days rest, Belanov's ribs were less sore and he was now ready to complete his contract.

Suzie Drake's address on the outskirts of Bosham Hoe in West Sussex, had been supplied by Crossman after he obtained it from Lefty. Arriving at nine o'clock in the evening as the last vestiges of daylight gave way to the night sky, Belanov discovered the house was surrounded by a ten foot high wall, enabling him to keep an eye on it only through the bars in the wrought iron gates. After watching for several hours from his car parked nearby he quickly realised the sequence of lights turning on and off in each room followed a pattern. He was soon capable of predicting which rooms would have their lights extinguished or lit, confirming the house at that time was almost certainly unoccupied.

'With a high wall surrounding this house and with a light switching sequence in evidence, they are obviously security minded and would have installed a burglar alarm system,' Belanov reasoned to himself. 'And I can see floodlights dotted around the house, probably activated by movement. I'll sit and wait – I'm sure the house is empty at the moment, but someone may return later.'

Belanov had a long wait. He sat in his car until dawn arrived. The sky lightened from black to charcoal grey, changed to blue-grey and finally to a cerulean blue with a few wispy clouds drifting across the heavens. Belanov watched all the lights in the house switch off as daylight emerged with no one returning and no sign of life. He gave a satisfactory pat on the back to himself that his assessment of the situation was correct. Glancing at the notes Phadkar had provided him with when he first telephoned him for information, he calculated his next move would be to ring SMJ Boatyard. They should be able to tell him where Suzie Drake was.

He glanced at his watch. 'Six o'clock. It is too early for me to ring the boatyard. I will wait until around nine o'clock. As I am sure the house empty, now is a good time to do some exploring,' he concluded.

If Belanov wanted to enter the house without being detected when Suzie Drake was present, it would be useful to have a better idea of how to get into the building unseen and have some indication of the layout.

Wandering around the high wall that surrounded both the house and gardens, Belanov looked at the branch of the oak tree that overhung the edge of the wall. The nearest house was over 200 yards away and was surrounded by a tall hedge and several trees, making it highly unlikely he could be seen from there.

'This is the easiest way in,' Balanov told himself. He ran at the wall, took two steps up it and launched himself skywards. Grabbing the branch, he pulled himself to the top of the wall. Clambering over, he dropped to the ground, crouched low and scampered to the rear entrance to check the door and windows to the utility room. Belanov examined the window carefully.

'These windows have a metal plate on the opening and the frame, which makes the alarm contact. If it is broken the alarm will start to ring, but it is easy to overcome. I know what I need to do in order to get into this house. It will be no problem,' he muttered.

Belanov wandered around the house glancing through the windows to get an idea of the layout, but did not want to break into it at this time for fear of it being detected and putting the occupants more on guard. He returned to his car and lowered the back of the seat to make comfortable and determined to snatch a couple of hours of much needed rest after his all night vigil. He drifted into a state of relaxation but not sleep, his senses ever vigilante.

A few hours passed before Belanov opened his eyes and flexed his neck muscles, which had gone a little stiff after his rest in the car. He glanced at his watch. It was a little after nine o'clock and he needed to stretch his legs. He grabbed his mobile phone and slammed the car door shut. The air was filled with the sound of waves lapping against the shore and seagulls squawking. Wandering through the trees, he emerged to a cliff edge above a tranquil bay where wooden steps led down to a picturesque sandy beach.

An elderly gentleman with a walking stick approached, smiled and said, 'Good morning. It's a lovely day for a stroll, isn't it?'

Belanov nodded. 'Yes, it is.'

'Come on Rex,' the man said to his Alsatian dog. It came bounding through the trees and dashed down the steps, reaching the beach before his owner had negotiated the first few rungs. Belanov watched the dog turn to see his owner slowly following before turning and running into the sea.

Pressing the buttons to ring SMJ Boatyard, Carol the receptionist answered the call. 'Good morning. SMJ Boatyard Ltd. Can I help you?'

'I would like to speak to Miss Suzie Drake, please,' Belanov said in his best English accent.

'I'm sorry, sir, but Miss Drake is away at the moment. Can Mr Sterling help you?'

'No, it is Miss Drake that I wish to speak to. I met her a while ago and she asked me to call on her if I was in the area.'

'Oh, I see.'

'Do you know when she is due to return?'

'No, not at the moment. She is abroad doing some filming and may be away for some time.'

'Abroad! Do you know where?'

'She is due to reach the island of Ibiza sometime soon. In the next day or two I believe.'

'Ibiza. Thank you.'

'Who shall I say was enquiring?'

The question remained hanging in the air as the line went dead. Belanov closed his mobile phone. The receptionist shrugged, made a note of the call in her log book, and went back to reading the newspaper until the next visitor or telephone call arrived.

With the information he had gathered, Belanov now had to make a decision whether to wait for Suzie Drake to return or try to seek her out.

'The receptionist said she may be away for some time,' he considered, so he made the decision to travel to Ibiza. 'Observing a person and remaining unseen in a crowded holiday resort is very easy,' he told himself. 'The Mediterranean is a nice place to visit, and I did state when negotiating my contract, that I could charge for any additional travel I might have to do should it become necessary. Visiting the island of Ibiza on my client's bill sounds like the best option to me,' he decided. 'And engineering an accident to kill Suzie Drake in a thronging holiday town will be no problem.'

Belanov rang the airline and booked a flight to Ibiza with murder his objective.

Chapter Twenty-Eight

Ibiza

On Tuesday, the morning after Jeremy Pendleton's party aboard *Julia* in Gibraltar marina, Alastaire Bignor talked to Suzie about his wish for her to take a small part in his production. He convinced her it would be very easy, and she and Mike would be proud in the future when they saw the production on television. It would also be a good advertising feature for their boatyard. A large coloured poster from the film, which he would send to her, would look good in the foyer of their offices to attract and interest potential customers. He sounded very convincing and after talking it over with Mike she agreed, albeit rather reluctantly.

When Suzie and Mike looked at the script of the scenes Suzie was to play, they were happy she had a relatively small part in the production with only a few lines to speak. After agreeing to Bignor's request, partly because of the pressure from Jeremy Pendleton, the filming took place in one of the larger bedrooms aboard *Quester II*. It took a little over an hour to complete and although Suzie wore shorts and a T-shirt for the filming, the fact that the whole scene took place in a bedroom worried her a little.

She spoke naturally when it became her turn to say her lines, and Bignor praised her for the professionalism and ease with which she delivered them. 'You are a natural, Miss Drake. I could include a few more scenes with you if you wish.'

'No, thank you, Mr Bignor. I have completed my obligation to you and to Jeremy. That is quite enough.'

He smiled reluctantly, realising he would not be able to persuade Suzie to agree to any further scenes.

With the filming at an end, both yachts set sail for the island of Ibiza. Alastaire Bignor had arranged to film several further scenes at a villa a few miles outside of San Antonio de Portmany, where the two yachts would tie up in the local marina.

They sailed from Gibraltar in mid-morning under a clear sky and on a calm Mediterranean Sea kissed by a gentle breeze. All the cast and film crew were aboard *Julia*, and Mike, Suzie and Jenny were thankful to get a few hours to themselves. Suzie was teaching Jenny how to pilot the yacht. She was enjoying the challenge, but for safety kept *Quester II* clear of Pendleton's yacht and sailed along 300 yards astern of his vessel. Even on this vast sea, loud music and the occasional screams from some of the women could be heard drifting across the deep blue, gently rolling waves.

After the first lesson was completed the autopilot on *Quester II* was engaged. Jenny kept an eye on the controls while Mike and Suzie took the opportunity to do some sunbathing.

'It sounds as if Jeremy is having one long party all the way to Ibiza,' Suzie remarked.

Mike was stretched out on a lounger to accommodate his awkwardness in lying down and rising again afterwards, due to his plasters. 'Why doesn't that surprise me? With all those lovely ladies aboard and Jeremy Pendleton around, I'm surprised Bignor gets any filming done at all.'

'He's already taken some at our boatyard, some on both yachts while we were sailing here and some in Gibraltar. If he's also filming when we get to Ibiza and the show only last about an hour, he can't need much more, surely?'

Mike glanced across Suzie, lying on a blanket on the top deck sunbathing topless. 'I gather he needs to film more than twice the length to what he requires, because a lot of it ends up edited out as unsuitable, or is saved for a later show or something like that, so he told me.'

'Sounds like a lot of waste to me.'

'Yeah. How's Jenny getting on with piloting *Quester*?'

'Good. She's picked it up very quickly. By the time we get back home she'll be able to handle the yacht as well as either of us.'

'Does that mean she'll want to be out and about more instead of staying in the office doing paperwork and telephone sales?'

'Probably. And until you are well enough to handle a yacht again, I'd say that was a good thing, wouldn't you?'

'I guess so,' Mike said, sounding none too convinced.

The two yachts sailed on into the night and approached Ibiza the following day when the sun was high in the sky at around noon. *Quester II* followed *Julia* into the San Antonio marina and both yachts tied up alongside each other. The crew and cast went ashore to explore, while Bignor and Pendleton journeyed to the villa to finalise arrangements for the filming there.

Mike continued sunbathing aboard their yacht on the top deck, while Suzie and Jenny prepared lunch for them all. Below a shaded area on the top deck masking them from the searing sun, a healthy salad lunch was served, which Mike complained about because it did not include chips with it.

Suzie asked him, 'Now that you've finished complaining about your lunch, and I see you haven't wasted any, would you like to go ashore?'

'Perhaps a bit later. It's too hot at the moment for you to have to wander around with me in this contraption. I think I'll stay here and get some rest, but don't let me stop you,' said Mike, hoping to limit the annoyance he caused with his complaint.

'That's very thoughtful of you. In that case, Jenny and I will go ashore to look around the shops. We need to restock some food and drink, including chips. I'll organise that and check out where we refuel as well.'

Mike acknowledged the slightly sarcastic comment from Suzie. 'Okay, luv. Be careful and leave my Whisky flask within reach, will you?'

'Okay, but remember your still taking those pills, and don't you go getting drunk. If you fall over and hurt yourself there'll be no one about to help you, and Mr Craig will be sorry he agreed to let you go on this trip with us to look after you.'

Mike gave her a 'I wouldn't be so silly' look, which she smiled at.

Suzie dressed in shorts, a scoop-neck T-shirt and sandals. She gave Mike a kiss, grabbed her handbag and dark glasses, and she and Jenny stepped ashore and disappeared towards the shopping area. It was crowded with mainly young holidaymakers searching for bargains in the plethora of souvenir shops, or simply drinking themselves into a state of total intoxication and generally making a nuisance. This all added to the poor reputation the area had for attracting 'lager louts' as young drunks were called.

As they left the yacht, none of them saw a lone figure standing at the far end of the jetty watching them. Viktor Belanov lowered his binoculars and smiled to himself. He had guessed correctly where the yachts would tie up and had seen his target leave *Quester II* and wander into town.

He wanted to make the death of Suzie Drake look like an accident as his employer had asked, but only if he could achieve it easily, otherwise she was to die any way he could manage – which usually meant with a bullet. This was the first time he had glimpsed the woman of his attentions. Previously, he possessed only a description of her and knew her fiancé was in a wheelchair. He watched Suzie kiss Mike goodbye on the top deck, and with him exhibiting his plaster casts and she with attractive features and shoulder length black hair, the identification of his target was confirmed.

'She is a good-looking woman. It is a pity she has to die,' Belanov pondered. 'But that is my contract and die she must.'

Jenny and Suzie wandered around the shops. They thronged with noisy young men and women. Suzie kept turning around to stare behind her.

'You keep looking around. What's the matter? Are you worried about Mike?' Jenny asked.

'No, it's not that. I've got this funny feeling in the back of my neck as if somebody is watching me. I don't like to ignore those feelings, they've been very useful in the past on more than one occasion.'

Suddenly, from among the crowds behind them, Jeremy Pendleton appeared. 'Good afternoon ladies. I trust you are enjoying yourselves and this glorious weather?'

'Oh, it's you Jeremy. I might have guessed,' said Suzie.

He frowned, not understanding her remark.

'I had a feeling somebody was watching me. I thought you were supposed to be checking on the villa with Alastaire?'

'We were. It didn't take very long to do that. All the arrangements were already in place. It was simply a case of making sure the production group were expected and everything was prepared and ready as previously agreed.'

'I see.'

'Is Mike not with you?' Pendleton asked, looking around for his wheelchair.

'No, he's having a rest and we girls are taking the opportunity to do some shopping.'

'Good. Would you two lovely ladies care for a drink? There's a hotel just along the road that I stay in sometimes, which is cool, quiet and where they serve very good cocktails.'

'It's a bit early for cocktails Jeremy and I don't think visiting a hotel with you is a good idea anyway. Somebody might see us and get the wrong idea ... or perhaps for you it would be the right idea?'

'I can't think what you mean,' suggested Pendleton with a smile playing on his lips.

'We'll see you back at the yachts,' stated Suzie, as she and Jenny moved on.

'Does he ever give up?' smiled Jenny.

'No, I don't think he ever will. Like I said, I quite enjoy our little exchanges and while he thinks there is a chance I might find myself in a position where it is difficult to refuse him, I'm sure he'll keep on trying.'

'He's very good-looking. I'm not surprised that women are attracted to him.'

'Yes, and to his vast riches as well no doubt.'

'No doubt.'

The pair continued their shopping, unaware that Belanov's eyes were following them from a safe distance. 'If they like shopping, and most women do, then it might provide me with an opportunity to complete my contract soon,' he considered. 'I must make a few arrangements first.' He had seen enough and left to set in motion a plan that would fulfil his contract.

Suzie and Jenny pushed their way through the crowded streets and spent an enjoyable afternoon looking at designer clothes, shoes, beachwear and jewellery. When they finally ran out of time after almost four hours and their shopping for that day was finished, they returned to *Quester II* where Mike was fast asleep on his bed, with an empty Whisky flask standing on the bedside cabinet. He awoke when Suzie entered the cabin. 'Hi. How did you get on?'

'Fine. I see you decided not to lounge outside in the sun.'

'No. It was getting a bit too hot and I didn't want to get sunburnt.'

'Very sensible. I also see you managed to finish your Whisky,' Suzie said, shaking the empty flask.

'It dulls the pain of these broken bones,' he said, looking for sympathy, which he did not get. 'And it helps me to sleep.'

'I bet it does.'

'What expensive items did you buy?'

'What makes you think I bought something expensive?'

'Because you always buy something expensive.'

'Well, as a matter of fact, we've both bought a few clothes and Jenny bought herself a pair of lovely shoes as well.'

'You've been spending all your pocket money then?'

'No, I haven't. Anyway, Alastaire Bignor is going to pay me for my part in his production.'

'Really?' Mike said in a surprised tone. 'How much?'

'Well, it's not exactly in money. I'll get a free ticket to the first viewing of his new production.'

'Cheat! That's not a payment. It won't cost him a penny.'

'Perhaps not, but I'll be able to wear the new outfit I've just bought,' said Suzie, smiling as she left the room.

'New outfit! What new outfit? How much did it cost?'

'I'll show you later. By the way, I've arranged to have some provisions delivered by van. They should be arriving soon,' called Suzie from the galley.

'You've been busy,' stated Mike, grabbing his crutches and wandering to the galley. Jenny joined them there.

'Yes, I have been busy. Would you both like a cup of tea. I'm thirsty after all that shopping,' said Suzie grabbing the kettle.

'Yes, please,' they both replied.

'I talked to Alastaire on the jetty, Mike. He wants to do some inside filming aboard *Quester* tonight. Apparently he's had to wait until we've docked and the yacht is not swaying, so that his actors aren't staggering about all over the place.'

'I don't see why. If you're aboard a yacht at sea, then it's likely you'll experience some movement. It should give some realism to the scene.'

'I agree, but that's obviously not how Bignor sees it.'

'So, what are we going to do tonight?' Mike asked. 'Stay in the bedroom?'

'No! Jenny and I thought we could all go out for a meal in a restaurant to get out of his way, if you agreed.'

'Sounds good to me,' stated Mike, always ready to eat.

'There's a nice looking place not far from here, which we checked out on the way back. I'll pop across to them and book a table for tonight after I've finished my cup of tea.'

'Okay. I'll start to get myself ready. It may take me a while.'

'Don't worry. I'll help you to get dressed when I return,' said Suzie.

Finishing her drink, Suzie picked up her handbag and stepped ashore to book the restaurant table and make certain they were able to accommodate Mike in his wheelchair.

Sitting in a car parked nearby and watching his target jump ashore and trot into town, was Viktor Belanov.

Chapter Twenty-Nine

Lights, Camera, Action

With Alastaire Bignor filming aboard *Quester II* that evening, Suzie booked a table in a nearby restaurant for her, Mike and Jenny to enjoy dining out while allowing the film director the freedom to continue his work.

At half past seven that evening Suzie and Jenny pushed Mike ashore and wheeled him to the nearby *Ricardo's Restaurant*. The owner, dressed in a smart dark suit, white shirt, black bow tie and shoes that had a shine he could see his face in, greeted them as they entered. He grabbed the handles on Mike's wheelchair and guided them to a table in a quiet corner where room had been made to accommodate the bulky wheelchair.

'Thank you, Ricardo. That's very good of you.'

'It is my pleasure, Miss Drake,' he gushed, in an accent familiar of English spoken by a smart, late thirties Spaniard with well-tanned features. He assisted the women to sit at the table before he returned with a menu for each of them.

The trio scanned the comprehensive menu, which listed their cuisine in both Spanish and English. The restaurant offered mainly traditional Spanish dishes with sea food and fresh produce top of the list, added to by meat, poultry and game cooked with garlic, olives and hot peppers.

'What's Jeremy doing tonight?' asked Mike, casting his eye down the list of choices on the menu.

'Having another party probably,' suggested Jenny.

'Is that why Bignor's filming aboard *Quester*?'

'No, I don't think so. One of Bignor's characters owns our yacht, so when they film scenes with him in his cabin it has to be done aboard *Quester*.'

'Right, I see,' said Mike.

'I understand Jeremy is going to a restaurant tonight that also has a casino. He likes to have a little flutter,' Suzie remarked.

'So I've heard,' said Mike, glancing at Suzie who gave him a 'don't you start that again' look.

After a request from Ricardo for his recommendation of a choice from the menu, the trio ordered their meals. Suzie and Jenny went for grilled shrimp and crabmeat as a starter, while Mike preferred pan fried oysters with cream. For a main course they each had grilled salmon with all the trimmings, and completed their meal with a refreshing dish of fruit and ice cream. Mike ordered one bottle of rosé wine and one bottle of white wine. The food was cooked to perfection and Ricardo hovered nearby to attend to his customer's every wish. The meal was completed with coffees, which were topped up as many times as his guests wanted.

The restaurant held only twenty-five tables and although it was not completely full, few tables remained empty after a steady flow of customers entered throughout the evening. Spanish music drifted from the restaurant's hidden loudspeakers quietly in the background, and subdued lighting added to the peaceful ambiance in marked contrast to the many noisy bars along the street.

By half past nine Mike, Suzie and Jenny had finished their meals and after accepting a liqueur drink from Ricardo as a parting gift, Mike paid the bill with his credit card and thanked the restaurant owner for a splendidly enjoyable meal. They were waved goodnight by their host, and wandered back to the yacht.

'That was a really good meal,' praised Mike.

'And not a sign of a chip,' teased Suzie.

'Yes, okay,' said Mike.

'He's a very nice restaurant owner,' suggested Jenny, phoning Jim on her mobile to let him know what they were doing and how the filming was progressing. 'I feel a bit mean, leaving Jim behind to manage everything on his own while we're out enjoying ourselves,' she confessed.

'I wouldn't worry about him. I expect the girls in the office are looking after most of the paperwork and I wouldn't mind betting you that Jim is ordering takeaways for his lunch, with chips,' smiled Mike.

'That's what I'm worried about. He needs to lose a bit of weight, not put it on with Chinese takeaways and the like,' Jenny said.

'Leave him alone. He'll be all right,' suggested Mike. 'I'm sure Mrs Charlie will see to it that he gets a healthy dinner each evening when he gets home.'

'He might have one when he gets home, but it's what he's eating for lunch that worries me. He's too fond of Chinese takeaways and pub fried foods.'

'Then you'll have to put him on a strict diet when you get home, won't you?'

'He wouldn't like that. And anyway, I'm not able to see what he's eating when he goes out to see our customers.'

'You'll have to make him work harder in your gym,' suggested Suzie.

'How do I do that?'

'I'm sure you could find a way,' she suggested giving her a knowing look, which she acknowledged and Mike noticed.

'Huh! Restricting his sexual activities eh? Just like Suzie does to me,' he maintained. 'You women are really sneaky.'

The two women smiled at each other, but said nothing.

The trio reached the quayside. 'I wonder if Bignor is still filming on our yacht,' pondered Suzie, stopping alongside *Quester II*. 'I'd better creep aboard quietly and find out. I don't want to upset our illustrious producer by interfering with his filming if he hasn't finished it yet.'

'Good idea,' said Mike. 'It's a warm evening. We could wait out here and watch the yachts coming and going through the marina, while listening to the rowdy noise drifting across from most of the bars.'

'At least there was nice quiet music in our restaurant,' said Jenny.

Suzie crept aboard their yacht and tiptoed down the steps to the cabins. She could see and hear the film crew busy filming in the bedroom, with bright lights issuing from the room illuminating the corridor. One of the film crew crept towards her and put a finger to his lips to indicate she should be quiet. Suzie came closer and could hear a lot of grunting going on, followed by what sounded like someone being slapped.

'What's happening?' she whispered.

'Err ... we're filming a love scene at the moment. We shouldn't be much longer,' he replied.

Suddenly a woman cried out, 'Oh! Yes! Yes! Yes!'

'What's going on here?' Suzie demanded to know, pushing her way past the man to peer into the bedroom.

A naked woman was on all fours on top of the bed with a naked man stood behind her with his hands on her backside and thrusting into her. The whole scene was being filmed by Bignor and his crew.

'Porn! Is that what you're filming, porn?' shouted Suzie.

Bignor turned to face her and pushed Suzie from the bedroom. 'I am doing a boy and girl film for a client of mine.'

'Not aboard my yacht you're not. You're supposed to be here doing a television project, not filming porn.'

'Television projects are all very well, and very useful, but they are few and far between. In order to keep filming these pilot shows I need to have finances coming in, and the easiest way to achieve that is to produce glamour films. All the producers that I know do it.'

'Glamour films! Is that what you call them? I'd call them pornographic, and you're not sullying our boatyard or the reputation we've tried so hard to build up over the past few years by releasing porn films taken aboard one of our yachts. I want you all off this vessel and that film destroyed and any other pornographic film you've taken aboard this yacht.'

'Surely there's no harm in me keeping what I've filmed? I'm sure that no one could recognise your yacht from the shots taken in the bedroom.'

'Maybe and maybe not. I'm not prepared to take that chance. If you won't assure me you will destroy those films, I'll be forced to take legal advice and tell the world what you are really up to,' spat Suzie.

Bignor shrugged. 'Oh! Very well. I'll do as you say.'

'I want you and your crew, and 'stars' off of this yacht in one hour.'

'One hour! That will be a bit difficult.'

'I don't care. Get 'em off! Hmm, I haven't said that in a while,' mused Suzie.

Bignor did not smile. He returned to the bedroom to stop the filming and ask his men to pack everything away.

Jenny came aboard. 'Is anything wrong? We heard a lot of shouting.'

'Felini here is shooting porn aboard our yacht.'

'What! Not for a television show, surely?'

'No. It's private stuff, done for a big payoff. I've told them to pack their bags, cameras and everything else and leave. We'll set sail for home tomorrow. I'll let Mike know what's happening.'

'Do you want to tell Jeremy Pendleton or shall I?' Jenny asked.

'I'd better do it. He probably won't like it, but that's his hard luck. I wouldn't mind betting he knows all about Bignor's other filming activities.'

'Why do you think they choose *Quester* to do this filming?'

'Probably because Sir Jeremy Pendleton MBE doesn't want the filming to be done aboard his yacht in case somebody recognises it. It's a very posh, distinctive yacht,' Suzie spat.

'Sounds plausible,' said Jenny. 'Would you like me to stay here?'

'Yes, please Jenny. I want you to make sure they all leave as quickly as possible. I've given them an hour. I'll take Mike for a wander around the town. There's no point in him sitting in his wheelchair on the quay for the next hour. I think I'll need that time to calm down.'

'Okay, Suzie. I'll see you in about an hour.'

Suzie explained to Mike what she discovered Bignor was filming aboard their yacht. 'In that case, wait for me here. I'd like to have a last look around *Julia* before we set sail.'

Mike grabbed his crutches and hobbled aboard the yacht while Suzie waited on the quayside and seethed. Ten minutes later he hobbled back.

'Happy now?' she asked him.

'Yes. I took a few photos on my mobile while the yacht is empty. There's nobody aboard and we might be able to use them in one of our brochures now it's fully equipped with Pendleton's luxurious extras.'

'Can we do that?'

'Of course we can. We built it,' he said, shoving the mobile phone back into his pocket and returning to his wheelchair. 'And if he complains about it, I'll remind him what his business partner Alastaire Bignor was filming aboard our yacht. That should shut him up.'

While Jenny watched Bignor organise his cast and crew to collect all their equipment and transfer it from *Quester II* to *Julia*, Suzie accompanied Mike around the town enabling him to have a brief look at the shops before they departed. All were brightly lit and shone out in the darkening evening, with many of the owners standing in their doorway encouraging the tourists to stop and peruse their wares in the hope of enticing them to make a purchase. Most of the bars were blaring out loud music and were crowded with young noisy holidaymakers who spilled out on to the street, and were determined to get drunk and have what they saw as a good time shouting and singing.

One young man, well-built but with a boozer's potbelly hanging over his belt, who was clearly drunk, grabbed Mike's wheelchair. 'Whas a matter wiv you then? Get beaten up by your ol' lady, did you?' he laughed, encouraging his mates and their girlfriends to laugh along with him, all of them hanging on to a glass or tankard of alcohol.

'No, but she could take you apart with one hand tied behind her back.'

'Ish that so,' he remarked, grabbing Suzie's left arm.

'Let go of my arm or you'll find out exactly what I am capable of and you won't like it one little bit,' warned Suzie.

'I'd like to see you try it,' he boasted, pulling harder on Suzie's arm.

Suzie lashed out a straight right fist, hitting him in the nose and propelling him into his mates, most of them spilling their drink. He crashed to the ground, his nose bleeding. Wiping the blood from his face with the back of his hand, the young man got sharply to his feet, threw his tankard of beer aside and rushed at Suzie with gritted teeth and a snarl on his face. Suzie swivelled on her left foot and banged a right foot into his chest as he charged at her, knocking him back down to the ground. Two more of his mates rushed forward to help him. Suzie grabbed one by the arm and swung him into the other onrushing youth. They clashed heads and slumped to the ground alongside their mate, nursing a head that fast turned into a nasty headache.

'Anybody else fancy their chances?' asked Suzie, looking at the rest of them. Nobody said anything or moved. 'I thought not,' she said, grabbing the handle of Mike's wheelchair and pushing it forward. The youths moved out of her way and Mike and Suzie continued their look around the town.

'They were all drunk,' she said.

'Yes. It was only the drink that made them so brave, and so foolish. It's good to see you haven't lost your touch,' said Mike.

'Even so it hurt my fist when I punched him. He's probably got a broken nose now.'

'Serves him right,' said Mike. 'That'll teach him not to be so cheeky. Perhaps he'll think twice about drinking quite so much in future.'

'Perhaps, but I doubt it. He's more likely to make up a story and brag about it to mates who weren't here to see what really happened.'

It was almost eleven o'clock when Mike and Suzie returned to *Quester II*. Jenny was sitting in the lounge. All was quiet in the yacht.

'Has everyone gone?' asked Suzie.

'Yes, everyone's gone. They've taken all their equipment across to Pendleton's yacht.'

'Good.'

'Suzie told me she got quite angry with Bignor when she found out what he was up to,' Mike admitted to Jenny.

'Yes, and I'm not surprised,' she replied.

'I saw red when I discovered what they were really filming,' Suzie added. 'The cheek of the man, thinking he could use our yacht to record his smutty films. If anyone saw those and recognised it as filmed aboard our yacht, it could do the reputation of our boatyard a lot of damage with our important clients.'

'Has Jeremy tried to persuade you to change your mind about throwing Bignor off and banning him from any more filming?' Jenny asked.

'No, not yet, though I expect him to. I imagine he's still out this evening at that restaurant with the casino. He probably playing roulette. It's the game he likes.'

'Well, at least there haven't been any problems with sailing the yacht. She's handled her new maiden voyage with ease, so far,' said Jenny. 'Let's hope the return journey is as problem free.'

'Yes, I'll drink to that,' said Mike, looking at Suzie.

'Yes, all right,' she smiled. 'I guess we could all do with a nightcap to round off this eventful evening, especially after I had to defend us from rowdy youths.'

'Why? What happened?' asked Jenny, her eyes widening in expectation of a juicy tale emerging.

'It was just a couple of drunk youths getting a bit over enthusiastic,' she stated, rubbing the fingers of her bruised hand.

'Suzie soon showed them who's boss. And mine's a large Whisky,' stated Mike.

'Of course, your favourite tipple.' Suzie looked at Jenny questioningly.

'I'll have a Brandy and Coke please.'

'Okay. I think I'll have the same. I'll make it a big one as well. I feel like celebrating.'

'What are you celebrating?' asked Mike. 'Buying a new outfit?'

'Yes. That and finding out about Bignor's underhanded filming before copies got into general circulation. I wonder how much more of that sort of filming he's done aboard *Quester* on this trip,' considered Suzie, handing out the drinks.

'We may never know,' stated Mike, taking a large swallow of his Whisky.

'I hope he keeps to his word and destroys all of those films.'

They sat and chatted about the evening's revelations while sipping their drinks and having a top-up. After almost an hour they began to yawn and agreed it was time to retire for the night.

'I don't want Jeremy Pendleton barging in here at two in the morning when he finds out what's happened,' Suzie stated, bolting the cabin entrance doors.

Most of the throbbing music from the town's bars was far enough away from the marina to fade into a distant rumble in the background, enabling the owners of *Quester II* to settle down for a quiet nights sleep, induced by the restaurant wine and a couple of large drinks that each of them had consumed.

Chapter Thirty

Rejection

The early morning sun rose above the horizon in a light blue sky devoid of anything but the smallest wisp of a cloud on the morning after Bignor and his crew were evicted from *Quester II* for filming pornographic films in the bedroom. Aboard the yacht, Mike and Suzie were stirring as the sun's golden rays streamed through the cabin window to light their bedroom in a warm glow. The digital numbers on the clock flicked past, showing the time was approaching 6 a.m.

Breaking the tranquil peace of the early morning came a vigorous hammering on the cabin entrance doors. Sitting up in bed, Suzie muttered, 'Oh God! I bet that's Jeremy banging on the door to talk to us about throwing Bignor off our yacht last night.' She yawned and stretched. 'I'd better let him in before he knocks the blinking door down.'

'Tell him to come back at a sensible time after we've had breakfast,' Mike grumbled, glancing at the clock.

'I doubt very much he'll want to do that,' she replied, slipping out of bed and grabbing her white towelling dressing gown. Suzie tied the belt around her slim waist as she hurried to the entrance door and unbolted it.

'I hope I'm not disturbing you,' said Pendleton peering in, still dressed in his evening suit.

'You are. And I imagine from your dress you've come straight here from your gambling casino, via your yacht and a chat with Alastaire Bignor no doubt,' said Suzie, turning to stroll into the galley area.

Pendleton followed her. 'Yes, that's quite right. I wanted to have a word with you about the outcome of last night's activity.'

Lifting the kettle, Suzie filled it with water. 'Cup of tea?'

'No thanks. Too early for me.'

'Last night's activity eh? Is that what you call filming pornographic scenes in our yacht's bedroom?'

'Alastaire has to produce these in order to keep enough capital coming in for him to finance these pilot shows. There's the equipment, the cast, the crew and the hire of the yachts. It all costs a lot of money to do this filming.'

'Judging by the fee he first offered our financial advisers for the hire of this yacht, he doesn't pay out a lot of money.'

'That's because he's on a tight budget. Alastaire is forced to make these films in order to keep his projects alive.'

The unmistakable sound of Mike hobbling along the corridor on his crutches preceded him arriving in the galley, bare-chested and wearing trousers only. 'Is that so? Nobody forced Bignor to film that stuff,' he declared, plonking himself down on the galley seat and allowing his crutches to clatter to the floor.

'That's right,' agreed Suzie. 'Cup of tea, Mike?'

'Yes please, luv.'

'Perhaps forced is not the correct word to use, but Alastaire does need the money to continue his other work. Would you all please reconsider your decision to stop him using your yacht for his pilot show.'

'He seems to be shooting rather a lot for a one hour programme,' said Suzie. 'Hasn't he taken enough film already?'

'Possibly. He tells me he could rearrange the story, so the shots he has are enough to finish the film, but it would not be what he planned. It would take longer and cost more, and the finished episode would not be to his high artistic standard and would suffer.'

'Then his high artistic standard will have to suffer. Won't it?' Mike said. 'And if Bignor doesn't destroy all the porno film taken aboard our yacht, we'll stop him using any of his footage taken aboard *Quester* both inside and outside. The three of us talked about it last night and we have all agreed on our actions.'

'If you did that it would ruin everything. His whole production would have to be scrapped,' suggested Pendleton.

'It serves him right for doing his private filming behind our backs.'

'If he had asked your permission would you have said yes?'

'No. He would have had to film it aboard your yacht, Jeremy,' countered Suzie. 'Would you allow him to do that?'

Pendleton smiled but said nothing. They all knew he would not allow it as his luxury yacht was unique and could be easily recognised.

Suzie handed Mike his cup of tea and sat down beside him. 'Anything else you want to ask?'

'Are you sure you will not change you minds?'

'No. Our minds are made up. Our decision is unanimous and final.'

Shaking his head, Pendleton said, 'So be it. I can see you are determined to prevent Alastaire from shooting any more film aboard your vessel. It's a pity though; if the series becomes a hit, there could have been a lot more business and publicity in it for your boatyard.'

'And if the porno film had become a success and somebody recognised this yacht, we could have lost many of our business customers,' stated Suzie.

'Others might have liked the kudos of hiring a yacht that was instrumental in taking part in such a film.'

'I doubt that very much and we are not prepared to take that chance,' said Mike.

'Very well,' sighed Pendleton. 'Alastaire will have to write a new yacht into his script if a series is commissioned; unless you change you mind that is.'

'Has he taken any of this type of film aboard your yacht, Jeremy?' Suzie pointedly asked.

'No, not to my knowledge.'

'And did you know he was going to shoot his smutty films aboard our yacht?'

'Not exactly. I have to confess that I knew he was forced … that is obliged, to produce these films in order to stay solvent, but I was not privy to where and when he did the filming.'

'I see. A very diplomatic reply,' said Suzie, sounding as if she was unsure whether to believe him or not.

Heading for the exit, Pendleton put one foot on the bottom step before turning to face them. 'I do understand your reasons for being annoyed and I hope this little episode doesn't harm the good friendship we enjoy.'

'Good friendship, eh? We'll think about that,' said Mike, pleased to see Pendleton not getting his way for once.

A resigned looking Jeremy Pendleton took a longing look at Suzie, sitting on the galley seat in her white dressing gown showing her long bronzed legs and suntanned cleavage where the gown had drifted apart. Wearily he returned to his yacht with the bad news for Alastaire Bignor.

Turning to Mike, Suzie purred, 'You're looking very sexy with your tanned muscles showing. I could quite fancy taking you back to bed.'

Mike breathed in heavily expanding his chest. 'I won't stop you. You're looking pretty good yourself, as I saw Jeremy admiring.'

Suzie looked down. 'I hadn't realised my dressing gown had come open quite so far.'

'He did, and so had I,' Mike said, moving across to kiss Suzie's cleavage.

'Come on then Hopalong. Quietly, we don't want to wake Jenny if that banging hasn't already roused her.'

'I'm with you,' said Mike, taking his crutches from Suzie who collected them from the floor. He hobbled towards the bedroom at a faster rate than he left it a few minutes earlier.

Suzie remarked. 'It must be my turn on top again.'

Chapter Thirty-One

Sudden Death

Following the rejection of Jeremy Pendleton's plea for Mike and Suzie to change their minds about allowing Alastaire Bignor to complete his filming aboard their yacht, they returned to their bedroom to enjoy a sexual interlude. Suzie took her usual position on top again because of Mike's arms and leg in plaster. Both had difficulty in keeping their ecstatic groans and sensuous thrills quiet, knowing Jenny was in the next bedroom and may have been woken earlier by Pendleton's banging on their entrance door. After their pleasurable union, they snatched a short nap before rising again for breakfast.

After an 8 a.m. breakfast fry-up – which Suzie only allowed Mike on rare occasions, *Quester II* was made ready to sail. Jenny was woken by Pendleton's banging on the door but told Suzie she returned to the land of slumber again quickly afterwards. She did not want to embarrass them by revealing that she listened to their bedroom activity and muffled cries in an attempt to avoid being heard. It made her more aware of how she was missing her husband Jim, and was pleased the trip was being cut short and they were returning home.

The supplies Suzie ordered were delivered and Jenny was encouraged to pilot the yacht out of the marina, watched carefully by Suzie. After *Quester II* was refuelled, they sailed into the open sea and headed for home.

'You managed that very well,' praised Suzie.

'Yes, I do seem to have got the hang of it,' remarked Jenny, spinning the wheel. 'Does this mean I'll be able to accompany you on more trips to deliver our yachts to their clients, instead of being stuck in the office?' she probed.

'I don't see why not. It's always useful to have more than one person aboard who can handle the yacht.'

'Good.'

'I'll have to persuade Mike and Jim to agree to that of course.'

'Of course. I'm sure Jim will be okay about it.'

'Got him twisted around you little finger then, have you?'

'More or less. Like you, I too can use my body to get what I want when I need to, though up to now I haven't thought about using it to get Jim fit. I will now.'

'It's a jolly good job that men are so desperate to get us into bed with them they'll agree to almost anything.'

'Yes, isn't it? They don't seem to realise we want to make love just as much as they do.'

The women giggled. 'Let's keep it that way.'

While *Quester II* was sailing out of the marina on the start of her leisurely voyage back to England, Jeremy Pendleton watched from his yacht with a touch of sadness. He had not been able to get any closer to Suzie or Mike. He worried that the unhappy episode with Alastaire Bignor would be a setback on the small advance he began to make with them, though he was more concerned with the effect it may have on his relationship with Suzie.

Meanwhile, Bignor was reorganising his schedule to meet the unforeseen situation he now found himself immersed in. 'It'll take me a while to sort this mess out,' he told Pendleton. 'I've got quite a lot of rewriting to do. The cast and crew might as well go ashore and enjoy themselves for the rest of the day while I get on with this revised shooting schedule.'

'I'm sure they'll all be happy to oblige and will be ready to work twice as hard when they return. I'll give them the news before I retire for a short nap. I've had a long night,' Pendleton declared.

'And found a new friend to impress?' suggested Bignor, who had seen an attractive, suntanned red-head escorted into his bedroom.

'I'll see you later,' Pendleton said, ignoring the comment.

The cast and crew were delighted to have another day off to explore the town. Those who were not taking part in Bignor's glamour films soon discovered why *Quester II* had left and they had been given an unexpected leave for the day. Several of them grouped together to visit the town, while Rachel stayed behind on the yacht expecting to spend her time with Jeremy Pendleton after missing the previous night out with him.

She quietly entered his bedroom. After his long gambling night, accompanied by a female he had met, Rachel discovered this redhead was now sharing his bed. Departing in disgust, she deliberately banged the door shut and went ashore to find the other cast members.

Leaving the marina, she dodged the traffic and crossed the street, unaware of Belanov, seated behind the wheel of a car watching her closely, mistakenly thinking she was Suzie Drake. 'I though I might have missed her now that one of the yachts has left, but she is still here. This is my chance,' he breathed, slipping the car into gear and moving slowly forward.

He shadowed Rachel twenty yards behind her as she walked along the pavement. The town held only a few tourists who had risen early that morning wandering through the shopping area. Majority of them were still sleeping the previous night's rowdy entertainment off and would not see the light of day until the afternoon. Rachel glanced behind her, saw no traffic coming her way and stepped into the road to cross it. At that instant, Belanov rammed the accelerator to the floor and the car gathered speed fast.

With the roar of the engine approaching, Rachel turned to see the vehicle charging towards her and a look of horror crossed her face. She screamed out loud as the car smashed into her, sending her flying over the top and crashing to the ground with a deathly thud. Motoring down the street as fast as he could, Belanov sped away and turned on to the road to Ibiza town. He left a twisted and battered Rachel lying in the road with blood oozing from a large gash in her skull.

Reaching Ibiza, Belanov drove his car to the remotest corner of a car park, collected his belongings from the boot and walked briskly to the terminal and caught a ferry to Valencia. He knew he had to move quickly before the police could mount a search for the hit-and-run driver. From Valencia he caught a flight home to Moscow in his carefully planned escape route.

In San Antonio, the police and ambulance were quickly on the scene of the accident and Rachel was rushed to hospital. Despite the speedy attention she received there was nothing the medical staff could do for her, the injury to her head was too severe and she was pronounced dead on arrival.

Later that day, the police broadcast an appeal for witnesses on both local radio and television, and a holidaymaker came forward to tell them he was taking a video at the time of the accident and filmed some of it with his camera. The recording was examined and showed Rachel as she started to cross the road before the camera was panned back quickly past Belanov's car and towards the marina. A slightly blurred image of the driver was extracted from the video, and copies were sent to the television broadcast company and local newspapers in the hope that somebody would recognise and identify the driver.

The incident made headline news in the islands newspapers the following morning. It was picked up by the British press when they discovered Rachel was English and was working on a film for an English director and cast, which was expected to be screened on British television.

Alastaire Bignor took the opportunity to speak to the press in order to publicise his pilot show. 'I am shocked at the loss of one of my brightest and talented stars. Rachel was one of the leading ladies in my forthcoming episode and will be greatly missed. I will have to do a lot of re-shooting but I will continue filming this blockbuster show, which I am certain will be greatly admired by the television public when it is broadcast. Rachel, I know, would have wanted it this way and a dedication to her will be included in the credits.'

'Do you have any idea why she was the victim of a hit-and-run incident?' asked one young man reporting for the tabloids in England.

'I cannot say for sure, but there are many jealous producers and directors who go to extraordinary lengths to prevent rival entrepreneurs like myself from marketing their productions.'

'Are you saying she was deliberately killed to try and prevent you from completing your film?'

'No, I'm not saying that. I'm merely suggesting there are other jealous filmmakers who would be happy to see me fail. But I'm not going to. This dynamic production will be filmed and dedicated to the memory of Rachel – a lovely lady.'

'And what do you say to the rumour that you've had a falling out with the owners of a yacht where you were filming and they've now left to return to England?'

'I do not know where you heard that vicious rumour from,' bluffed Bignor, 'but I can assure you it is not true. The owners had to return home for personal reasons. I have completed filming on their yacht, so I gave my blessing for them to leave.'

'I see. Thank you, Mr Bignor,' the reporter said, scribbling down the final sentences in his note pad.

* * *

The following day saw graphic headlines in England from several of the tabloids. STAR KILLED TO PREVENT FILMING, read one. HIT & RUN TO STOP HIT TV PRODUCTION, read another. The articles were accompanied by photographs of the dead girl and her killer driver with the question, 'Have you seen this man?' posed by them. One article also suggested the producer of the film, Mr Alastaire Bignor, after a blazing row with one of the yacht owners, had been thrown off and quoted an anonymous 'star' of his production as the source of the information.

The story also appeared on many of the newspapers web sites where it was seen by a late thirties Ukrainian hit man named Zenon Horak, who regularly scanned the internet for information. His path had crossed the affairs of Mike Randle and Suzie Drake in the past and he recognised the resemblance that Rachel had to Suzie. When he saw the photograph of the car driver he drew a sharp intake of breath. It was a little blurred, but was clear enough for him to recognise the man.

'Belanov!' he cried. 'So that is what you are up to theses days. And what will your next move be? I wonder ...'

Horak scanned through the emails he had received in the previous few weeks and eventually found the one he was looking for. He reread the brief. 'I should have realised this contract was to kill Suzie Drake and one other person – presumably her black co-director,' he correctly assumed. 'So, Belanov thinks he has killed Suzie Drake, and when he discovers his mistake, he will have to rectify it or his reputation will suffer.'

*   *   *

In the meantime, Belanov had boarded a flight from Valencia to Moscow and returned to his native Russia. As always, he was pleased to be back on home soil and knew he was safe again. Travelling the world to undertake various contracts had quickly lost its glamour and home was where he wanted to be, enforced by thoughts of settling down to a more normal life. To his annoyance, he received an email from Crossman stating he had killed the wrong person by mistake and asking if he still intend to fulfil his contract or otherwise refund the money? Belanov's enquiries confirmed the newspaper reports that it was Rachel he killed and Suzie Drake was still alive and aboard her yacht sailing back to their Hamble boatyard in England.

Belanov's ribs were starting to ache again and he wanted to take a longer rest before considering whether to take on another job or not, but had no option other than to search out Suzie Drake again. He would lose the extra travelling money he sought for his trip to Ibiza by having to return to England to finished the contract. He cursed at the thought, picked up the telephone and booked a flight to London Heathrow Airport.

When the tickets were confirmed he rang Crossman. 'I will complete the contract I agreed with you.'

'Good. I understand the Drake women is sailing back to England at the moment in her yacht.'

'That is my information also. I will need the same items you provided for me on my last visit.'

'I understand,' agreed Crossman. 'And if Mike Randle happens to be with her when you make the hit and can eliminate him as well, there'll be a bonus in it for you,' he agreed, though failed to stipulate exactly how much the bonus would be.

'Good.'

Crossman made arrangements to provide a car and a gun, the same Yarygin PYa pistol as before. They were left in the Heathrow long stay car park with the ignition key hidden and the location emailed to him. Crossman instructed Lefty to carry out the task, which he did, stealing a car from a nearby multistory car park and driving it to Heathrow. He left the parking ticket in the ashtray and hid the ignition key on the top of one of the wheels.

Everything was in place for the reluctant Belanov to return and carry out his murderous task to eliminate Suzie Drake and possibly Mike Randle as well.

Chapter Thirty-Two

Return

The unhurried trip back to England for Mike, Suzie and Jenny gave them time to reflect on Alastaire Bignor's behaviour and their decision to end the agreement for him to film aboard their yacht.

'Do you think we did the right thing?' Suzie asked Mike.

'Yes, of course we did. We're not that desperate for the money or the publicity, though both would have been a nice bonus for us.'

'I hope he destroys those films or we could end up with a nasty legal wrangle that could be expensive.'

'I'm sure he will, in order to keep the rest of the filming aboard *Quester* for his TV production. If he's that strapped for cash he probably couldn't afford to do otherwise.'

'Time will tell.'

The three of them were lounging on the top deck sunbathing, basking in the glorious warm sunshine of the day below a cloud free sky with a gentle breeze blowing to cool the air. The yacht was gliding through a calm sea hindered by the occasional wave throwing up a salt spray that drifted across her bows. With the yacht on autopilot, all three of the passengers were able to relax. Suzie, as usual was topless under a hot sun beating down. Jenny was encouraged to do the same, after extracting a promise from them both they would not tell her husband. Jenny had a fuller figure than Suzie and Mike had a job to take his eyes from her, an interest that was not missed by Suzie.

Jenny had once slept with Mike in the distant past, before she was married, and seeing her topless again reminded him of that time and the sexual enjoyment they shared as strangers. The episode was now long past, but did not stop Mike from thinking about it from time to time, though he still worried that Jim would somehow find out. If he did, it could be very awkward for him and for Jenny, and could make things difficult in their boatyard partnership.

Mike talked to Reg on the radio to let him know when they expected to reach home. 'We had a few problems and decided to cut our visit short and return.'

'So I've been hearing.'

'Oh, how's that?'

'Haven't you been listening to the news?'

'No, we haven't turned the radio or the television on. We're all simply chilling out and sunbathing in this glorious weather. Why, what's happened?'

'Your film producer's had a bit more trouble. One of his girls, named Rachel, was the victim of a hit-and-run driver in Ibiza. She was killed.'

'That's terrible! I remember her. She was the attractive girl who Jeremy Pendleton had in his clutches. She resembled Suzie.'

'I though that when I saw the picture of her in the newspaper. The article also stated that Alastaire Bignor had a row with the owner of a yacht he was using for his film, and they left Ibiza. Pendleton was also interviewed, so he was still there with his yacht. It confirmed that it was you and Miss Drake who'd had the disagreement and left.'

'Hmm, that's right. Did they catch the person who was driving the hit-and-run car?'

'No, I don't think so.'

'Well, thanks Reg. We should be home sometime on Tuesday afternoon, I reckon.'

'Okay. We'll be waiting for you to arrive.'

Quester II docked in Gibraltar to break-up the journey before the longest leg of their trip home began. With bright sunshine and a calm sea with a good breeze, they sailed home to their Hamble River boatyard without rushing, taking five lazy days.

*   *   *

In Moscow, Belanov boarded a plane bound for London still fuming that he was obliged to return to England after thinking his work for the client was finished. The four hour flight arrived at London's Heathrow airport at 10.30 p.m. and after passing through passport control he located his car.

Belanov drove to Brighton and booked back into the 'Carrington Hotel', the same one he left almost two weeks previously. The receptionist recognised him and welcomed him back. It went against his best instincts to use the same hotel twice in such a short space of time, but it saved him from searching for another suitable hotel. It was far enough away from SMJ Boatyard and Suzie Drake's house for it to be safe, and it was a hotel that had a convenient fire escape. This lead to a rear alleyway that served as a possible escape route in case of trouble, an element all those who were trained by the Soviet Government were taught to look for.

Belanov's home town beckoned him, and he was anxious to get the job over and finished with as quickly as possible. After resting during the day and with the sun dipping down to the horizon, he drove to Suzie Drake's house to check it out. He found the same intruder alarm light sequence working, indicating she had not yet arrived home. He drove to SMJ Boatyard to establish its location and find a good position to survey the premises without being seen. Suzie Drake was returning by yacht, so would dock at the company's boatyard.

*   *   *

By Tuesday, with their journey almost at an end, *Quester II* sailed up The Solent into Southampton Water and along to SMJ Boatyard at Hamble in the early afternoon. Reg, George and Jim were all waiting by the quayside.

'Steady ... steady ... cut the engines, Jenny,' Suzie said, watching the quayside gently approaching as the yacht slowly drifted towards it. *Quester II* bumped to a gentle stop. 'Great! That's very good, Jenny. At least this trip's had a positive outcome for you,' she said, throwing a line ashore for George to secure the motor yacht after a trouble free trial.

The ramp was pushed into place and Jenny dashed down into the arms of her husband and they hugged and kissed. 'Missed me?' she asked.

'Just a bit. It's been almost two weeks since you left but it feels much longer. It looks as if you've learned to pilot the yacht very well. Did you enjoy the trip?' Jim asked.

'I did. I've learned a lot about filming a television adventure as well as learning how to pilot a yacht.'

'You'll be wanting to go along when the yachts are delivered next.'

'It's strange you should mention it, because that's exactly what I was thinking as well.'

Jim lifted his eyebrows. 'Did you now? Have you spoken to Mike and Suzie about this revelation?'

'Suzie thinks it's a good idea. She'll speak with Mike about it later. She's sure she can persuade him.'

'And do you intend to persuade me as well.'

'You'll have to wait until we get home to find that out,' Jenny cheekily smiled.

George and Suzie helped Mike to hobble ashore and his wheelchair was lowered down the steep ramp. 'Thanks, George. I'll be glad to get these damn plasters off and get mobile again.'

'All in good time, Mr Randle. I see you've managed to top up your suntan.'

'Yes, the weather's been excellent, and a quiet unrushed trip home was very relaxing.'

'You stay out here in the sunshine while I take a look at any correspondence that's come in while we've been away,' Suzie told Mike.

He dumped his muscular frame down in the wheelchair and surveyed the yard. 'It's good to be back,' he declared. George escorted him into the workshop for a look at progress on two yachts they were refurbishing before they moved to a sunny spot where the pair chatted for a while.

Suzie entered their office and took a quick look through the recent paperwork and with nothing needing her immediate attention she returned to the yard. 'You've done a very good job of looking after the place, Jim. Thank you.'

'It's not been too hectic. The girls did most of the paperwork. I've just answered a few questions and kept in touch with our clients and I've good news about the Calizares job. He's happy with our estimates and should be placing a firm order any time now.'

'That's very good news, and one in the eye for Harman's boatyard. Well done again.'

George folded up Mike's wheelchair and stowed it in the boot of their car. They said goodbye to Jim and Jenny and Suzie drove Mike home. As they left the boatyard, Belanov watched them from his car, parked in a nearby waiting area.

'So, you are very much alive, Miss Drake,' he told himself. He knew where they were heading for, home, so there was no need for him to follow them closely and chance the possibility of being seen, putting them on their guard. 'Well, the holiday is over, I will not make the same mistake again. I am not going to mess about trying to make it look like an accident this time. Tonight Miss Drake, with your man on crutches and not able to protect you, I will put a bullet into both of you and neither of you will see tomorrow's light of day.'

Chapter Thirty-Three

Home

Following their trip back to England from the island of Ibiza, the four co-directors travelled home; Mike and Suzie to Bosham Hoe, and Jim and Jenny to Weybridge. Shadowing Mike and Suzie at a safe distance keeping well out of sight was Viktor Belanov, intent on fulfilling his original contract to Khurram Phadkar by killing Suzie Drake and earning himself a bonus by also eliminating Mike Randle. Belanov had travelled to Ibiza in pursuit of Suzie, but killed Rachel by mistake. He was now obliged to complete his contract and had returned to England to achieve it.

Pressing the button on the remote to open the wrought iron gates to their home, Suzie declared, 'You see, the gates have been fixed and so has the alarm system.'

'I bet that cost a bob or two.'

'I wish you'd stop worrying about the cost of everything. We can easily afford it, and in any case, the insurance took care of most of it.'

'Sorry about that. It stems from me and my sister having to live with Gracie when mum and dad died. We were still very young, so she gave up work to look after us, and had to be very careful with finances until we were old enough to allow her to go back to work.'

'I know that. Your Aunt did a very good job of bringing you and Tracy up, but we are in a much better financial position than she was. We pay our insurance company so that when we've a problem, they take care of it.'

'We seemed to have relied on our insurance a lot these past few weeks.'

'That's what it's for,' Suzie said, collecting their letters from the post box fixed to the wall. 'The alarm company has mended our burglar

204

alarm and I've asked them to quote us for a better system. Our present one is a bit old and it seems to be rather ineffective against the more sophisticated burglars of today.'

The gate clanged shut behind them and Suzie drove up to the triple garage and workshop. The garage door rose, revealing a shiny, new Jubilee Special Triumph Bonneville motorcycle. Mike's eyes opened wide in surprise.

'This is a coming home present for you – *Bonnie II*.'

'Not the original one?'

'Some of it is, but a lot had to be replaced,' said Suzie, not wishing to disappoint Mike by telling him there was virtually nothing left unbroken that could be repaired. The original ignition lock and key were replaced on the new bike at Suzie's request, so Mike could continue to use his existing key.

Struggling to get out of the car, Mike hobbled to the bike, twisted the ignition key and pressed the starter button. The bike roared into life. 'Doesn't she sound sweet?'

'She certainly does, and it will be an incentive for you to get yourself fit and well so that we can go for a ride on her.'

'That day can't come soon enough for me,' Mike said, finding it awkward to rev up the bike with his wrist in plaster.

'It'll be a few weeks yet. You'll need some physiotherapy treatment on your wrists and leg before you're fit and able to ride your bike again.'

Mike gave a long sigh. 'I guess you're right.'

'In the meantime, you'll simply have to rely on me ferrying you everywhere.'

Turning the ignition key to shut the engine off, Mike muttered, 'Hmm.'

Garaging the car, the pair entered their house and Suzie punched in the code to turn the beeping alarm off. She dumped the letters on the hall table. 'They're mostly bills. I'll take a look at them later on.'

'It's good to be home,' declared Mike, standing in the hallway surveying the scene. He gave a sniff. 'Have you had the place painted?'

'Of course I have. All the bullet holes in the wall by the stairs and in the living room had to be filled in and I couldn't leave it all patched up, so I've had the hallway and living room repainted, and before you ask the insurance paid for it.'

'Is the hall a different colour?'

'Men! Don't you notice anything?'

'It looks different.'

'That's because it used to be cream, and it's now a pale green.'

'Oh, right. It looks nice,' declared Mike, trying hard to recover some pride over his lack of observation.

'I'm glad you think so, because we're stuck with it for a while. I've also had the living room doorframe replaced. It had a few lumps gouged out of it.'

'It must have been quite a battle.'

'It was. It's lucky I haven't lost my touch or my aim, otherwise it might have been very different for Jenny and me.'

'In that case, we'd better join the local gun club and make sure we don't lose our touch.'

'With the number of dangerous jobs that Sir Joseph keeps asking us to do, it may not be necessary,' suggested Suzie as the pair stepped into the living room.

'True, unless he takes note of the fact we keep telling him each job is the last one.'

'Have you noticed how he always seems to come up with a very good reason why we should do one more job for him?'

'Yes. He's good at that and is very persuasive.'

'I was jolly pleased he was able to help us with that man's body. I didn't fancy ringing the police about it,' said Suzie.

'No, I don't imagine you did.'

'You sit down and I'll make us a nice cup of tea.'

Mike plonked himself down on the settee and put his plastered leg up on the coffee table. Suzie gave him a hard stare when she came in the room and Mike moved his leg on to a stool. She handed him his cup of tea.

'Noticed anything different in here?' she asked.

Mike looked around. 'Nothing jumps out at me.'

'What about the carpet?'

Mike looked at it. 'What about the carpet? It looks new.'

'It is new. I had to have it replaced because of all the blood stains.'

'Oh! Right. It's the same colour, isn't it?'

'Yes, it is. Well done for remembering that.'

Mike ignored her slightly sarcastic remark and sipped his tea.

While they were settling in, Belanov arrived in his car and park it across the road from the house among the trees where he had waited before. With his telescope, and using the trees as cover, he scanned the windows of their home through the open framework of the gate.

He pulled up sharply when he caught a glimpse of Suzie passing a window in the living room. 'So, you are now home and feeling safe. Your alarm system will not prevent me from getting to you, Miss Drake. Make the most of the few hours of life you have left,' he said closing his telescope.

Belanov had a few hours to wait before dark, so he wandered down the wooden steps to the empty beach where he strolled on his last visit. He lit a cigarette, sat on a salt rotting tree trunk lying near the back of the beach, and breathed in the salt laden air as he watched the tide bringing in the rolling waves with seagulls squawking overhead. Turning at the distant barking of a dog, he saw the man and his Alsatian dog that he had previously seen walking along the sand.

The man approached. 'Oh, it's you again. Good evening,' said Mr Lockhart.

'Good evening,' Belanov replied, trying hard to disguise his Russian accent.

'You're back again, so are you thinking of buying a property near here?'

'No. No, I'm not,' replied Belanov, thinking this man was becoming a nuisance, and could be a witness who had seen a stranger in the area. He stood and put a hand on the gun in his pocket. Suddenly the dog began to growl in a low controlled manner with piercing eyes staring at him and showing his sharp teeth. He looked ready to spring into action.

'Down boy,' said the man, patting the dog's back. 'I'm sorry. I don't know what's got into him today. He's not usually like this, even with strangers.'

'That's okay,' Belanov replied, relaxing his grip on the gun.

'Come on Rex, it's time to go home,' Mr Lockhart said, moving towards the steps.

Rex followed and stayed alongside his master as he climbed the steps instead of bounding to the top and waiting for him as he usually did. Only the dog had sensed the danger, and his master continued to walk home oblivious of the close escape his life had been threatened with.

Looking at his watch, Belanov blew out a lungful of smoke, looked skywards and knew he had several more hours to wait until it was dark and the female of his attention was asleep and could be caught totally unaware. He returned to his car and closed his eyes. In his chosen profession there were many times when he had to sit and wait for the right time to arrive. It was a frustrating part of his job, but one he had no choice but to endure. His thoughts turned to home and the quiet life he could enjoy once this job was over. The problems this job had brought helped him to make his mind up – this would be his last job. He would take a holiday to relax, wind down and let his ribs fully heal and then he would retire. He had saved enough money to live a comfortable life in semi-luxury.

Darkness slowly descended. The orange ball in the sky sank below the horizon and stars began to appear as the bright sky faded until only the moon and millions of twinkling pinpoints of lights in a grey heaven were visible. With few vehicles passing, noises of the day subsided. Only the occasional seagull squawked over waves that lapped on to the shore, and rolled in their constant ebb and flow as they advanced up the sand, until the hour came for them to recede once more. The sound of a distant electric train rattled its way past on the line, fading into the night.

Opening his eyes, Belanov noted that lights were on in the living room. With his telescope he could see Mike and Suzie sitting side-by-side on the settee chatting. He wondered what they were saying to each other and pondered that whatever it was, by tomorrow it would be of no consequence any longer, because both of them would be dead.

'My wrists are giving me a bit of jip,' complained Mike.

'That's probably because you were revving up your motorbike,' suggested Suzie. 'I'll bring you a hot water bottle to place on them, that should help,' she said, stepping into the kitchen and filling the kettle. 'Did you see that letter from the hospital?' she asked, flipping the switch on.

'No, what's it about?'

'You have to get in touch with them to make an appointment to have some physiotherapy.'

'Oh, okay. I'll do that in the morning.'

Suzie brought Mike in a hot water bottle and placed it over the plasters on his aching wrists. 'Is that better?'

'Yes, thanks, luv. I think I'll go to bed in a minute.'

'Okay. Would you like a cup of hot milk with a little brandy in it to help you sleep?' she asked.

'I'm not so keen on hot milk. Can't I just have the brandy?'

'No, you can't. It's all or nothing.'

'Okay, I'll have the milk and Brandy then,' Mike decided.

'It will help you to sleep. I promise.'

'I know a better way. Using up my energy helps me to sleep.'

'I bet you do, but it's milk for you tonight. We'll see about your other method in the morning.'

'Is that a promise?'

'You'll find that out in the morning,' said Suzie, returning to the kitchen to prepare the drink. She switched the light on.

Outside, Belanov watched her through his telescope. 'Ah, she is probably preparing supper. It will not be long before they retire for the night. If I had my rifle with the telescopic sights, I could kill her now right where she stands, and disappear before anyone could do anything about it.'

Suzie shivered and looked up, but could see nothing but darkness and the dim outline of the gates lit by two lamps, each mounted on one of the gate's upright pillars. She returned to the living room with their drinks.

Mike drunk his milk and Brandy and pulled a face while swallowing it, but secretly enjoyed the drink.

'There's a good boy. I'll tuck you up in bed now,' said Suzie taking his glass.

Getting wearily to his feet, Mike confessed, 'I must admit, I am a bit tired.'

'We're both tired. It's been a long day.'

The grandfather clock in the hall chimed eleven times as Suzie activated the intruder alarm before helping Mike to climb the stairs to their bedroom. She had a quick shower, donned her kimono robe and gave Mike a strip-down wash. Despite being tired, when she washed him his natural urges took over and he displayed an erection.

'I see you don't want to wait until the morning.'

'It's not my fault you're a gorgeous, desirable woman and I can't wait to taste the fruits of your delightful sexy charms. After all …'

'Okay, okay,' interrupted Suzie, 'I give in. Perhaps you'll sleep better afterwards.'

'I'm bound to,' Mike agreed.

'Then I guess it's my turn on top yet again.'

'Until I get theses plasters removed, it's the easiest way for us to manage. I'll make it up to you afterwards and I'll go on top every night.'

'Will you now? I wouldn't bet on that if I were you.'

'Okay, every other night then.'

Suzie smiled. Their loving relationship continued to blossom and their sexual desires complimented each other. She had at last got an engagement ring out of Mike, and the next step was to get him to name their wedding date. That was proving to be a little difficult, and though she thought about using his sexual desires of her to persuade him to name the day, while he was recovering from the accident was not the right time to pressurise him too much.

They went to bed and discovered renewed energy to make love. This time they were able to call out loud in abandon at their climaxes, instead of having to muffle them as they had done on the yacht with Jenny in the bedroom next door.

Belanov watched the downstairs lights go out. The landing and front bedroom lights came on, and he waited. A little over half an hour later the bedroom light also went out, leaving a dim light on the upstairs landing showing. He continued to wait another hour before making his move. He wanted to be sure both of them were well asleep.

His previous visit to the house had gained him the knowledge that scaling the wall at the side of the house by an oak tree was the easiest way to get on to the property, and even if security spotlights came on, their activation was unlikely to be seen from his victim's front bedroom. He was unaware Mike and Suzie had disconnected them, maintaining that a high wall and security spotlights were more than they required. Suzie even talked about reducing the front wall in height so she could see more from the kitchen window.

After scrambling over the wall, Belanov hurried to the outdoor utility room and prized a window open just enough to see the alarm plates. He bridged them with a piece of wire connected to a crocodile clip at each end to avoid breaking the circuit, in the way he had anticipated on his first visit. Once inside he opened the back door with a lock pick and crept into the hall. It was bathed in moonlight cascading through the hallway windows situated on each side of the front door, added to by the dim light illuminating the stairs from the first floor landing. All was quiet apart from the ticking of the grandfather clock.

Belanov screwed the silencer on his gun as he backed down the hallway while watching the stairs and the balcony above for movement. He had seen the lights go out in the front bedroom, so was certain he knew which room his victims were asleep in.

Creeping up the stairs, Belanov put his weight carefully on each step one at a time to avoid making a noise if one of the treads was loose or squeaked. Approaching silently was imperative and was an art he had mastered when he was a member of the Russia *Shturmovana Gruppa*, an assault group of the antiterrorist commando forces.

Reaching the balcony on the top landing, Belanov glanced in both directions before moving to his left and gliding silently towards the main bedroom, his breathing slow and controlled. The door was wide open and inside, bathed in moonlight seeping through the window, was the outline of Mike and Suzie sleeping beneath a single cotton sheet on a large waterbed.

Creeping cautiously into the room, Belanov raised his gun.

Chapter Thirty-Four

The End

Viktor Belanov was intent on fulfilling his contract to kill Suzie Drake and Mike Randle. After running down Rachel by mistake, he was obliged to return to England to complete the contract. When Mike and Suzie docked in Hamble on return from their trip to Ibiza, he followed the pair home and waited outside until they went to bed. Belanov sneaked into their house after disabling the alarm and tiptoed into their bedroom.

He raised his gun when suddenly Mike and Suzie's eyes opened wide. Both had sensed the presence of another person entering the room and Suzie sat up in bed, holding the sheet to cover her naked body.

'Who are you? What do you want?' she asked of the shadowy outline of a figure standing in the doorway, while she slowly slipping her hand beneath her pillow to retrieve the gun hidden there. Keeping a gun close by was a habit she acquired when she was a mercenary, but stopped using until the recent break in.

'If you move your hand any closer to that pillow I will shoot you now,' Belanov warned.

Suzie pulled her hand away.

'I take it you are the real Suzie Drake?' he asked.

Mike turned on to his elbow to push himself up to a sitting position, grunting as he did with the effort and discomfort of the movement.

'Who wants to know?'

'I wouldn't want to kill the wrong person again.'

'Ah! So you're the hit-and-run driver,' said Suzie, desperately trying to think of a way to overcome the dire situation they were faced with.

'This time there will be no mistake.'

'Why do you want to kill me? What have I done to deserve this?' she asked.

She considered the possibility of snatching her gun while rolling out of the bed. She knew the odds of success were not good. By the time she grabbed the weapon he could have shot her, but it was better than sitting there and doing nothing. She tried to keep him talking while assessing her chances and considering what might distract him for a split second.

'There is no harm in telling you why I am here. I am a professional problem solver hired by the boss of 'The Rosy Cheeks Nightclub' in London.'

'You mean you are a professional assassin?'

'Something like that. The nightclub owner was a little upset when you shot his twin brother and he hired me to even things up.'

'Ah! The man who broke in here looking for the drugs and smashed everything in sight. He tried to kill me and I shot him in self defence.'

'Perhaps so, perhaps not. I do not make a judgement on these things.'

'But you are prepared to kill someone for money, even though it may be for something that is a lie.'

'It is not a lie. You have just admitted to killing him.'

'In the defence of my life.'

'That is not my concern. Enough of this chatter. You are the one I was hired to kill and you must die.'

Belanov levelled his gun at Suzie, who dropped the sheet to show her naked figure and prepared to make her move. She had used the tactic to distract an opponent once before and it had worked.

Belanov froze for a moment but before Suzie could move, he reacted to a rustle behind him. He span round sharply and his eyes opened wide in astonishment as he instantly recognised the shadowy figure before him. Without a word being spoken, the puff of a silenced weapon resounded in the air and a bullet drove into Belanov's forehead. Blood spattered over the bed as his body crashed to the floor, with Mike and Suzie wondering for a moment what had happened.

Drifting cordite evaporated into the air as the shadowy figure melted back into the darkness and the sound of someone leaping down the stairway several steps at a time, echoed from the hallway. Suzie jumped out of bed, grabbed the gun and her kimono, and ran to the landing balcony as she tied the sash. She arrived in time to see a man open the front door and dash away, triggering the burglar alarm.

Suzie smelt a distinct fragrance in the air. 'I recognise that aroma. Is it Horak?' She dashed down the stairs, quickly banged in the code on the alarm console to stop the loud clanging and stepped through the open front doorway. In the moonlight, she saw the man vault over the ten-foot-high gate. 'And I've seen you do that same trick before. Now I know it's Zenon Horak.'

The man jumped to the ground, turned and peered through the gate. He saw Suzie standing on the doorstep bathed in moonlight. She could see the outline of a man stood there, watching her. She released the sash on her kimono and opened it wide to show him her naked body. Horak smiled. He had seen the same attractive body once before and knew she had guessed it was him who had intervened. He dashed to his Volvo car and Suzie heard the roar as it motored down the coast road towards the motorway.

She returned to the bedroom. Mike had switched the light on and was searching through the pockets of Belanov's body. 'Has our anonymous rescuer gone?'

'Yes. It was Zenon Horak. I'm sure of it.'

'Horak! That's a surprise. Why did he come here? And how did he know this man was coming here to kill you?'

'I don't know the answer to either of those questions, but I'm very grateful he did.'

'So am I. There's nothing on this man to identify him, but he had a Russian accent. I think we'd better ring Sir Joseph again rather than the police and ask him to remove the body. I'm sure he'd want to have first hand knowledge about assassins who visit this country.'

'This will be the second time we've asked him to do that in the last few weeks. He'll be wondering what on earth's going on here.'

'I'll give him a ring,' said Mike.

'No, that's okay, I'll do it. I don't want him to know I think it was Horak who was here.'

'Why not?'

'There's still a warrant out for his arrest on a murder charge, and he did save both our lives. I'm sure this gunman would have killed you as well. He wouldn't want to leave you as a witness,' Suzie maintained.

'I guess your right.'

Suzie deliberately omitted telling Mike about opening her kimono on the steps.

She added, 'Although apart from my speculation, we could tell him what happened, except he would almost certainly guess it was Horak. Perhaps we'd better say I shot him.'

'So, we'd better get our story straight before you ring him. Sir Joseph's a clever man and will pick up on any discrepancies.'

Suzie nodded. They agreed their story and Suzie rang Sir Joseph at home. 'I'm sorry to ring you at this early hour,' she said, when he picked up the telephone on his bedside cabinet.

'That's all right, Suzie, I'm used to it. I imagine it must be something fairly important for you to ring me at this hour. What is it?'

'A gunman broke into our house and I was forced to shoot him.'

'Another one?'

'Yes, I'm sorry to say.'

'Do you know who he was?'

'No, but he had a foreign accent. Russian we believe.'

'Is it Zenon Horak?'

'No, it's not him. Not unless he's changed his height and build as well as his facial appearance.'

'Do you know why the gunman targeted you?'

'He told us the owner of 'The Rosy Cheeks Nightclub' in London hired him to kill me because I shot his twin brother a few weeks ago when he broke into our house.'

'I see.'

'He also told me he was the hit-and-run driver who killed poor Rachel in Ibiza because he mistook her for me.'

'Well at least it clears that mystery up. It also means he was prepared to go globetrotting to find you and has been after you for quite a while.'

'Yes. That's quite scary.'

'I'm amazed how these people manage to get into this country so easily. I must have a word with the immigration authorities and try to get things tightened up. I'll send Sandy round to pick up the body and I'll sort things out with the authorities about it tomorrow.'

'Thank you, Sir Joseph.'

'Goodnight, Suzie.'

'Goodnight.'

'We've definitely got to get a new burglar alarm,' stated Mike. 'It seems any bugger can get past our present one.'

'I'll ring the alarm company in the morning and find out what's happening about that quote they promised me.'

After their disturbed nights sleep, the adrenaline was still high in them. Mike and Suzie sat in their kitchen and discussed what had happened over a cup of coffee while they waited for Sandy to arrive. It was half past three in the morning when he reached their house and removed the body.

Eventually, Mike and Suzie were tired enough to go back to bed and grab a few hours sleep, though they slept in the spare bedroom, not wanting to use their own bed until the blood in the room had been cleaned away. Their delight at coming home, was dampened by the unexpected brush with death that burst into their lives. It made them thankful another hit man had come to their rescue, though the explanation of how Horak knew what was about to happen and be there in time to kill the assassin, was a mystery to them. It would remain that way, unless and until they met him again.

Chapter Thirty-Five

Home To Roost

Driving along the coast road at 1 a.m. towards the motorway in his favourite car - a Volvo, Zenon Horak smiled to himself. He had killed Viktor Belanov and saved the lives of Mike Randle and Suzie Drake. He was pleased at the outcome of his night's work, as was Mike and Suzie, though they were surprised at his appearance and were unable to understand how or why he arrived at a most opportune moment.

'It has taken me a long time get my revenge,' Horak said to himself. 'And I am pleased to have saved Mike Randle and Suzie Drake from the murderous clutches of Viktor Belanov. They did not deserve to die at the hands of a thug like him, like my poor Natasha did.'

The circumstances Mike and Suzie were not aware of, was that in the past when Horak, who at the time was a member of the Russia *Shturmovana Gruppa*, deserted to become a freelance agent, the Russian Federal Security Service sent two men after him. They had orders to kill him as an example to others who might have similar ideas. The men discovered the address of his girlfriend Natasha and in their brutal questioning to persuade her to divulge Horak's whereabouts, she died from her injuries. When they located Horak, he killed one of his pursuers but was hit by a bullet fired by the second man before he was able to make his escape. That second man was Viktor Belanov, who was a member of the same Russian assault group as Horak. He swore then, that he would get his revenge on Belanov one day for killing his girl friend. Today he kept that promise to himself.

Since that time he had purposely kept away from forming any close relationships with anyone to avoid a similar tragedy occurring. The attractive Suzie Drake had reminded him of his girlfriend, which had softened the hard exterior towards her that he tried to maintain because of the profession he had undertaken. Their paths crossed twice before and he admired her fighting skills as well as the beautiful sight of her naked body.

Horak drove on to the A3 and headed straight for London. 'I heard Belanov mention that the boss of 'The Rosy Cheeks Nightclub' in London was the man who put out the contract. I think I will go and see him,' he said to himself.

Punching the nightclub's name into his satellite navigator, Horak followed the directions to Brixton and parked outside the nightclub. It was 2.45 a.m. and members were drifting away after a night's entertainment. Scouting around the back of the nightclub, Horak entered through the rear entrance. Loud music filled the air coming from the bar area with the girls doing their final erotic acts of the night. Horak saw the obliging sign on a door of 'The Boss. Knock and wait' and entered the office without knocking.

In the dimly lit room, Crossman looked up from his desk and saw the outline of the tall wiry framed stranger. 'Who are you, and what the hell do you want?'

Standing in shadows Horak asked, 'You are the boss?' in his Ukrainian accent.

'Oh, it's you,' Crossman said, recognising the accent and thinking it was his hit man. 'You did a good job on Deven. Mo's behaving himself now, or at least it seems that way. We had a little chat and everything appears to be sorted out. Only time will tell if he's truthful about his intentions. He was a little too ready to give in rather quickly. I may yet need your services again. All you have to do at the moment, is to eliminate that Drake woman.'

'I am sorry to inform you, but that will not now be possible.'

'Oh, and why's that?'

'Because your tame killer is dead.'

'Dead? Who are you? You're not my man.'

'No, I am not. But you are the boss, are you not?'

'Yes, I am the boss. Why?' asked Crossman, not liking what he was hearing. He slowly moved his hand towards the desk middle drawer where he kept his loaded gun.

'I am a sort of friend of Suzie Drake. She is an attractive female who does not deserve to die at the hands of a mad killer like Viktor Belanov.'

'Who?' Crossman asked, keeping the man talking while inching his hand towards his gun.

'Viktor Belanov, your hired killer. I shot him.'

A flush coloured Crossman's face. 'And what do you want with me?'

'You are the boss who hired him.'

'No, I didn't actually hire him. It was the previous boss Mr Phadkar who hired him to kill Miss Drake. It's all a big mistake.'

'You are the boss?' Horak repeated.

'Yes, but I didn't hire him.'

'Belanov said the boss of this nightclub hired him, and I heard you say all he had to do now was to eliminate the Drake woman. You are condemned out of your own mouth.'

Horak's keen senses detected a noise in the passageway outside the door and he stood to one side. The door crashed open and Mo, along with two other men, burst into the room brandishing guns.

'What do you want?' a frightened looking Crossman asked, staring at the three guns pointing at him.

'Revenge. People on the street know what you did and it is bad for my reputation to let a white dealer like you dictate to me and my men. Did you really think I would give in so easily?'

'No. I have to say I had my doubts about your real intentions.'

'You sent a hit man after Deven and he killed him and two of my men. For that you have to die, unless ...'

'Unless what?' asked Crossman, seeing the door drift slowly shut to reveal a shadowy Horak.

'Unless you tell me who your supplier is. Then we can go direct to them and cut you out. Your money making spree will be over and you will no longer have a hold over us.'

'Well, if it's the killer of Deven you want, he's standing right behind you.'

The three men did not move. 'Do you expect me to fall for a silly old trick like that while you grab the gun in your desk?'

Crossman raised his hands to show he had no gun. 'It's no trick. Why doesn't one of you turn and look? You may be surprised.'

Mo nodded to one of his men who turned to stare and the dark outline of Horak standing by the door with a gun in his hand.

'He ain't kidding boss,' the man said, raising his gun to fire.

Suddenly, Crossman grabbed the gun from his desk drawer expecting Mo to turn as well, as the second man span round. Before Crossman could pull the trigger, Mo's gun spat out its lethal slug of metal hitting him in the chest, crashing Crossman back into his chair where he slumped sideways with his head at a grotesque angle.

Simultaneously, Horak's silenced gun spat twice in quick succession killing both of Mo's men with shots to the head. Mo span round to be met by a third bullet from Horak's weapon, propelling him into the desk where he slid to the floor alongside his two dead gang members.

At that moment, Angie, who had heard Mo's gun fire, rushed into the room, saw Crossman's body slumped in the chair and the three drug gang members lying on the floor. She turned to see Horak standing in the shadows, half-smiled and looked at his gun pointing at her.

'Are you going to shoot me as well?'

'No. I do not kill innocent defenceless women.'

'I'm pleased to hear that. Nobody will worry about Crossman's death. He was a cruel, viscous man, who murdered his way to riches but got too greedy.'

'Most of them do,' said Horak.

'And Mo and his men sell drugs to stupid addicts on the streets. Only they will miss them.'

'There will be other dealers to take their places,' suggested Horak.

'Perhaps so, but getting rid of one drug dealer is better than letting him continue to sell his misery to silly young kids who regret it after it's too late and are hooked.'

Horak nodded.

'Now that Crossman is dead, I will run this nightclub. There'll be no more drug dealings. I'll keep the girls doing their stripping but stop the private meetings for prostitution, and I'll have live bands and music in here. It's what I've always thought was how the nightclub should be run and now I have the opportunity to do it. I'm sure I can make a success of it.'

'Good,' said Horak lowering his gun. 'You have not seen me.'

'I came in here and found Crossman and the other men dead. They must have shot each other.'

'In about fifteen minute's time.'

'As you say, in about fifteen minute's time.'

Horak left Angie standing there and departed the same way he came in and melted into the night.

* * *

Suzie rang Jim and Jenny at 7 a.m. on Wednesday morning to tell them what had happened in the early hours of the morning. She explained that she had shot the intruder, and Mike and her had only slept for a few hours after Sandy had removed yet another body from their home.

'Are you both okay?'

'We are. It's all been a bit of a shock and we are both rather tired still, so we will not be coming in to work today.'

'That's fine. Jim and I will look after things for today. Let's hope that is the end of it. You don't want to be looking over your shoulder all the time wondering if somebody is going to put a bullet in you,' Jenny stated.

'Amen to that. I'll see you tomorrow morning.'

Later that morning, a little before ten o'clock, Sir Joseph Sterling rang Suzie. 'Jenny told me you were having the day off work. I'd like to pay you and Mike a visit this afternoon, if it's convenient?' he requested.

'Yes, of course. Would you like to tell me what it's concerned with, though I imagine it's about what happened here last night?' Suzie asked.

'I'd rather discuss the matter with you face to face, if you don't mind. What time would suit you?'

'Around three o'clock?'

'Three would suit me admirably.'

'We'll see you at three then. Goodbye.'

Mike and Suzie pondered on what Sir Joseph wanted to speak to them about, and assumed it was probably about the gunman who had so rudely disturbed them in the early hours of that morning. They went over their story again to make sure they both agreed about what had happened.

At precisely three o'clock, Sir Joseph's car entered through the gateway to their house. It crunched along the gravel driveway and halted outside their front door. Suzie went out to greet him while Mike stood by the front door.

'No chauffer today, Sir Joseph?' Suzie asked.

'No, not today. I want our talk to be private.'

Suzie gave an expectant nod. They climbed the three steps to the front door, entered the house and went into the living room.

'How are you getting on?' Sir Joseph asked Mike.

'Fine, thanks. The cruise to the Med was good. I was able to rest most of the time. But I'll be a lot happier when these plasters come off and I can get rid of these blasted crutches.'

'Of course, they must be very inconvenient. How long before that happens?'

'Probably another couple of months.'

'Would you like a cup of tea or coffee, Sir Joseph?' Suzie asked.

'Yes, please. Tea, no sugar.'

Mike nodded his agreement to Suzie's enquiring look and she stepped into the kitchen to brew a pot of tea. She brought them in on a tray with a plate of biscuits, including some plain chocolate digestives, which everyone knew were Sir Joseph's favourite.

Sipping his tea, Mike asked, 'We're always pleased to see you, especially when you occasionally consent to visit us at our home. We assume you have a specific reason for this visit today, presumably connected with what happened to us last night.'

'Thank you. Yes, I have. I wanted to bring you up to date with certain events and ask a few questions … unofficially, off the record.'

'Why off the record?' asked Suzie.

'Because I'm hoping I may get some answers you might otherwise be reluctant to give me, and I received some news this morning I think you may be interested in.'

'Oh, what's that?'

'I'll save that until later,' Sir Joseph indicated, grabbing a chocolate biscuit. 'First of all I want to talk to you about the gunman who visited you here early this morning.'

'Not a nice fellow,' remarked Mike.

'Quite. He was Viktor Belanov, a Russian who turned hit man when he left the Russian security service, and he used a Yarygin PYa pistol, the one Sandy collected from you along with the body. We matched the bullets from his gun to the killing of three men in London two weeks ago. We believe they were mixed up in drug dealing. You said Mr Belanov stated he was hired to kill you and you shot him while he stood in your bedroom.'

'That's right. Your man Sandy collected his body from there.'

'So he told me.'

'Since we had a break-in here and another one at the boatyard, I started to keep a gun under my pillow again. We kept him chatting while I quietly reached for it.'

'And you shot him?'

'Yes, that's right. I shot him in the head.'

'Hmm,' mused Sir Joseph. 'And I don't suppose you are aware that a gunman shot and killed Mr Jake Crossman, the new owner of 'The Rosy Cheeks Nightclub' in London.'

'No. We didn't know that,' said Mike, glancing across to Suzie. 'Not that I'm very upset about it. He was obviously mixed up with the sale of drugs, and was responsible for smashing me and my motorbike and tried to finish the job at the hospital.'

'Three other suspected drugs dealers were also killed with him. One of the men named Mo, was injured in the previous killings I just mentioned, and his gun matched the bullet that killed Mr Crossman.'

'It sounds like a revenge killing.'

'Yes, the police thought that as well. We have also matched the bullets from the gun you retrieved at the hospital to the killings aboard your yacht *Quester*, which you pointed out was dropped by Mr Crossman.'

'Right. The picture becomes clearer. He tried to steal his boss's drugs so he could take over the nightclub and the drugs trade, but the dealer's didn't like it.'

'That's what it looks like. We haven't found out what happened to his former bosses brother yet. The twin of the one you shot, Suzie.'

'Crossman probably killed him as well to get his hands on the nightclub,' she postulated.

'Possibly. We received an anonymous tip-off from a woman about the location of the body in a disused quarry, but we've not discovered it yet. It's quite a big quarry, so it may take some time.'

'There can't be many women who were privy to that sort of information,' suggested Mike.

'No, my thoughts as well. We talked to a woman named Angie at the nightclub, but she denies making the call.'

'I remember her,' said Mike. 'She's the one who copied my credit card.'

'She said she was forced to do that by the owners. She now plans to run the nightclub and has assured me it will be a legitimate entertainment nightclub, with no drugs and no reason for the police to worry about anything that goes on there.'

'Good for her,' declared Suzie.

'Is your gun still under the pillow, Suzie?' asked Sir Joseph.

'Yes, it is.'

'And what make is it?'

Suzie looked at Mike. 'It's a Walther PPK pistol.'

'I believe your weapon fires a 7.65mm calibre bullet?'

'Err, yes, that's right. How well informed you are.'

'That was the calibre of bullet taken from Mr Phadkar after you shot him.'

'I see.'

'Mr Belanov however, was killed with a 9mm calibre Russian bullet. Forensics have matched the bullet that killed him with the ones that killed the three gang members in Crossman's office. They are identical, so the same person must have killed them both, or at least the same gun must have been used to shoot them with. As you said you killed Mr Belanov, did you also go rushing off to London to kill the three drugs dealers as well, Suzie?'

'Well … no, I didn't.'

'I didn't think so. In fact, I knew you hadn't. Sandy tells me you were here when he collected Viktor Belanov's body at around 3.30 a.m., so you could not possibly have been in London killing anyone in Mr Crossman office at approximately 3 a.m.'

'No, that's right.'

'DI Brooke had a man posted outside the nightclub entrance to keep an eye on any dealings that went on there with the drugs. I'm sorry to say he missed our drug dealers and gunman going in, and the gunman coming out again afterwards, so they probably used the back entrance.'

'Or your man went to sleep,' suggested Mike.

'That is possible, but he says not.'

'Hmm,' muttered Mike.

'We really needed two men to watch the nightclub. One at the front and one at the back. Colin tried to get agreement for that, but it seems that resources wouldn't stretch that far.'

'They would probably have spotted them anyway and still sneaked in.'

'Possibly, but that still doesn't explain why you stated that you killed Viktor Belanov, which the forensics evidence shows is not true.'

'So, we need to amend our story,' suggested Mike.

'I would say so. Go on. I'm listening,' stated Sir Joseph.

'Off the record?'

'Off the record, as long as you've not committed a serious offence.'

'That may depend on your opinion of what is a serious offence,' challenged Mike.

'You'll have to trust me on that one. What is your amended story?'

Suzie related the details of how they looked certain to be killed, when another gunman intervened to save them both.

'And who was this other gunman? Zenon Horak?'

'We don't know for sure. He stood in the darkened doorway and dashed out of the house straight away after killing our would-be assassin. We didn't see his face.'

'But it still puzzles me why or how a gunman, perhaps Mr Horak, came here and shot Mr Belanov before going to 'The Rosy Cheeks Nightclub' and shooting dead three drug dealers.'

'He must have overheard Belanov saying it was the boss of the nightclub who hired him to kill us.'

'But that still doesn't answer why he went to the nightclub to kill them.'

'Perhaps he's got a crush on Suzie?' suggested Mike.

Sir Joseph was unable to conceal a half-smile. 'Perhaps you're right. Why did you try to protect this gunman?'

'Simple. He saved our lives. We felt he deserved that much. I believe it was Horak, but neither of us saw his face and he was gone within seconds.'

'I understand. I've issued Mr Horak's photograph to all the ports and airports with instructions to look out for him, but like last time I'm not hopeful of catching the man.'

'He may have changed his appearance now that you've got photos of him,' added Suzie.

'Quite possible,' agreed Sir Joseph, unaware that Horak had undergone plastic surgery to his face performed by Dr Leonard Shevchenko, a man who was a friend of his father and who took the bullet from Horak after his near fatal encounter with Belanov the first time.

'So, what's this other item of interest to us?' asked Mike, trying to steer the conversation away from awkward questions and hoping it was the last they heard of their attempted cover up.

'The coastguard has caught another vessel trying to smuggle drugs into the country early this morning, also after a woman made an anonymous telephone call to them.'

'Angie again?' suggested Mike.

'Who knows? The information was valuable, so I'm not too bothered about where it came from, though like you I have my suspicions.'

'Is it the same lot that used *Quester*, do you know?' asked Suzie.

'We think so. This time we were able to arrest both the crew and yacht bringing the drugs into this country, and also the supply ship that brought the drugs from South America.'

'Sounds like a good night's work,' Suzie maintained.

'Yes. Inspector Fairbourne took part in the raid and is highly delighted with the outcome.'

'I hope they didn't use another yacht from our boatyard,' quipped Mike.

'No, they didn't. They used one from Harman's Yard in Devon, and apparently the yacht was severely damaged in the fight that took place between the gang and the police when they boarded her. The gang's leader, a left handed Irish safe-breaker by the name of Lefty, ended up in Southampton Hospital with a few broken bones.'

'There is some justice after all,' said Mike, with a broad smile across his face.

'I have one other bit of news for you as well,' said Sir Joseph.

'Good news?' asked Suzie.

'I'm not sure you would exactly call it good news, but after having spoken to Jim and Jenny about why you returned from Ibiza early, I'm sure you will find it interesting and possibly amusing.'

Mike and Suzie looked at each other. 'So, go on, don't keep us in suspension, tell us what it is,' he said.

'The Spanish police on Ibiza were patrolling the beaches two nights ago, when they came across Mr Alastaire Bignor and some of his crew filming couples having sex on the beach by the side of a blazing fire. He was arrested and charged with promoting couples to engage in an indecent act in a public place.'

Suzie smiled. Mike laughed out loud. 'Ha, ha, ha. It serves him right.'

'You know why he had to do that, don't you?' asked Suzie.

Sir Joseph shook his head. 'No. Do tell.'

'Because Sir Jeremy Pendleton MBE wouldn't let him film his 'glamour films' as he calls them, aboard his yacht *Julia*, in case someone recognised the vessel as his.'

'What do you think that will do to Bignor's television pilot production?' wondered Mike. 'Will it kill it?'

'If what I heard this morning is correct, two television companies are eager to sign up his production for a series. It seems that publicity, whether good or bad, is good for the ratings,' Sir Joseph stated.

'So Bignor got what he wanted after all,' he said. 'And *Quester* will be seen in the pilot film along with Suzie's first acting part.'

'I didn't know you inspired to be an actress,' said Sir Joseph.

'I don't. It was a very small part and will probably be cut out of the finished film.'

'You could be right,' suggested Mike.

Sir Joseph finished his tea and biscuits, bade them farewell and left to return to London certain that Zenon Horak had killed Viktor Belanov and the three drugs dealers, and he had a sneaking suspicion why.

Sat in his wheelchair, Mike produced several DVD discs. 'Bignor won't be needing these then.'

Suzie stared at them. 'What are they?'

'Bignor's DVD discs.'

'And where did you get those from?'

'I borrowed them from his cabin when I was taking the photographs of Jeremy's yacht, just before you threw him and his crew off *Quester.*'

'What's on them?'

'This one's got the scene with you in it,' he said, holding it up. 'That's why you are not likely to be in the final film. You're very good, but I didn't know you went naked for the bedroom scene and had sex with the local stud.'

'What! I didn't. I wouldn't do that for Bignor's film.'

'I know. I could see it wasn't your body. I know your attractive shape only too well. I reckon Bignor used Rachel and spliced the scenes together to make it look like it was you. He probably had a crush on you as well.'

'The bastard!'

'The DVD also has scenes of you cavorting around the top deck of *Quester* sunbathing topless. It must have been taken with a jolly good telephoto lens.'

'What! Let me see that,' Suzie said, snatching the DVD. 'I'm going to destroy these. And what's on the rest of them?'

'I don't know. I haven't had time to look at them all yet.'

Grabbing the rest of them, Suzie stated, 'I'll take a look at these first, just in case they're more of Bignor's 'glamour films' he shot.' She marched off to hide them.

'Okay, luv,' Mike said. 'It's a good job that Bignor made two copies of your acting,' Mike whispered, tapping a DVD in his top pocket.

About the Author

Anthony J Broughton is a keen photographer, and an avid fan of comedy and the Good Show. Now retired from a career as a design draughtsman, he and his wife, Linda, reside in a small village in the Sussex countryside. Pleasure Cruise is his sixth novel. To read more about Anthony, visit his web site at www.anthonyjbroughton.co.uk.

Printed in the United States
By Bookmasters